*This novel is dedicated to the memory of
Doris Pauline Berkenbosch Blood.*

ACKNOWLEDGMENTS

I'm not sure if anyone has publicly thanked a pandemic, but when the world came to a screeching halt in March of 2020, I did what I could do from my little sunshine-yellow office—I wrote a story. Without the shadow of COVID 19, this story may never have been birthed.

Although a story may be written in quarantine, it never becomes a book that way. Thank you to my faithful critique groups: Sharpened Pencils and Word Weavers International, Des Moines Chapter. Your polishing always makes me shine.

Thank you to my dear friends who lived in Des Moines in the 1930s—Bert Borg and Rowena Arnold. Your answers to my questions were always helpful.

Thanks always to my best friend and husband, Gary. From supporting me in the writing to listening to the final product, you have been my helpmate.

Thank you to Scrivenings Press for striving to make my work better, and for the hard work of publication. I truly appreciate all of you.

Thank you to my readers. You are the ones who make this all worthwhile.

Lastly, thank you to the Good Shepherd who has been my faithful and loving guide through writing and life.

ABOUT THIS BOOK

In 1934, a young girl bought cheap dimestore notebooks to use as diaries. She spent her days working long hours as a housekeeper for wealthy home-owners in Des Moines, Iowa. But every night, she would record her thoughts and activities before she slept. Those diaries were hidden away as she married, raised a family, and became elderly.

When my mother died in 2003, I became the owner of the numerous diaries spanning her lifetime. I read them and became enchanted with the idea of a novel, set in the 1930s, with a protagonist who worked as a maid.

Flight of the Red-winged Blackbird is not my mother's story, but I drew greedily from those diaries for authenticity. This novel is dedicated to the memory of Doris Pauline Berkenbosch Blood, the writer who filled those precious, old notebooks.

~ Susan R. Lawrence

PART ONE

1

Grantsville, Iowa, 1932

R uth pushed aside the bedroom curtains and watched as the black truck rattled down the dirt lane, trailing a cloud of dust. If she hurried, she could be at the station in time to catch the four o'clock train to Des Moines.

She pulled a battered plaid suitcase from under her bed. Inside, she'd already stuffed a few underclothes. She folded two dresses, a faded nightgown, and a warm sweater, and laid them on top. Then she tucked in the only items she'd brought with her to the farm three years before—a Bible and a small photograph, cracked and worn, of the mother she barely remembered. Kneeling, she pried the loose board between her bed and the wall, removed a coin purse, and slid it into her dress pocket.

With a firm hand, Ruth snapped the clasps of the suitcase and lifted it. She shut the bedroom door, stopping only to jam a straw hat over her mass of curls, and strode out of the house without a backward look.

Her long legs carried her quickly down the lane and into the cornfield. She walked between the rows, far enough into the field that no one could see her from the road. The sharp edges of the leaves scraped her arms, but she didn't slow her pace. She could not miss the train. The heat and humidity from the nearly six-foot-tall plants soon left her dripping with perspiration. She wished she had a wet rag to sponge off her face.

The field ended at the crossroad. She looked both ways before scurrying across the road and into the next field. A barbedwire fence protected it, so she set her suitcase down, pried apart the strands and stepped through, carefully lifting her skirts to prevent catching and tearing the fabric. At the opposite end of the field, she brushed the last of the cornstalk leaves aside. A flashy red-winged blackbird swished up from his cattail perch in the ditch, calling "*ka-chee, ka-chee.*" Ruth gasped and nearly dropped her suitcase. She watched the bird fly across the sharp blue sky. A yearning flooded her heart, and she gazed upward until she could no longer observe his flight.

Then she crawled between the strands of barbed wire and waded through towering weeds on the railroad embankment. After reaching the tracks, she picked off the burrs and seeds that stuck to her skirt. If she followed the tracks to the Grantsville depot, she could purchase a ticket. Her ticket to freedom.

Ruth tugged the straw hat farther down on her face and kept her eyes on the wooden railroad ties as she stepped from one to another, taking care not to trip. As she neared Grantsville, she could hear traffic. A sputtering *chug-chug* of a motorcar, the muffled *clop, clop* of a horse, and the rhythmic squeak of wagon wheels. She resisted the temptation to raise her head and look. If someone recognized her, the entire plan could fail.

She walked faster, and her heart kept pace with her feet as she neared the depot. No one stood on the platform. She let out the breath she had been holding, set her suitcase down, and took a moment to still her racing heart. Then, reaching into her pocket, she drew out the coin purse and clutched it to her chest as she stepped inside.

Mr. Van Gundy, a man she knew only by name, was behind the ticket window. He glanced up from his newspaper. "May I help you, ma'am?"

"I'd like one ticket to Des Moines," Ruth whispered.

Mr. Van Gundy frowned and stroked a bristly mustache, but he must have heard her because he asked, "Round-trip or one-way?"

"One-way." She answered firmly and nodded to confirm it.

Few people left Grantsville without plans to return as soon as possible. Those who lived here couldn't imagine making their home anywhere else. But not Ruth. She hadn't found a home here, she'd found a house of horrors. But Mr. Van Gundy didn't question her.

"That will be seventy-five cents."

Ruth carefully counted coins and slid them under the metal barrier across the window. He pushed the ticket back to her and muttered, "Thank you. The train will arrive," he pulled a round, gold watch from his pocket and looked at it, "in twenty minutes. You may have a seat in the waiting area. I'll announce the train's arrival." He gave a vague wave toward the wooden benches lining the station's perimeter and turned his attention back to his newspaper.

Ruth smiled. As if anyone in the small building would miss the arrival of the smoking, roaring dragon. She looked around for a sign.

"The ladies' room is down that hall." Mr. Van Gundy pointed without looking up.

"Thank you." Ruth's cheeks warmed, but she hurried in the direction he pointed. In the small room, she splashed water on her sweaty face and patted it dry with the towel provided, marveling at water running from a faucet inside the building. She tucked some loose curls back behind her ear. Then she looked at the straw hat in her hand. She would never again work in a field. She stuffed the hat deep into the trashcan, tossed back her freed tresses, and held her head high as she made her way through the depot to a bench.

Twenty minutes later, she heard the train whistle. It seemed to be calling her name. She stood, even before Mr. Van Gundy's voice announced, "The train for Des Moines is now arriving. All passengers need to make their way to the platform for boarding. Please have your tickets ready."

Ruth clutched her ticket in one hand, her suitcase in the other. She followed two men and a woman to the platform and watched as the train hissed and squealed to a stop. The conductor held the handle on the side of the train as he stepped onto the platform.

A rush of memories flooded over her. Coming from New York City, a fifteen-year-old orphan on the train. The night on the stage at the operahouse when the Schmidts chose her. The excitement of having a family in Grantsville, Iowa. She'd thought it was a dream come true, but the dream turned into a nightmare. She shook her head and stepped up to the train.

The conductor punched a hole in her ticket and handed it back. "Welcome, miss. Enjoy your train ride."

Ruth made her way to a car with only a few people, all strangers. She lifted her suitcase to the overhead storage area and sat in an empty row by the window. Within a few minutes the whistle sounded again, and with a jerk, the car moved.

As the train pulled out of Grantsville, it picked up speed.

The wheels sang a sweet song to Ruth. *Free. Free. You're finally free.*

2

The rhythmic song of the train's wheels on the tracks and the warm, late-afternoon sun slanting through the window weighed heavy on Ruth's eyelids. She blinked, and the cornfields blurred past. In some fields, the corn was beginning to fire—the bottoms of the stalks and the leaves had turned brown, dry and brittle, one of the first signs of fall's advent and the nearing harvest time in Iowa.

Today's temperatures were summery, but they would change quickly in the coming months. Her small suitcase wouldn't accommodate a winter coat, even if she'd had one to bring. Ruth rolled her eyes at the irony. A coat was the least of her problems.

She pulled out her coin purse and checked the contents. The small piece of paper with a Des Moines address scrawled on it was still folded safely inside. She tucked the purse back in her pocket and allowed herself the luxury of closing her eyes.

"Next stop, Des Moines, Iowa. Arriving now. Des Moines. Please gather all your belongings." The conductor's voice in the aisle startled Ruth awake. She stood and pulled her suitcase down as the train swayed and slid to a stop.

Ruth eased down the metal steps, her heart hammering. Buildings towered around her, and motorcars sped up and down the crisscross of streets. She clutched her suitcase while people jostled past. She'd lived in New York City as a child, but it had been three years since she'd been anywhere other than the farm or the village of Grantsville, and the noise and bustle made a sliver of fear creep up her spine. A glance at the sun told her she had less than two hours of daylight. She needed to go. But which direction? She had no idea where Cottage Grove Avenue was, and everyone on the platform seemed too busy to ask.

Ruth let the stream of people move her along the platform to the station. She could use the facilities inside and then find someone to ask for directions. After enjoying her second indoor toilet in one day, she washed her hands, dried them on the roller towel on the wall, and walked into the lobby.

Compared to the depot in Grantsville, it was huge. Everyone rushed past, bags clutched in their hands. A woman in a huge, gaudy hat bumped into Ruth and hurried on without apology. Ruth edged toward one of the ticket windows when a voice at her elbow said, "Are you lost, kitten?"

She turned and nearly bumped into a well-dressed young man with dark hair combed in a wave to the side.

"Ummm. No. Well, maybe." She held out the scrap of paper. "I need to get to this address."

A little frown creased his brow as he read the address. "Do you have a car?"

She shook her head. "No." *Did she look like someone who could afford a car?*

"Can you take a cab?"

Again, she shook her head. "I can walk. I'm used to walking

long distances." She must have walked several miles every day just taking care of the house and the farm.

He studied her for a moment, then pointed. "Okay, then. Go straight west on this street to 6th Avenue. Then turn north until you get to Woodland. Go west on Woodland to 19th, and north on 19th to Cottage Grove."

Ruth repeated. "West to 6th, north to Woodland, west to 19th, and north to Cottage Grove. I can do it."

He glanced at the clock on the depot wall. "I'd take you myself, but I'm going the opposite direction—to Indianola with a friend in his car. I'll walk you to the street, though."

"That's not necessary. I appreciate the information, and I'm confident I can find this place." She tucked the paper in the pocket of her dress and gave him what she hoped was a pleasant but dismissive smile.

He ran fingers through the thick wave of his hair, then tucked his hands in his pockets. "Hey. I get to Des Moines about once a week. How about we go to a hop? Or a picture show? Can I ring you up?" He gazed at her with a winsome smile.

Ruth picked up her suitcase and straightened her shoulders. "No, that's not possible." She strode out of the depot and knew without looking that he stared at her until the door closed.

The sun had slid behind the tall buildings of the city when she set the suitcase down and rubbed her shoulders. There wasn't much in the case, but it had become heavier and heavier with each block. She pulled the paper out of her pocket again and checked. The black numbers on the gray three-story home in front of her matched. A neat little sign informed passersby: *Sisters of Mercy Home for Unwed Mothers.*

Behind the house, facing the street on the next block and rising even taller, stood a massive stone church. Ruth tipped her head back and followed the spire to its very peak, where a cross seemed to scrape the clouds and maybe Heaven. Surely a place in the shadows of the house of God would be safe.

She trudged up the wide steps to a wraparound porch. Several wicker chairs and a swing made it warm and welcoming. She hoped the people inside were as well. With a deep breath, she lifted her hand and knocked.

Light footsteps clacked on a wooden floor. The door swung open. A tiny, bird-like woman dressed in the black and white habit of a nun appraised her from head to toe with bright, beady eyes. "May I help you?" she chirped.

Ruth dropped the suitcase and covered her face with her hands as a sob escaped her lips. "Can—can I stay here?" She felt like she was fifteen again, standing on the operahouse stage and hoping for a family.

The nun reached for Ruth's suitcase with one hand, and with the other took hold of her arm and guided her inside to a parlor with pale blue upholstered chairs, a striped sofa, and a fireplace. She set the suitcase down and patted the seat of a chair. "Sit here."

Ruth's knees buckled, and she sank onto the cushion.

The nun perched on the edge of a chair opposite Ruth's. "My name is Sister Jean Marie. Now tell me what's going on with you. Where have you come from?"

Fear rushed in and strangled Ruth's words. What if they traced her and sent her back to Grantsville? What if *he* found her? She couldn't let that happen. "My name is Emma, and I—I came from Indianola," she blurted out.

The little nun's head bobbed, and the habit moved with it. "And you're in a family way?"

No one had yet put it in words. Ruth looked at her dust-covered shoes and nodded.

A small hand patted hers. "God can forgive even this and

use it for his glory. We love babies here. We can help you, Emma. How did you get here?"

Ruth raised her head. Did she dare hope? "I walked from the train depot."

"Oh, my. That is a long way. I'm guessing you haven't had dinner, have you, dear?"

"No." Nor had she had anyone speak soothingly to her, or care for her, in a very long time.

"Come on. Follow me. I'll show you where you can sleep tonight, and then I'll take you to the dining room and introduce you to some of the girls. Tomorrow, you will meet with Mother Superior. She makes the final decisions regarding new admissions."

Despite the nervousness of meeting Mother Superior, Ruth felt safe. Hope spread through her and gave her new strength. She picked up her suitcase and followed Sister Jean Marie up the wide wooden staircase.

3

I f Sister Jean Marie reminded Ruth of a bird, Mother Superior was a hawk. The woman's piercing ice-blue gaze trapped Ruth and held her firm on the seat of an uncomfortably stiff wooden chair.

"Your full name?"

"Emma Ruth Russo." The name rolled easily off her tongue. The Italian name she'd not been allowed to use for three years. And the borrowed first name she hoped they could not track.

"Your age?"

"Nineteen." She would be in a few weeks, anyway.

"And your family?" Mother Superior held a fountain pen poised over the paper. As soon as Ruth talked, the pen sprang to life, scratching her answers.

Ruth studied her hands. "I'm an orphan. My mother died when I was eleven. Papa was killed in an accident when I was young."

"Where were you born?"

"New York City. After my mother died, I lived with an aunt for a little while, but she barely earned enough to keep herself alive. So, she took me to the Children's Aid Society. I stayed there until they put me on an orphan train and brought me to Iowa. I was fifteen." Speaking aloud of the heartache of those years suddenly made old griefs resurface, and tears filled Ruth's eyes. She blinked hard and swallowed.

Mother Superior's blue eyes registered no compassion. She continued jabbing Ruth with questions. "Where is the father of the baby?"

Ruth's hands twisted in her lap. A tear spilled over and landed on her skirt. Her thumb rubbed at the spot. "He's dead."

Mother Superior's pen quivered, but she didn't write. "Cause of death?"

How could she continue these lies? Surely, she would trip up somewhere. Ruth blurted the first thing that came to her. "Polio. He contracted polio."

The questions were relentless. "And the father's family? Would they not support you?"

Ruth shook her head. "They're very poor people."

As the pen scratched again, Ruth sat up a little straighter. "I just need a place to live. I can work. I'll find a job."

Mother Superior sniffed just a tiny bit. "An employer would not hire someone in your condition, Emma. We will take you in. You may live here until you have given birth and recovered. You will work at the home and attend Mass at the cathedral on Sundays. We will try to find a suitable place for you after your baby is born and adopted. But you must live by the rules here at Sisters of Mercy."

Ruth shivered as a chill swept over her. "But—I don't want my baby to be adopted. I want to keep her—or him. I don't want her to be an orphan too."

Mother Superior's eyebrows drew together as she glared at Ruth. "That would not be the best choice for your baby. He deserves a home with both a mother and a father. You have no way of supporting yourself, let alone a child. I know you are upset and emotional right now. But in the coming months, you will see the foolishness of trying to keep the baby. Have you seen a doctor yet?"

Ruth shook her head. She couldn't speak.

"We will make an appointment with Doctor Osborne. He tends to all our mothers. When we know your due date, I will help you make a plan. Now, Sister Jean Marie will take you on a tour of our facility and instruct you on our house rules. And I will let the other sisters know you will be with us until your baby is born. Welcome to Sisters of Mercy."

When Mother Superior stood, she towered over Ruth, and her shoulders were as broad as many of the farmers around Grantsville. Ruth trembled but stood, arms folded across her middle, and followed the nun down the hall.

It was a relief to be with Sister Jean Marie. Ruth hurried to keep up as the tiny woman scurried up and down the halls and in and out of rooms in the mammoth old home. They saw almost every room, from the dank and dimly lit basement to the tiny bedrooms on the third floor, where mothers stayed after giving birth. In each area, Sister Jean Marie spouted so many dos and don'ts that Ruth's head began to hurt.

Sister Jean Marie guided Ruth through the kitchen with floor-to-ceiling cabinets, long counters, and a white enamel electric stove. One burner held a huge pot. A short girl with pretty waved hair stood over it, stirring the contents. She paused to greet Ruth with a shy "hello."

They concluded the tour in the dining room, where women lined up at a pass-through window into the kitchen to receive a bowl of soup. They carried the bowls to the table and set them beside a glass of water, a napkin, and a soup spoon already in place.

"Go ahead and get your lunch." Sister Jean Marie urged Ruth.

After receiving her steaming vegetable soup, Ruth sat at the table next to a woman she'd met the previous evening. Lydia had long freckled arms, dark red hair, and looked like she was ready to give birth any moment. "Hi. How was your meeting with Mother Superior?" Lydia whispered.

Ruth shook her head and whispered back. "I'll tell you later."

The nuns took their soup bowls to a separate table. Mother Superior went through the line last. When she set her bowl at her place, everyone stood while she prayed.

We don't have to worry about the soup being too hot to eat, thought Ruth, as Mother Superior finally concluded her prayer, and they sank to their chairs.

Lydia passed a basket of crackers to Ruth. "Will you be staying with us?"

"Yes. Until my baby is born." Ruth took four of the saltines and passed the basket across the table.

"Who are you rooming with?"

Sister Jean Marie had shown her the room, but she didn't know who the other bed belonged to. "It's the first bedroom on the right."

"Oh, that's my room." A short, round-faced girl with pale, limp hair extended a hand across the table. "I'm Doris."

Ruth set her spoon down and shook the proffered hand. "My name is Emma."

"Hi, Emma. And welcome to Sisters of Mercy. It will be good to have someone in the room again. My previous roommate left right after the birth. Her mother and father took her back home to Newton."

"And her baby?" Soup dribbled from Ruth's spoon as she waited for the answer.

"Oh. I suppose it was adopted. We never hear about the babies."

"You don't even know if it was a boy or girl?"

Doris gave a little shrug. "No. Sometimes a baby will stay here for a few days, and one of the nuns cares for it, but most of the time, babies go to their adoptive home right away."

Ruth ate the rest of her soup without talking, listening to the girls chatting around her. She watched as some of them stacked bowls and spoons on the counter at the pass-through window. How was she supposed to spend her afternoon? According to the house rules, everyone had chores, but none had been assigned to her yet.

She needn't have worried. When she stood, Sister Jean Marie appeared at her elbow. "Come, dear. I'm going to introduce you to Frances. She's the resident in charge of our cleaning crew and will show you what your duties will be."

She led Ruth to a tall, angular woman with a protruding belly. "Frances, this is Emma. She's been assigned to your crew. Please give her instructions and put her to work."

Sister Jean Marie patted Ruth's hand as one might pat a small child's. Somehow, Ruth didn't find it the least offensive. The nun smiled. "You'll do fine. I'm glad you're here." Then she darted across the dining room to another cluster of women.

Frances tossed her perfectly-styled waves of brown hair. "First day?"

Ruth nodded. "I came last night, but I had my interview with Mother Superior this morning."

"And you passed the inspection?" Frances's laugh was friendly. "When are you due?"

"I'm not sure. I haven't seen the doctor yet."

As she talked, Frances led her up the broad stairs to the second level. "I'm going to assign you the third floor. The girl who cleaned it moved out." She turned to look at Ruth. "I think you can handle it."

The third floor held five bedrooms—three for mothers who had delivered, and two for the nuns, sisters Jean Marie and Catherine. Mother Superior's bedroom was on the first floor, near the labor and birthing room. A large closet held cleaning rags, brooms, dust mops, rug beaters, and everything necessary to keep the third floor pristine. If the room was occupied by a resident, Ruth was not required to clean it. But sitting areas, hallways, the bathroom, and the nun's rooms must be cleaned daily. Some jobs, such as rug beating, would only need to be done weekly.

"So that's the lowdown. Do you have any questions?" Frances shifted from one foot to another, no doubt eager to get started on her own afternoon chores.

"When we finish, what do we do?"

"Oh, that's our own time. We can write letters home or do laundry or clean our rooms. There isn't much free time. Guess they don't want us to spend time thinking about how we ruined our lives." Frances shrugged and headed for the stairs. "I will inspect your work. If it isn't clean enough, I get into trouble as well as you. So, don't get me into trouble." Although her tone seemed friendly now, Ruth guessed Frances was the type she wouldn't want to cross.

Ruth pulled a duster off the shelf and headed to the empty room where she'd spent her first night. She'd moved her suitcase with its meager contents to the second-floor room she would share with Doris. Where the expectant mothers lived. She paused a moment with a hand on her barely rounding abdomen. The rollercoaster of events leading up to today had not given her many moments to consider. In a few short months, she would become a mother.

4

From far downstairs, the dinner bell clanged sharply. Ruth stowed the broom she'd been using in the closet and hurried down.

Frances stood behind her in the line at the window. "Did you finish?"

"All but the rugs. I should have time to do them tomorrow."

"Swell. I didn't know how I was going to get all that done. I'm glad you're here. So, what's your story, morning glory?"

Story? How could she answer? "I'm having a baby. My husband died."

"Oh?" Frances's eyebrow shot up. "You were married, then? What's that like?"

Ruth took a step as the line began to move. "We weren't married that long before he became ill." She turned and took the plate of meatloaf, corn, and mashed potatoes, hoping Frances's questions were over.

They weren't. Frances followed her to the table and set her

plate at the spot next to Ruth's. "What happened? How did he die?"

Ruth hung her head and mumbled. "Polio. He had polio. I don't like to talk about it." The first honest thing out of her mouth in the entire conversation.

"Oh. I'm sorry. I understand." Frances nodded and turned to the woman on her other side.

After Mother Superior's lengthy prayer, Ruth dug into the meatloaf, listening to the conversation ebb and flow around her but not joining in. The meal was delicious, and she'd not had to cook one thing. At the Schmidt's, cooking had been her first duty. Thelma, her foster mother, suffered from an illness that made her nauseated, so Ruth made breakfast before she left for school in the morning and an evening meal when she returned. Thelma's husband, Otto, complained that they didn't have the traditional large dinner at noon.

He seemed happy when Thelma's health deteriorated, and Ruth dropped out of school to care for her. Ruth's teacher, Miss Jones, had been disappointed that her best pupil couldn't continue her schooling, but not more so than the pupil herself. Ruth loved the interaction and competition with the other students at the country school. Especially the only other student in the upper grades, a boy one year older than her— Jack Meyer.

When a twitter of laughter surrounded her, Ruth looked up from her plate.

Frances gave her a nudge with her elbow. "Doris has been asking you a question, and you just kept on with your daydream."

"Sorry." Ruth used her napkin and dotted her mouth. "What did you ask, Doris?"

"Where did you live before you came to Sisters of Mercy?"

She just couldn't escape the web of lies she'd woven. "We had a small farm near Indianola."

As she turned back to her dinner, she could see Frances's eyebrows knitting together in a frown. Had she said something wrong?

Farther down the table, a woman who didn't look any more pregnant than Ruth stood and picked up her dishes. "Are you Emma? I'm Pearl. I think you're scheduled in the kitchen with me tonight."

Ruth bounced up, happy to leave the table and Frances's questions. She'd forgotten about mealtime duties. Sister Jean Marie had told her about the schedule posted beside the kitchen door, but she hadn't checked it. She followed Pearl into the kitchen and away from the interrogations.

Pearl and Ruth worked well together, washing and drying the dishes and putting things away. By the time they hung up the dishtowels, Ruth knew the outlay of the kitchen well. Best of all, Pearl kept up a steady stream of chatter about herself and asked no questions.

"That's it." Pearl turned off the kitchen light and closed the door. "I'm going to bed early. I'm not working any harder than I did in Ames, but I tire faster. Must be—" She looked down at her still flat abdomen.

Ruth nodded. "I'm ready for bed, too. What did you do in Ames?"

"I was a student at Iowa State College. The first in my family to graduate from high school. I wanted to design clothes. I messed that up." Pearl's lips tightened as if she were fighting tears, her blue eyes filled, but none spilled over. She turned and called, "Good night," as she fled up the stairs.

When Ruth entered her room, Doris sat at the small wooden desk writing what appeared to be a letter. She draped an arm across it as if she didn't want Ruth to see what she was writing.

Ruth opened her suitcase, pulled out a dress, and shook it, hoping the wrinkles would smooth away.

"My clothes are on the left in the closet," Doris spoke up. "You can hang yours on the right. And I kept the bottom drawer of the chest empty for you."

"Thanks," Ruth replied. As she hung the dresses in the closet and laid her underwear in the drawer, Doris's pen scratched across the paper again.

Ruth placed her worn nightgown on the chair and slid the suitcase under the bed. Then she put sheets on, tucking the bottom corners in tightly. The colorful crazy quilt went on last. As she smoothed it over, she wondered who had taken the time to put the many little pieces of fabric together and fasten them with such neat, tiny stitches.

With one last look at Doris, still working on her letter, Ruth draped her nightgown over her arm and went down the hall to the bathroom. She used the toilet, washed herself, brushed out her heavy dark curls, and put on her nightgown. When she came out of the bathroom, Frances waited outside.

Ruth nodded at her and smiled. "Good night."

Frances leaned close and whispered. "Not sure what you're hiding, but you didn't come from Indianola. It's not that big of a town, and there's never been any Russos there. Not an Italian anywhere near. The farmers are Dutch or German."

Ruth's breath caught in her throat and her face flushed. "Please, please, don't speak of it."

When Frances didn't answer, Ruth dashed down the hall and into her bedroom. She slid under the warm quilt and pulled it up to her nose. Not long after, Doris pulled the cord that turned off the light, but Ruth lay for a long time before sleep came.

Much later, she heard someone shout, "Emma! Emma!" When a hand shook her shoulder, Ruth opened her eyes. She panted like she'd been running and trembled all over.

Doris stood over her, a look of alarm on her face. "You were shouting in your sleep. You kept saying, 'No. No. Please go away.'"

Ruth propped up on her elbow. "I'm sorry for waking you. I had a bad dream."

"It must have been a nightmare, the way you were carrying on. You really sounded frightened. Scared me to death. You okay now?"

"I'm fine. I hope you can go back to sleep." Ruth lay back on her pillow and tried to calm her trembling body.

Doris climbed into the twin bed against the wall opposite Ruth's. "I can always sleep. Night," she called cheerfully as she pulled her quilt up and rolled over.

Ruth closed her eyes, but she fought to stay awake. She didn't want to dream again.

5

R uth stirred her tea, wishing for a cup of steaming, strong coffee. Mother Superior didn't believe coffee was good for anyone, especially pregnant women. After Doris woke her from her dream, she'd eventually fallen into a fitful sleep, tossing and turning until the morning bell sounded. She and Doris had dressed and made their beds without much conversation.

Ruth scraped up the last bite of oatmeal. She no longer had any traces of morning sickness and instead felt constantly hungry. She stacked and carried her dishes to the window. She'd get an early start cleaning the third floor.

"Emma, dear," Sister Jean Marie called from the nun's table.

Ruth walked over, hoping the summons didn't mean she'd broken a rule. "Yes, Sister?"

"Doctor Osborne will be here at nine today. You will be his first appointment, so be in the health and delivery wing a few minutes before then."

"Yes. I'll be there." Ruth felt a flutter of excitement. The doctor could tell her when the tiny baby growing inside her would be born. She hurried up the stairs. An hour before her appointment would be enough time to get at least one room cleaned.

Shortly after nine, Ruth sat facing a man who looked like he should be handing out candy canes or Christmas presents. A bush of white hair, a well-trimmed white beard, and a short, portly physique all reminded her of the drawings she'd seen depicting Santa Claus. He even had a little ho-ho chuckle as he introduced himself.

He asked her many of the same questions the nuns had, and she hoped she gave the same answers. She'd been married, her husband had died, and there was no one to take care of her. At least the last one was true.

"And Mrs. Russo, what was the date of your last menstrual cycle?"

For a brief moment, Ruth wondered who Mrs. Russo was. Then, when she realized it was her, she frowned as she tried to remember. "The spring. Sometime in the spring. Maybe May? No. The morning we were planting corn in the far field, I woke up feeling ill. I thought I wouldn't be able to drive the team. Then after some crackers and tea, I was fine. I think that's when I first thought I might be—expecting. So, my last cycle must have been in April some time."

Dr. Osborne watched her intently. Then, he scribbled more notes. He pulled out a well-worn paper with what appeared to be a chart. His finger traced a line, then he looked up at her and smiled. "Well, Mrs. Russo, it looks like you will deliver in January. Maybe the last week. Sometimes first babies are stubborn, though. They might come early, they might come late. What are your plans after you deliver?"

Ruth sat up straighter. "To raise my baby. I plan on getting a job and supporting both of us. Maybe here in Des Moines. Maybe Ames."

Dr. Osborne's bushy white eyebrows rose. "You plan on keeping the child? Does Mother Superior know?"

Ruth slumped again. "I told her. She doesn't approve."

Dr. Osborne's face lost the jolly Santa look. His eyebrows bushed together. "It would be a hard thing to do. There are not many job opportunities for a woman with a child. Is there no family anywhere?"

Ruth shook her head, looking at the threadbare skirt of her dress. "My mother died when I was eleven. I came from New York on an orphan train when I was fifteen."

Dr. Osborne glanced at his notes. "You lived with your husband on a farm near Indianola? Is that where you lived before you were married?"

The doctor's gentle demeanor had been an ambush. She'd talked herself into a trap. She nodded and whispered, "Yes," praying the questions would cease.

Dr. Osborne didn't respond until she looked up. "I feel that I am not getting the whole story here. I understand that you may be protecting someone, even yourself. But—the sisters who work here can't help you go forward without knowing the truth, and neither can I. As your doctor, I want you to know that what you say remains confidential. So, if you want to talk, I will listen."

Tears filled Ruth's eyes, and for a moment she was tempted to tell the kind man everything, starting with the moment the Schmidts walked up to the stage at the operahouse in Grantsville and promised her a home. Then, the shame of it all washed over her again, and she knew she could not share her story with anyone. Ever. "Thanks." She blinked away tears, looked up, and tried to smile at him.

Dr. Osborne set Ruth's chart to one side. "You appear to be

in good health and should have no problems in your pregnancy. Get plenty of rest and eat the good food provided. If you have questions or anything unusual happens, talk to Sister Jean Marie, and we'll set up another appointment. Otherwise, I will put you on the schedule for your next appointment in October."

Ruth nodded and left his office to finish her cleaning chores.

At supper that evening, Ruth sat next to Pearl. Dr. Osborne had told her to eat. She would have no problem with this plate of chicken and mashed potatoes and the slices of pie on the buffet.

After Mother Superior's prayer, Ruth asked Pearl, "No kitchen duty tonight?"

"No. It looks like you and I are every other night this week. Share the fun, you know."

Ruth felt like conversing. It had been a long time since she'd been around others her age, and she hardly knew what to say. The usual first topic at the dinner table—where you were from—was not one she wanted to broach. Fantasizing would be safe. "If you weren't here, what would you want to do tonight?"

Pearl smiled broadly, showing a dimple in one cheek. "I'd go to the closest wingding and dance the night away. I miss dancing. Of course, if I had stayed away from the dances and out of the coupes, I might not have this problem." She glanced down at her belly.

Ruth giggled a little. "I've never been to a dance for young people. I went to a barn raising once, and we all square danced in the barn that night. It was fun."

"Oh, you should try the turkey trot. Now that's what I call fun. Square dancing is for the old folks. When this is all over, we can go to a dance. Where are you going to live after you deliver?"

Ruth shrugged. "Maybe in Des Moines. The capital city. I can't believe I'm here. I'll need to find a job, though."

Margaret, across the table from Ruth, leaned forward. "I work in Des Moines. I mean, I did. I worked for the Hamiltons on Grand Avenue."

Ruth swallowed another spoonful of mashed potatoes. "What did you do?"

Margaret grimaced. "Everything. I kept the house running. I cleaned, I cooked, I did the washing, and I watched the baby. All the rich people need girls. Then they can go play golf or shop or visit."

Ruth's spoon rested against the chicken wing on her plate. She could do that kind of work. She'd been running a farmhouse for over three years. She'd cooked, she'd cleaned—as well as milking, taking care of the animals, tending crops in the fields, and a multitude of other tasks. Caring for a home in Des Moines actually sounded easier. But would anyone hire a woman with a baby?

Pearl leaned close and asked in a hushed tone, "Do you have plans after dinner?"

Ruth turned to look at her. "I was going to hand-wash some of my clothes."

Pearl's little nose wrinkled. "Doll, you need to learn how kick up your heels a bit. Lydia has a deck of cards. We can play a few games. We take turns watching for the nuns, but they usually don't come to the second floor."

Ruth hesitated. She didn't want to do anything that would jeopardize her stay here. She had no other options. But an evening playing games sounded like fun. "What would they do if they caught you?"

Pearl shrugged. "Probably take away a privilege or give us

extra chores. We would have to go to confession for sure. We are supposed to use our evenings to read, study, do something to improve our lives." Pearl stood and picked up her dishes. "Our room is at the end of the hall on the right. See you later." She winked and left.

Ruth finished her dinner in silence. She didn't want to get into trouble, but she longed to have a friend. And Pearl was bubbly and fun. She chewed the last bit of chicken off the wing, stood, and took her dishes to the window. Then she headed upstairs.

She had no trouble finding Pearl and Lydia's room. Bits of conversation and laughter floated down the hall. It looked like almost everyone had gathered there. Frances, Margaret, Evelyn, and Mildred were seated on the floor with a deck of Flinch cards. Lydia and a girl Ruth hadn't yet met had cards spread out on the bed with piles of buttons. Pearl was obviously standing watch by the door. She smiled when she saw Ruth. "Come on in. The wingding's here. Glad you could come."

Several girls looked up and greeted her. Margaret scooted over and made a place for her on the floor. "You can take my place in Flinch as soon as this game is over. Do you know how to play?"

"No." Ruth stepped back.

"Sit down. It's easy. I'll teach you." Margaret explained the purpose of the game—to be the first to empty the Flinch pile. While she was busy explaining, Frances hollered, "Flinch!"

Margaret protested. "Not fair. I was explaining the game to Emma." But she took the penalty card and put it at the bottom of her pile. Within a few more rounds, Frances won the game and gathered the cards to reshuffle them.

Lydia asked from her perch on the bed. "Any of you want to switch and join the poker game?"

Pearl responded. "No, I couldn't risk losing any more buttons." The girls roared with laughter.

Ruth played Flinch and talked and laughed until nearly ten o'clock. Finally, Pearl, who had quit standing guard and joined the Flinch game, yawned. "Hey, the morning bell will come all too soon. Maybe we better retire."

Ruth helped gather the Flinch cards and store them inside a cloth bag Lydia hung in her closet. "Good night, everyone," she called softly as she made her way down the hall to her room. Doris was already in bed and looked like she was asleep. Ruth undressed quietly in the dark, slid her nightgown over her head, and slipped into her bed.

The conversation and laughter had chased away any thoughts of sleep. She was grateful the girls' chatter had simply been silly and not full of questions. Ruth had loved the card games and saw nothing wrong with them. Why did the nuns object? Having fun with other girls her age certainly did improve her life.

6

The bell for breakfast broke through Ruth's gray drowsiness. She yawned and propped herself up on her elbows. Doris was dressing quietly by her bed.

"What time is it?"

"Six." She whispered as if Ruth were still asleep.

"Why did the breakfast bell ring so early?"

"It's Sunday. We go to Mass."

Ruth sat up and pushed her hair out of her eyes. "I don't think I've ever been to Mass. What's it like?"

"A lot of sitting, standing, and kneeling."

Ruth tossed the quilt aside and slid out of bed. Then she turned and pulled up the covers, tugging until the bed appeared smooth and neat. She took a clean dress from the hook and slipped out of her nightgown and into her clothes.

After using the bathroom, she joined the other girls as they streamed downstairs to the dining room. Only cereal and milk were served. They had a choice between cornflakes, shredded wheat, and one Ruth had never tried, Rice Krispies. She read the information on the front of the box, then poured a small amount into her bowl.

Sister Catherine was the only nun with them, and her prayer was brief. Perhaps because of the early hour, the conversation at the table seemed subdued, and Ruth finished her bowl of the strange, crackling cereal without talking.

Another bell rang. Before Ruth could ask what it was for, the girls at the table took their dishes to the kitchen and lined up behind Sister Catherine in the hall. Ruth followed Doris as they marched down the hall and out a back door that Ruth hadn't known existed. A narrow gravel path led through the yard and to the stone church Ruth had noticed the day she arrived. The group entered the sanctuary by a side door and followed Sister Catherine to a pew at the very back. A few heads turned and watched as they entered, but most people kept their eyes to the front. Mother Superior and Sister Jean Marie sat on the opposite side of the church.

Ruth blinked as her eyes adjusted to the church's dim interior. Sunlight shone on the stained-glass windows, but did little to dispel the shadows in the cavernous room. A huge cross bearing the figure of Jesus dominated the front wall. An ornate table draped with white cloths stretched across the raised stage. And everywhere, candles cast flickering light over the dark wooden pews and floor.

Ruth breathed in deeply. The sanctuary smelled of wood polish, warm candles, and a sweet fragrance she couldn't quite identify. Although slightly nervous about behaving properly in this unfamiliar setting, she relaxed. It felt good to sit and be still.

Sister Catherine passed a few worn books down the row. Doris handed one to Ruth and whispered, "This is the missal, if you want to follow along."

A white-robed priest entered from a door at the front. A

dark-green, shorter robe draped about his shoulders, and he carried a gold cross in his hand. He walked to the front of the table and knelt for a moment before turning to the congregation.

When he first spoke, Ruth thought something was wrong with her hearing. She could understand nothing. After hearing a few more sentences, she realized he spoke in a foreign language. She glanced at the other girls, but none seemed startled. She thumbed through the missal, but was lost already.

Suddenly everyone around her knelt on the cushioned platform at their feet. By the time Ruth gathered her skirt and knelt, the people stood and chanted something undecipherable—maybe the same language the priest used.

Ruth flipped through the book again to see what they were saying, and the people sat. For the rest of the Mass, Ruth fumbled her way through, always one step behind and feeling miserably embarrassed. At one point, Margaret and Lydia stood, along with most of the other people in the congregation, and walked to the table in the front. Ruth looked at Sister Catherine, but she shook her head at Ruth before rising and going to the table herself. The priest offered each one something to eat from a gold tray and gave them a drink from a cup. They must be taking communion.

Finally, the priest spoke in English, and they sat down. He talked about the need to be cleansed of sin through confession, repentance, and absolution. Ruth bowed her head. If she'd felt uncomfortable before, this man's words really made her squirm. She glanced down the row at the other residents of Sisters of Mercy Home for Unwed Mothers. Each of them wore their disgrace in the form of a protruding belly. No need to confess—their sin was evident. Waves of shame blocked the meaning of any further words from the priest.

At last, there was a final prayer and the congregation drifted to the aisles, greeting one another. Talk and laughter floated over the pews.

Sister Catherine gathered up the missals before leading the girls through the side door back to their temporary lodging. No one acknowledged them. When they stepped through the door of the Home, the church felt miles away.

The lunch of bean soup warmed not only their stomachs but the atmosphere at the table as well, and the women chatted and joked.

During a lull in the conversation, Ruth asked, "How do you figure out what to do in the Mass?"

Margaret laid down her spoon and turned blue eyes toward Ruth. "You must not be Catholic?"

Ruth shook her head. "I don't think so. I don't know. Maybe my mother was, but she died when I was young."

Margaret brushed frizzy brown hair out of her eyes. "Just keep following what everyone else does, and you'll get the hang of it. The Mass is the same every week. Did Sister Catherine give you a missal to look at?"

"Yes, but I got lost and couldn't find my place, so it was no help."

"I'll sit by you next week and show you how to read the English when the priest is speaking Latin. It makes the service so much more meaningful. I love Mass. It keeps my mind focused on God's goodness instead of my mistakes."

Ruth smiled. "Thanks. That's kind of you." She ate the rest of her soup in silence. If she wasn't Catholic, what was she?

When she was very little, her mother prayed with her and read from the Bible that Ruth still had tucked away in her suitcase under the bed. Her aunt may have taken her to Mass once, but she only lived with her a short time. Thelma Schmidt took her to the small country church near their farm a few times. But when Thelma's illness made the walk too difficult for her, they stopped going. Ruth would not leave Thelma, and Otto refused to harness the horse for church. He said even an animal deserved a day off.

She glanced down. Maybe the priest was right, she should confess her sin. But if she didn't belong to a church, how did she contact God?

7

R uth woke to moaning outside her door. For a brief moment, she thought she was back in the farmhouse, and Otto was outside her door with a hangover. Fear swept over her, and her entire body tensed before she remembered she was safe with the Sisters of Mercy. She slipped out of bed and pushed open the door.

Pearl half-carried, half-dragged a whimpering Lydia down the hall. Lydia held one hand on her belly while the other arm was draped around Pearl's neck.

"Emma!" Pearl looked relieved to see her.

"What's wrong?" Ruth stepped out into the hall.

"It's her time. Help me take her to the birthing wing. Then we can go get one of the sisters."

"I only have my nightgown on."

"For heaven's sake," Pearl sputtered. "This is not a time to be modest. Lydia needs our help."

"Ohhh …" Lydia clutched her belly and doubled over, nearly falling to the floor.

Ruth hurried to Lydia's other side and lifted her free arm

around her shoulders. Slowly, the trio made their way down the stairs to the first floor and turned right. When Lydia stopped again for a contraction, Ruth ran ahead and held open the door. By the time they got Lydia to the room, Sister Catherine had appeared. She helped Lydia to the bed. Then, from a closet, she took out a gown that fastened with ties only at the back of the neck.

She looked up briefly at Pearl and Ruth. "Please wait in the hall while I help her change."

They stepped into the hall and waited without speaking. Pearl was wide-eyed and flushed from the effort to help Lydia, and Ruth knew she must be too.

Sister Catherine closed the door as she came out into the hall. "Thank you for helping her get down to the birthing room. Has she been having contractions for long?"

Pearl's cheerful face frowned in thought. "I don't think so. She woke me up moaning. And I walked her down the stairs." She looked at Ruth and smiled. "Emma heard us and came out to help. It was maybe fifteen minutes ago. But I don't know how long Lydia was awake."

Another loud groan sounded from behind the closed door. Ruth wished she dared cover her ears like a child. "Will she be okay?"

Sister Catherine smiled at her. "She'll be fine, but she has several hours of hard work ahead of her. And then we'll have another sweet baby."

Someone would have a sweet baby, but it would not be Lydia.

Ruth glanced down at her nightgown. "I need to go dress before the breakfast bell rings."

"Good idea." Pearl turned to Sister Catherine. "Will you let us know how she is?"

"Certainly." The sister stepped quietly inside the birthing room, firmly closing the door behind her.

By the time the breakfast bell sounded, everyone knew that Lydia was in labor. As the girls took their plates and sat, the impending birth became the topic of conversation. Everyone liked Lydia. But, after today, she would move to the third floor, and then, in a few days, she would leave Sisters of Mercy to resume her life.

"Is she going back to Iowa City?" Margaret asked as she dipped her spoon into the oatmeal.

"No. I don't believe so." Pearl answered. "Her parents don't want anything to do with her. I think she's going to try for a job here in Des Moines. She's applied for a room at the YWCA."

Ruth listened, but didn't join in the conversation. Her questions were of a much different variety. What was happening down the hall? She'd never been present at a human birth. She'd helped Otto last spring when a cow had a difficult time birthing. He made her stick her arm clear inside the cow, take hold of the calf's hooves, and pull him out. He said her arm was smaller than his. She hoped the doctor didn't have to do that to Lydia.

She wondered what it would be like if her mother hadn't died, and an aching wave of grief passed over her. A mother would explain birthing to her daughter, and she would be present when her time came. But if her mother were still alive, Ruth would not even be in Iowa with an overwhelming burden of shame.

"I wouldn't go back to my hometown, either. It would be hard to explain." Lilian, a quiet girl with a dark complexion and curly brown hair, spoke up.

Doris leaned forward. "I'm supposedly visiting my dad's sister, my Aunt Vivian. I want to go on to college, so moving back to my parents' home makes sense."

Frances, who sat across from Doris, suddenly turned and looked at Ruth, and her eyes narrowed. "How about you, Emma? Are you moving back to Indianola? What street do you live on?"

Ruth froze, only her heart bumping inside her chest. She slowly lowered her spoon to the bowl and looked around the table. No one knew. No one suspected she was caught in an immense web of lies.

"I think I'd like to stay in Des Moines, but I haven't made a decision yet."

The conversation continued to swirl around her, but Ruth took her dishes to the window and went upstairs to clean the third floor. She needed to get a room ready for Lydia.

At supper that night, the only news of Lydia was that she was "progressing well," according to Sister Jean Marie. The talk moved from Lydia to the possible repeal of Prohibition. Frances and Mildred were arguing over the dangers of alcohol. Frances maintained that a repeal of the 18th Amendment would make things safer, as people wouldn't break the law to get the drink they craved. Mildred pontificated on the consequences of being an alcoholic and the people hurt by chronic alcohol dependency.

The two girls' voices got higher and louder until a frown from the nuns' table elicited several "Shhhhs" from the other girls. Mildred resumed eating, but Frances turned to Ruth. "So, what are your feelings on Prohibition?"

Ruth shook her head. "I don't know. I haven't been around drinking much." She knew Otto had kept bottles in the barn, but she didn't know how or where he obtained them. He often came into the house smelling strongly of alcohol, and those were the nights Ruth hid in her bedroom, hoping he would pass out on the couch and not come to her room. Sometimes he woke with a hangover, but he didn't lie on the street the way the drunks in New York City did.

Frances snorted. "Of course, but who could believe anything you say? You said you lived in Indianola, and I know that's a lie."

Ruth's face flamed warmer than the slice of ham on her plate. Most of the girls weren't listening, but Mildred laid her fork on her plate and looked at her curiously as she wiped her mouth with a napkin.

"Please, Frances," Ruth pleaded. "Can we just not talk about it?"

Frances smiled triumphantly as she looked around at the other girls. "See? I knew she was lying. Why not talk about it, huh, Emma?"

Tears pooled in Ruth's eyes and a feeling of utter panic arose. Where could she run to? She was trapped.

Pearl, sitting beside Frances, nudged her arm. "Leave Emma alone. We all have our secrets."

"Not with each other. We don't keep secrets on second floor." Frances stood, and with a last hard look at Ruth, grabbed her dishes and left.

Pearl scooted down. "Don't pay her any mind. She's moody these days."

Ruth gave Pearl a grateful look, sniffed back tears, and finished her meal in silence.

She and Doris were in their room when Sister Jean Marie rang the bell to summon everyone. When they were all downstairs, she delivered the news. "Lydia has delivered a healthy baby boy. She is doing well and will probably be moved to the third floor tomorrow. Please pray for her healing from childbirth and that the parents of the baby will raise him in a godly home."

8

Two days later, Sister Jean Marie stopped at the breakfast table and asked to speak to Ruth privately. Swallowing feelings of dread, Ruth followed her to the room used primarily as Mother Superior's office.

Sister Jean Marie sat in a straight-back wooden chair on one side of the desk, Ruth sat opposite. The desk held tidy piles of official-looking papers, a typewriter, and a large, worn Bible. A telephone, which was to be used only by the nuns or for an approved emergency call, hung on the wall.

Sister Jean Marie gave Ruth a rather tight, little smile. "This is a conversation I'd rather not have."

Ruth's heart plummeted. She felt as vulnerable as that fifteen-year-old who stepped off the train three years ago into an unknown world called Iowa.

Sister Jean Marie twisted a handkerchief in her lap. She seemed so nervous Ruth almost felt sorry for her.

"Frances tells me that you are shirking your duties on the third floor. The bathroom has not been cleaned and she has had to clean some of the bedrooms herself. Is this true?"

Ruth opened her mouth, ready to protest. She kept the third floor spotless. Frances had nothing to say but praise when she checked her work. But she hung her head, staring at a stain on her skirt. If she called Frances a liar, Frances could come back and prove that Ruth had lied. She felt the tentacles of the lies wrap around her, squeezing the breath from her lungs.

She pressed her hand to her mouth and sat, unable to move, her surging emotions nearly overwhelming her.

"Emma? What do you have to say about this?"

Finally, she found her voice. "I can do better. Please give me another chance."

Sister Jean Marie's tight smile loosened into one that was more real. "Yes, of course we will give you another chance. You must realize that we're a large group here, and we all need to do our share, willingly, as if we were working for the Lord. Which we are, of course. This is His home and His work. Talk with Frances and find out what you need to do to improve. She's a good teacher, I'm certain she will be able to help you perform satisfactorily."

"Thank you, Sister. I do want to do a good job."

As soon as Sister Jean Marie said, "You may go now," Ruth fled the office. Instead of going immediately to the third floor to begin cleaning, she stopped at the room she shared with Doris. They'd made the beds, swept the floors and dusted the furniture before going down to breakfast. Ruth paced between the beds. How could she get out of this trap? When she left Grantsville, her only thought was to escape. Now her sanctuary had become a trap, and her safety was threatened.

She had to confront Frances. She knew Frances's routine never wavered. She began her day supervising those cleaning the kitchen. What that looked like was Frances drinking one more cup of tea while watching those on kitchen duty scrub sinks, counters, and floors.

Ruth trooped back downstairs. Because she'd met with Sister Jean Marie, she was now almost an hour late to begin cleaning. If she didn't hurry, she really could be accused of doing a poor job.

In the kitchen, Frances munched on a left-over piece of toast while Margaret scrubbed out a large pot used for cooking oatmeal. Doris knelt on the floor with a bucket and a scrub brush.

"May I speak with you?" Ruth kept her voice even and polite, even though she felt like screaming.

Frances smirked. "Well, if it isn't the pregnant girl from Indianola. Sure, I'll talk to you. What do you want?"

Ruth glanced at the two other girls in the kitchen who had stopped mid-scrub to stare at her and Frances. "Let's go into the dining room," she suggested.

Frances followed Ruth to the dining room and slouched in a chair, reaching down to rub one leg. "Darn kid, making my legs swell."

Ruth remained standing. "What can I do to get you to lay off? What you said to Sister Jean Marie isn't true, and you know it."

Frances shrugged. "What you told all of us isn't true either."

"I had my reasons for saying what I did. Can't you just accept that?"

"Well, I might be able to. What are you willing to do?"

"Anything." Ruth blurted an answer without thinking.

Frances's eyebrows raised. After a moment of thought, she leaned forward. "I want you to clean the office, Mother Superior's room, and the dining room downstairs."

That isn't fair! Ruth wanted to scream. Those were the main areas that Frances cleaned, and now Ruth had to do them in addition to the third floor? But if Frances would shut up about Indianola, it would be worth it.

Ruth nodded. "Okay. And you won't ever say another word about my lies—about living in Indianola or about my 'husband'? And you'll tell Sister Jean Marie that my work has improved and is now quite satisfactory?"

Frances sighed. "Yeah. I can do that. Just make sure you do a good job on the rooms downstairs. The nuns really look at those."

And what was Frances going to do while Ruth did her own work and most of Frances's as well? It didn't matter. She trudged up to the third floor and started cleaning. She was glad the weariness of the first trimester was over. A job kept the body busy and the mind from working overtime.

As Ruth put the dust mop away, she heard the bell ring for supper. If she took time to wash up or comb her hair before going to the dining room, she'd be late. The nuns frowned on that. She closed the closet door, tucked stray curls behind her ears, and hurried downstairs.

The stew Doris ladled out in large bowls smelled delicious. Someone had baked bread today, and thick slices were stacked on plates on the tables.

"This looks wonderful," Ruth commented as she carried her plate to the table. She intentionally took a seat by Pearl and far from Frances at the end. Frances had been first in line for supper, and she seemed to be sporting new pink nail polish.

Pearl had news. "Lydia has been moved to the third floor. I got to see her, and she's doing fine. The—the delivery went well. No complications."

Evelyn, a tiny girl who had just arrived the day before, asked, "How did they get her up all those stairs?"

"There's an elevator clear at the end of the hall. It's a

creepy, clanky old thing, and we're not allowed to use it, but it helps get girls who have delivered up to the third floor where they can recover."

"Where's her baby boy?" Ruth asked.

Pearl shrugged like it didn't matter. "He's probably gone to his new family. Unless he's with one of the nuns or Doctor Osborne is still checking him out."

"We never even got to see him." Ruth stirred the vegetables in her bowl.

"Oh, that's not allowed." Pearl dipped her bread into the stew and chewed it thoughtfully.

During the remainder of the meal, Pearl and Ruth talked about Pearl's upcoming visit from her mother and father. Evelyn, who sat across from them, shared that she was from Missouri. She'd traveled to Des Moines by bus to live with an aunt, but the aunt could not take her in and had dropped her at the Sisters of Mercy instead.

Before taking her dishes, Pearl stopped and whispered in Ruth's ear, "Card games tonight in my room. We have more space now that Lydia's gone."

Ruth nodded. "I'll try to come."

When she entered her room, Doris was already writing a letter, her ink pen scratching on the paper as she leaned over it and smiled.

"You certainly write a lot of letters." Ruth lay back on her bed, suddenly feeling weary.

Doris swiveled in her chair to look at her. "It's how I keep in touch."

"Who do you write?"

"My mom and dad. Sometimes I write my little sister, too. She likes to get one addressed just to her. And I write Thomas."

Ruth sat up. "Thomas?"

Doris's eyes filled with tears and her voice dropped to a whisper. "He's the father of my baby."

"Why didn't you marry him?"

"We wanted to get married. My father wouldn't allow it. Thomas says he'll wait for me. I'll turn eighteen in six months. And then maybe we'll run away and get married." Doris's hand flew to her mouth as if she'd said more than she intended.

Ruth tried to put her at ease. "I would never break your confidence."

Doris's head snapped up. "Or I yours. I don't care if you lived in Indianola or Timbuktu before you came here. I'm just glad you're my roommate." She shuffled around under the desk for a minute and then emerged clutching a magazine. "I have the September issue of *Ladies Home Journal*. Would you like to read it with me?"

Later, when Doris pulled the cord to turn out the light, Ruth remembered she'd been invited to play cards. She'd never gone down to Pearl's room. And she wasn't even disappointed.

9

Ruth settled into a routine. If she worked efficiently, she could clean all her rooms and the extra rooms Frances had given her before supper. It meant she couldn't rest as most of the women did after the noon meal, but she wasn't tired anyway. She spent evenings in her room, visiting with Doris and reading or playing games. Doris had found an old Uncle Wiggily game and a worn copy of *Black Beauty* in the closet in the dining room.

They always turned out the lights early. But sometimes they talked in the dark until one or both of them fell asleep. Doris loved to talk about her family and Thomas—what life had been like before she arrived at Sisters of Mercy. Ruth shared nothing of her life on the farm, choosing instead to listen to Doris or talk about what they would do after their babies were born.

Frances kept a cool, polite distance. When Ruth confronted her once, she reluctantly agreed that the rooms were cleaned well and promised to inform Sister Jean Marie that Emma was doing an adequate job. Ruth knew Frances had kept her word when Sister Jean Marie stopped her after breakfast one morning and complimented her on her "vastly improved performance."

Monday mornings were the hardest. The beds had to be stripped and clean sheets put on. As Ruth carried a bundle of dirty sheets to the stairs, she heard a sound in the bedroom where Lydia was recovering. She stopped and listened. Muffled sobs came from behind the closed door.

Should she get one of the nuns? Ask if she could help? She dropped the wad of bedding at the top of the stairs, knocked softly on Lydia's door, and entered. Lydia lay under the covers, her face buried in the pillow, crying.

Ruth took a step toward the bed. "Lydia? Is something wrong? Are you in pain? Shall I get Sister Jean Marie?"

Lydia did not lift her head. "No. I'll be okay." Another hiccupping sob.

Ruth stood still, not knowing whether to offer comfort or solitude. Then she stepped toward the bed and patted Lydia's back. "I'm a good listener."

Lydia rolled to face Ruth. "I never knew it would be so hard," she whispered.

"What?" Ruth thought of how Lydia had moaned and cried out in pain. "The labor?"

"No. The labor wasn't that bad. Don't let that scare you. But I miss my baby. He was so little and—and he had red hair, like mine."

Ruth swallowed her urge to sob along with Lydia. "The nuns found a good home for him. He'll have a mother and a father."

"But he was *mine*. He belonged to me. And I just turned my back and let them take him away."

Ruth patted Lydia again, little massaging pats she hoped were comforting. "You're young. You'll fall in love, get married and have a whole passel of kids." As Ruth spoke, she wondered if this would be true.

Lydia propped up on her elbow. "Yes. That might happen. But I will always miss this one. He'll always be my first."

Ruth turned her head, so Lydia wouldn't see the tears that had sprung to her own eyes. "I need to get back to my cleaning. It's the day to change bedding. Your bed doesn't need changed since you just came upstairs yesterday, but I'll come back later to see how you are and if you need anything."

She closed Lydia's door softly behind her. She leaned against the wall for a moment, but didn't hear any more crying. As she carried the dirty bedding downstairs to the basement, she resolved to have a conversation with Sister Jean Marie. The nuns needed to know she was determined to keep her baby. She would not be the woman lying in bed, consumed with grief, five days after giving birth.

At lunch, Ruth sat next to Pearl. "I saw Lydia this morning."

Pearl lifted the bread and scrutinized the contents of her sandwich. She pulled a pickle out and laid it on her plate. "How much longer until they use up that jar of donated pickles? They put them on everything. So, how is she? Ready to go?"

"She was really sad."

"About what?" Pearl took a big bite of her sandwich.

"Giving up her baby."

"You're kidding, right?"

Ruth shook her head. "No, I'm not."

"She's free. She can go back to Iowa City or stay in Des Moines and start her life again like nothing happened. Just a few months gone from her life. I'm not gonna be sad when this is all over."

Ruth put her sandwich back on her plate. "The baby grows

inside of you, is a part of you, for nine months, and you won't miss him even just a little?"

Pearl's mouth tightened into a firm line. "No. Not even a little. I've got big plans, and a baby would ruin everything. I'm grateful the sisters are finding a good home for it. I'm not ready to be a mother. Hey, we've missed you at cards. Coming tonight?"

Ruth shrugged. "Not sure. Is Doris welcome?"

"Well, yeah. We don't turn anyone away. But she won't come. She thinks cards are the devil's game."

Ruth finished her sandwich. She had to get busy or she'd still be cleaning after supper, not playing cards with the other girls or a game with Doris.

That night, when she got upstairs, Doris was writing—probably another letter to Thomas.

"Pearl invited me down to her room to play cards."

Doris laid down her fountain pen and looked at Ruth. "Well, go if you want."

Ruth hesitated, leaning against the door frame. "Why don't you come with me?"

Doris shook her head and laughed. "Even if I thought playing cards was okay, I'd feel my mama's eyes on me and never get over the shame." Her eyes dropped to her belly, and she sighed. "As if I don't already have enough to be ashamed of."

Ruth took one step inside the room. "You believe in God, don't you? Won't He forgive you?"

Doris's eyes were large in the glow of the hanging electric light. "I don't know."

"The nuns teach us about penance. Isn't there something you can do to make it up to God? You know, confess and say some Hail Marys or something?"

Doris frowned, one hand toying with the edge of her paper.

"I'm not sure. I'm not Catholic, and my pastor doesn't talk about what to do if you make a big mistake. He just talks about how we're not to make them. Righteous living, he calls it."

Just then, Pearl stuck her head in the door. "Are you coming, Emma?"

"Yeah, I'll be there in a minute." She asked Doris, "Sure you don't mind if I go?"

"Of course not. We're not married." Doris picked up her pen and turned back to her letter.

Ruth walked down the hall. She didn't know God very well, but she couldn't imagine that He would think having a baby was unforgivable. She wished she could ask someone about it.

In Pearl's room, they were just forming groups. Frances and Pearl began a poker game with buttons as the stakes. Margaret shuffled the Flinch cards. Ruth joined her and Lilian sitting on Lydia's former bed. While Margaret dealt the cards, Ruth remarked, "Lydia said to tell all of you hi. I think they're going to let her get out of bed tomorrow and walk a little. She can't come downstairs yet for meals, but she's healing."

Frances looked up from her handful of cards. "Lucky gal. She's got it all over with and now she can live it up." Her voice dropped to a whisper. "No more being told what to do."

Pearl giggled. "Or being forced to go to confession."

Margaret chimed in. "And doing penance."

Frances chuckled. "Like any of us actually do those silly prayers."

Pearl laid down her cards and grabbed the pile of buttons to add to her stash. "I bet Doris does."

Ruth's stomach tightened, but she didn't respond. After winning the first hand of Flinch, she yawned and stood. "Guess I better turn in for the night. Seems like I need to sleep more."

Margaret nodded. "Approaching the third trimester. You'll be getting swollen ankles and night sweats and sore ribs."

"Great. I can't wait." Ruth laughed. "Good night, everyone."

Instead of going directly to her room, she climbed the stairs to the third floor and knocked softly on Lydia's door.

"Come in," Lydia called. She sat up in bed, a book open on her lap. Although she smiled, her eyes were red and swollen.

"Just came to see if you needed anything." Ruth hesitated in the doorway.

"No. I'm okay. I read until I get sleepy." Lydia smiled, but it didn't reach her eyes. "Thanks, Emma."

Ruth trudged downstairs. Before crawling under her blankets, she sat on the bed and bowed her head. She wasn't sure if she said the correct words or not, but she prayed for Lydia's comfort. Her penance seemed heavy.

10

Ruth tried again, but she could no longer button her dress. The fabric would not stretch around her middle. She pulled out an apron, slipped it around her neck, and tied the strings in the back. At least she was covered.

After breakfast, she stood politely by the nun's table until Sister Jean Marie stood and carried her plate to the window. When she noticed Ruth, she asked, "Did you want something, Emma?"

"Yes. I have a request."

"Let's go to the office, and we can talk." Sister Jean Marie set out briskly, and Ruth hurried to catch up. In the small room, Sister Jean Marie sat behind the desk and folded her hands neatly on the polished wood surface.

Ruth stood, tugging at the apron so her gaping dress underneath didn't show. "My clothes don't fit me anymore."

"Have you checked in the donations closet? There might be some dresses in there that will fit."

Ruth nodded. "Yes, I did look. That's where I found this apron, and I'm grateful for it." She smoothed the skirt and sat.

"But I have an idea. I'd like to alter some of my clothes to fit me as the baby grows. I saw some pictures of what they called maternity clothes in a magazine. I think I could make something like those if I had a sewing machine."

"A sewing machine!" Sister Jean Marie's eyes widened, her mouth a perfect O.

"It would be very helpful. I could mend sheets and other girls' clothes, and even make clothes for my baby."

The nun frowned. "A sewing machine would be a rather expensive purchase."

"I have a little money saved from before I left—Indianola. If Sisters of Mercy could help me with the rest of the cost, I'm sure I could pay it back in a few weeks. There are lots of girls here who could use alterations."

The tips of Sister Jean Marie's fingers tented and tapped together. "And when would you do all this sewing?"

Ruth leaned forward in her chair, and her voice rose. "I could sew before bed, or I could get up early in the mornings. I promise I'd continue to get all my cleaning done."

"Well." The tent collapsed, and the nun laid her hands palm-down on the desk. "This is an interesting request. Let me look into the cost of a used machine. And I'll talk to Sister Catherine about it. I'll try to have an answer for you by the end of the day." She stood, and Ruth knew she was dismissed.

"Thanks for listening." Ruth pushed open the office door and headed for the stairs. All day as she went about her cleaning chores, she thought about the magic she could work with a sewing machine. Thelma had taught her to sew when she had first come to Grantsville. She loved the feel of smooth new fabric, loved slicing into it with scissors, cutting the pieces, and then stitching them together to make clothing.

After Thelma died, Ruth begged Otto to take her to Grantsville to buy fabric so she could sew, but he always said,

"You got too many clothes now. All of yours and all of Thelma's too. We got no money for extras."

So, she satisfied her creative urges by remaking clothes, altering Thelma's to fit her more-petite figure, and adding a bow or a belt or a ruffle to make them more stylish.

At supper, she tried to catch Sister Jean Marie's eye, but she was busy visiting with the other nuns and didn't look Ruth's way. She half-listened to Pearl talking about an article she'd read about Fred Astaire. Lydia, who was joining them for the first time since her baby had been born, looked up from her plate of food. "He's so dreamy."

Pearl nodded her head. "He is. I would give anything to dance with him. Dance with anybody. Here we are in the capital city, and we are forbidden to even go to a dance to watch."

Margaret passed a basket of crackers to Lydia. "Where are you going when you leave here?"

Lydia smiled at all of them. "I've decided to stay in Des Moines."

Pearl's eyes widened. "Why? I thought your plan was to go back to Iowa City."

"That was my original plan. But there's nothing there for me. I might as well get a job here, make some money, go to all those dances." She smiled at Pearl. "And maybe meet Mr. Right."

Ruth leaned over. "Where will you work?"

"I'm hoping to get a job at the canning factory. If that doesn't pan out, I'll get work in one of the big houses south of Grand. They're always looking for a girl." Lydia speared a bite of ham with her fork and chewed slowly. Her eyes were no longer red and swollen and her voice was cheerful and upbeat, but her eyes held hidden pain.

"That's great." Ruth truly felt excited for Lydia. "Do you think I could get a job working in someone's house?"

Pearl snorted. "Not if you keep your baby. No one wants someone else's kid in their home. They want you to watch theirs."

Ruth's chin lifted slightly. Since she'd been ten years old, she'd been fighting her own battles. She figured she could handle this one too.

"Emma, may I speak with you, please?" Mother Superior's stern voice startled her.

"Of course. Let me put my dishes away." Ruth stood and hurried over to stand in line at the window. The other women looked at her curiously, perhaps wondering what she had done to merit a one-on-one with the head nun.

Ruth followed Mother Superior down the hall to the office. They were both silent until they were in the small room and seated.

"Close the door, please." Mother Superior commanded from her chair behind the desk.

Ruth hopped up quickly and closed the door. After she was seated again, she waited, her heart pounding and mouth dry. What had she done? Was she to be kicked out on the streets? Surely the nun could hear the hammering of her heart.

Mother Superior's mouth twitched. Could she possibly be trying to smile? Or was it simply a reflex before uttering words of doom?

"I understand you have requested a sewing machine."

The sigh of relief escaped before Ruth could capture it. "Yes, Mother Superior. I can no longer fasten my clothes. If I had a machine, I could remake them to accommodate my ... my growth. And I could do alterations for the other women, or the nuns. I like to sew."

"And you don't feel this will interfere with your assigned duties?"

Ruth's hands, which had been clenched in her lap, unfurled. "No, ma'am. We have time in the evening. I would spend it sewing instead of playing games or reading."

"I've been saying we need more opportunities to teach our women skills they can use. I think a sewing machine would be an excellent idea." Now Ruth was sure the twitch was meant to be a smile. "We will ask for a donation from the Saint John's congregation. If we don't receive one, we can purchase a used one. Sister Jean Marie said you were willing to use some of your own money. But I think we will buy the machine, so we can use it for other girls after you're gone."

Ruth nodded. "That's wise."

"I will keep you updated on our purchase. Since it was your idea, and no one else has expressed a desire to have a sewing machine, I think we will let you keep it in your room as long as you are with us."

"Thank you, Mother Superior." Ruth didn't have to force her sincere gratitude, she could hardly control her bubbling excitement. She started to stand, thinking the meeting was over.

The nun gestured. "Don't leave yet. We need to discuss your plans. What is your due date?"

"Dr. Osborne said probably the last week of January." Ruth squirmed, knowing what direction the discussion was headed.

"And have you given up the idea of keeping the child?"

Ruth swallowed, looking down at her lap and her hands clenched around her growing abdomen. "No, Mother Superior," she whispered. "I plan to keep my baby."

"Emma. How will you support yourself and a baby? You have no one stepping forward to support you now, let alone when you are responsible for an innocent child. Can't you see how selfish that is? Your child needs both a mother and a father."

Her voice rose with each word, the syllables pounding at Ruth like blows from a hammer. Ruth could not answer, not even with a nod or a shake.

Ruth studied the floral pattern in the apron until Mother Superior grew quiet. As the silence in the room lengthened, Ruth mumbled, "I'll keep thinking about it."

Mother Superior rose to her full height. "That's good. You think long and hard about the right thing to do."

Ruth nodded, not trusting her voice to speak again. She scurried from the room, much as a mouse would escape from the hawk's talons. She didn't need to think about it, and she knew the right thing to do. She needed to formulate another plan, a plan to escape with her baby. Because keeping her baby —no matter how difficult—was right.

11

The used Singer sewing machine arrived a week later. It took four girls to carry the machine in its heavy oak cabinet up the stairs to Ruth's room. Within minutes, at least ten girls crowded into the small room to admire the shiny black machine.

"Emma," Pearl spoke around the wad of bubble gum she was chewing. "How you gonna have time to sew on top of all your work?" Most of the girls knew that Ruth was always busy cleaning somewhere, but not that she did Frances's chores as well as her own.

Ruth patted the cabinet as if it were a puppy. "I'll find time to do this. I love to sew."

Slowly, the girls drifted back to their scheduled duties or free time. Ruth pulled over the chair from the desk and sat. She didn't have any material or thread. But she pressed on the treadle with her foot and watched the needle bob up and down. She could picture the thread moving through some pretty print fabric. Or maybe some soft yellow flannel cut into pieces for an infant's nightslip.

She started when Sister Jean Marie poked her head in the door. "Emma? I found some things for you." She laid several folds of new fabric on Ruth's bed and held out a small wicker basket.

Ruth opened it and couldn't believe her eyes. It contained several spools of thread, a pair of scissors, a measuring tape, and a pincushion bristling with straight pins. "For me? Thank you, oh, thank you." She ran her hand over the bright new fabric and clutched the small basket to her as if it contained jewels.

"Yes, they are for you. My mother gave me the sewing basket before I joined the convent. She had dreams of me being a homemaker. If you can use them, it would be much better than leaving them sitting in my closet."

Ruth's eyes filled with tears at the nun's kindness. "Please, if you need anything mended, let me know."

"Certainly." Sister Jean Marie nodded and left.

Ruth unfolded the fabric— a couple of yards of a blue cotton print, some stiff black material such as was used in the nun's habits, and, hidden in between the other material, a few yards of soft white flannel.

Ruth made room on a shelf in the closet for the fabric and unloaded the spools of thread into one of the narrow drawers in the sewing machine cabinet. Then she hurried up to the third floor to finish her cleaning duties.

After she ate dinner, Ruth didn't linger at the table with a cup of tea and conversation with her tablemates. She carried her dishes to the window and skipped upstairs to her room. Then, she threaded the machine with black thread, filled a bobbin, and altered one of her dresses, using the apron as an insert at the sides. She smiled as the machine hummed and clicked and the needle flashed through the material.

When Doris came upstairs, Ruth showed her the remade dress. "What do you think?"

Doris held it up to her shoulders and smiled. "It would fit me. Could you ... would you ... remake one of my dresses?"

"Sure. Which one?"

Doris went to her closet and came back with a red polka-dotted dress.

Ruth looked at the waist and skirt. "I could remake this using the black material. But then you couldn't wear it after the baby. Are you sure that's what you want?"

Doris nodded. Then she sat on the bed close to Ruth's chair. She leaned over and whispered. "I'm meeting Thomas in downtown Des Moines next week. I want something nice to wear."

"The nuns let you do that?" Ruth gasped.

"Oh, they don't know. I told them my parents were in town and wanted to buy me a pair of new shoes. Since my parents are generous donators to Sisters of Mercy, they don't question me quite as much."

Ruth held up the polka-dotted dress. "Then we better get this remade to fit you."

Only when the laughter and talking had quieted in the hallway, and Doris could no longer contain her yawns, did Ruth stop snipping and stitching. Doris hung the almost-completed dress in her side of the closet, and Ruth cleaned up the scraps and put her tools away.

The next morning Ruth feared she might be tired from the long night of sewing, but she woke with a sense of renewed energy and purpose. She finished the dress for Doris and remade another one for herself.

As the week went on, a slow trickle of residents appeared at her door to ask for her services. Evelyn shyly requested a remake of a favorite dress. Pearl joked she would pay for her mending job in buttons. When Frances came with an armload of dresses, Ruth decided to set up some restrictions.

"I'd be glad to fix these for you, but I have limited time to sew."

Frances glowered at her. "Fine." She dropped the dresses on Ruth's bed. "I'll do the dining room and Mother Superior's room this week."

Ruth fingered the dresses. "There are three dresses here. It will take me longer than a week to do them."

Frances grimaced. "Okay. I'll do them for three weeks."

Ruth gave Frances her sweetest smile. "Thank you so much. That's very kind of you."

Frances stomped out of the bedroom and down the hall, but she kept her end of the bargain.

Saturday, Ruth made another deal. Lilian would take over her duties on the third floor for a week in return for repairing her nightgown and remaking a house dress.

When Doris returned from her meeting with Thomas, Ruth had spent the entire day at her machine, and it was nearly dinnertime. Ruth didn't need to ask Doris about her day. She had a glow about her that could only come from a girl in love. Ruth felt a twinge of envy. Not once had anyone made her glow, and now, no one ever would. A man wouldn't want a woman with a child that wasn't his. Or a woman who'd had a child out of wedlock. She was damaged goods.

After dinner, Ruth and Doris sat on the bed. They kept the worn copy of *The Ladies Home Journal* in front of them, so if one of the other girls or one of the nuns entered, they would look like they were reading.

"Did Thomas like the dress?" Ruth asked.

Doris grinned. "He called me his 'sweet patootie,' and said I was 'cute as a bug's ear.' I think he liked it."

"What did you do all day?"

"We ate lunch at Woolworth's downtown. And we walked up and down the streets. Most of the time I wasn't even aware where we were. We went to a matinee at the Orpheum."

"A moving picture? Keen! What was it like?"

Doris cocked her head. "You know, Emma, I don't even remember what happened up on the screen. I just remember Thomas holding my hand and giving me a kiss when the show ended." Her voice trailed off, her face dreamy, as she stared out the small window. Turning back to Ruth, she spoke almost angrily. "I wish I didn't have to be here. I wish we could just run away and get married now."

"Why don't you?"

"Thomas wants to wait till I turn eighteen. Then my parents can't do anything to sabotage the marriage."

Ruth wanted to hear more, but Doris stood up and stretched. When she moved to her desk and pulled out paper to write a letter, Ruth whispered, "But if you wait until your birthday, your baby will have been born. And you'll have lost him."

Doris sat hunched over her desk for a moment. When she turned, it looked like she had tears in her eyes. "But I'll have found a husband."

12

R uth watched out the window as cold wind gusts sent tiny tornadoes of dried leaves skittering down the street. Her thoughts turned to the farm in Grantsville. The corn would be picked and in the corncrib, the bright yellow ears making horizontal stripes in the slotted building. The animals would be growing fuzzy winter coats and spending more time huddled against the shelter of the barn. The red-winged blackbirds would have flown south.

When her mental tour brought her to the house, a wave of nausea flooded over her. She turned from the window to focus instead on the nightgown she was remaking for Mildred, and on the little nightslip pieces hidden in the closet. She had cut them out last night using a garment borrowed from the delivery wing as a pattern.

Early in the morning, Father O'Brien held a brief Thanksgiving Mass. They had cereal and toast for breakfast, and everyone helped with the dishes. There would be no cleaning of rooms today. It was a holiday, a day to give thanks. And Ruth planned to spend the rest of the day sewing.

On the past Monday, she had resumed her cleaning of the dining area and Mother Superior's room. Frances seemed pleased with the remake of her dresses, but once they were finished, she insisted Ruth do her work again, "... or I'll tell Mother Superior your little secret."

Frances wasn't due to deliver until January, so Ruth would not be able to escape her blackmail for weeks. But today was a gift, and she was thankful.

Ruth bent her head to the stitching. The hall was quiet. Doris was in the bathroom getting ready for a day with her parents. They had written their plans to take her out to eat in Des Moines. Ruth hoped Doris would remember all the day's details and share them with her when she returned.

Ruth had eaten in a restaurant only once, when she'd come on the orphan train to Grantsville. The Monarch Hotel served the children a meal before they went to the operahouse and were put on display for prospective families. She remembered the white tablecloths, the baskets of rolls, and the shiny silverware. She had been so awed by the fancy room she barely tasted her food.

Footsteps sounded in the hall, but Ruth didn't look up. Her foot rocked the treadle slowly as she finished the seam.

"Emma." Frances stood at the door with a scowl on her face.

Ruth carefully tied a knot and clipped the threads before she swiveled to face her. "Yes?"

"I'm scheduled to work in the kitchen at noon. You'll need to cover for me. I'm not feeling well."

"I'm sorry you're not feeling well, but I'm sewing. I'd really like to finish this nightgown today. And Pearl has asked me to mend a dress. Can't you find someone else to trade duties with you?"

Frances scowl darkened. "I'm not asking to trade. You do

this for me, and I won't reveal your secret. You act like you're special, saying you had a husband. But I think you made up that husband so you won't have a bastard baby. He's a lie to make you look better than the rest of us." She glared at Ruth through narrowed eyes.

Ruth laid Mildred's nightgown down on the cabinet with a sigh. "I'll take your duty, Frances."

Frances turned and smirked. "How nice of you. Thanks." Then she ambled down the hall to her room.

Ruth stood up so quickly, the chair almost tipped over. She paced back and forth across the small room. The web of lies she'd built was strangling her. Residents weren't allowed to leave without a reason, and with no way out, she was caught like a fly.

Doris stopped in the doorway. "Are you okay?"

What could she say that wouldn't destroy her life and the life of the baby she carried? Ruth leaned against Doris's desk. "I just needed to stretch my legs."

Doris's letter to Thomas lay on her desk. She would probably mail it while she was out. A letter! The key to unlock the door to freedom.

Ruth asked, "May I borrow a sheet of paper and an envelope? I need to write a letter to someone. And then will you mail it for me?"

"I'd be happy to do that." Doris opened a desk drawer and handed Ruth a sheet of stationery with a pretty floral design and an envelope.

Ruth cleared out a spot on the sewing cabinet. A few minutes later, she handed the envelope to her roommate along with three pennies for a stamp. Doris glanced at the envelope and looked up in surprise. "It's addressed to you."

"Yes. Please don't mention it to anyone. It's important, but I can't tell you why. Will you trust me?"

Doris shrugged. "Sure. I can keep my mouth shut. Don't know why you're mailing yourself a letter, though. Seems a waste of a stamp."

After the noon meal, Ruth dried the last of the dishes while Margaret wiped the counters clean. She glanced at the clock in the dining room. The time she thought she would have at the sewing machine had dissipated as quickly as the soap bubbles in the dishwater. She turned the dishpan over and watched as the water swirled down the drain. It still fascinated her that she could turn on a faucet inside the house and watch water gush out.

Maybe she should go to Mother Superior and confess her lies. Her hope of a sanctuary at Sisters of Mercy had evolved into a trap. She was comfortable being Emma Russo, but the girls often questioned her about her husband and how it felt to be married. When she was evasive, she hoped they believed she was grieving, not lying.

She remembered the nightmare months following Mrs. Schmidt's death. How Mr. Schmidt told her to call him Otto. How he called her pretty. How he came at night to her bedroom.

Suddenly, she struggled to breathe. She clutched the edge of the sink. Mother Superior could never know the truth, or anyone else. Her only hope would be to leave. But first she had to find a place for herself and the baby.

In the afternoon, she found time to sew for a few hours. But she had a hard time concentrating. She thought about the letter and her plan to leave. When she finally finished the nightgown, she took it to Mildred who threw her arms around Ruth. "You're so good to take care of our clothes. It's hard not to be able to wear fashionable garments, and to outgrow even our everyday ones. But you just stitch here and there and fix them so we can wear them."

The glow of Mildred's praise warmed Ruth as she returned to her room. She picked up the dress Pearl had dropped off and planned how she could remake it.

Doris came in so quietly Ruth didn't even know she was there until she paused in her sewing and looked up to see her sitting on her bed. "Did you have a nice day with your parents?" Ruth asked.

Doris's eyes filled with tears. "They told me they will move me to Coe College in Cedar Rapids after the baby is born. I won't even go back home."

"What about your plans with Thomas? Did you tell them you wanted to marry him?"

"No." Doris wailed, flopping back against her pillow. "I just couldn't. They are so excited about me being the first in my family to go to college."

Ruth laid Pearl's dress down, sat on the bed, and gently rubbed Doris's back. "I think if you're old enough to have a baby and a boyfriend, you're old enough to make decisions about your life."

Doris sniffled. "Easy for you to say. You've been married and lived on your own."

Ruth wished she could tell Doris the truth. That she'd never been married, never known the love of a man, and because of that, she carried more shame than all of them. Instead, she patted Doris's back until the tears had stopped.

Hours later, after both of them had retired, Ruth was shaken awake by Doris, her eyes wide and frightened, her face pale. "Emma, wake up. You're having a nightmare."

Ruth struggled to sit up. The sheets on her bed were tangled around her arms and legs. When she finally extracted herself from them, she whispered. "I'm so sorry I woke you."

"You scared me. Was it the same dream you had your first night here?"

Ruth rubbed her eyes and mumbled, "The same nightmare. I was running from him. He was about to catch me."

"Who?" Doris looked perplexed.

Ruth's hand went to her mouth. She'd said far too much. "It doesn't matter. It was just a dream." She slipped out from under the covers and stood, gasping as her bare feet touched the icy floor. "Brrrr. I'm going to use the restroom."

When she returned, Doris was snoring softly.

Ruth smoothed out the tangles and climbed under the blankets. She prayed for sleep, sleep with no nightmares.

13

Mail call occurred every day at lunchtime. Ruth waited expectantly as Mother Superior called out the names of the recipients and handed them their envelopes. When she called "Emma Russo" on Saturday, Ruth jumped to her feet and held out her hand.

Knowing what it contained, she was in no hurry to open it. The letter was just the first part of the plan.

On Monday morning, she asked Mother Superior if she could meet with her.

The nun scrutinized her as if to ascertain her motives before she replied. "I will be in my office after nine this morning."

"Swell." Ruth gulped as the nun glared at her use of slang. "I'll be there, Mother Superior."

Focusing on her cleaning duties was difficult. If the meeting with Mother Superior went well, she could escape the web and never have to lie again. Finally, the clock's hour hand crept toward nine. She stowed the mop, hurried down the stairs, and arrived outside Mother Superior's office at exactly nine o'clock. She took a deep breath and knocked.

"Come in." Mother Superior's invitation sounded more like a command.

Ruth entered and waited to sit until she was asked.

"What do you need, Emma? Is the sewing venture going well?"

"Yes, it is, Mother Superior. I love sewing, and everyone is keeping me busy with requests."

"You must consider each request carefully. If someone is asking you to sew something frivolous or unnecessary, you may deny them. If you have any doubts, consult Sister Jean Marie or me. But that isn't why you are here, is it?"

Ruth tugged at the fabric of her skirt. Even the remade clothes constricted around her ever-widening middle. "No, my request is unrelated to my sewing. I have received a letter from an aunt of my late husband. She lives in Missouri, but she will be in Des Moines in December. She'd like for me to take a bus and meet her for lunch." Ruth looked down at her hands, resting on her large midsection.

Mother Superior's mouth tightened in a grim line. "We don't believe it is proper for our young women to be on display so close to their time. But your case is a little different. And you do have so little family. What is the date of this luncheon?"

For a second, Ruth panicked. She hadn't considered when she could have her day of escape. "December fifteenth," she said firmly, knowing that two weeks would give her adequate time to prepare.

"I'm going to grant you permission. Before the time arrives, perhaps you can find a coat that will hide your condition?"

"I will do that. And thank you so much, Mother Superior. It means a lot to me to see Aunt Wanda." Ruth fled the room, grateful that this part of her plan was working.

A week later, Ruth was cleaning the dining room when Sister Jean Marie passed through with a young woman who walked with a pronounced limp. Ruth gave them a smile before she stooped to polish the legs of the long dining room table.

When Sister Jean Marie spoke, Ruth bumped her head as she stood. "Emma, this is Pauline. She will be living here at Sisters of Mercy until her baby is born. Oh, you two probably know each other. Pauline is from Indianola. Didn't you and your husband live there, Emma?"

Pauline and Ruth stood a moment, frozen. Then Ruth shook down the terror of being discovered and held out her hand. "I don't believe I've ever met you. We only lived in Indianola a short time, and our home was outside of town. We must not have run into each other."

Pauline shook her hand. "What is your last name, Emma?"

Ruth spoke in a rush of words. "I look forward to visiting with you at dinner. I'd better get back to my cleaning." She smiled and ducked back under the table, listening to the murmur of their voices as they continued their tour of the home.

As soon as she was certain they were gone and not coming back through, Ruth backed out carefully from under the table. She ran the dustmop over the floor without her usual attention to detail and fled upstairs. She sat on her bed, slightly winded from the stairs.

It was still a week until December fifteenth and her plan to escape. What if Pauline caused the whole web of lies she'd created to collapse, ensnaring her in the sticky strings?

Pearl appeared at her door and startled her from her thoughts. "Mother Superior would like to see you in her office, Emma."

With a sinking feeling of dread, Ruth stood. "What does she want? Am I in trouble?"

Pearl shrugged. "I was just coming back from the medical wing. She saw me pass her door and asked me to give you the message. She didn't look angry."

Ruth descended the stairs slowly, trying to plan what she would do when Mother Superior dismissed her. Would she have to leave immediately? Would she even get to tell the other residents goodbye? She hadn't been able to put her plan in place yet. So, where would she go?

Mother Superior sat at her desk bent over something, perhaps a letter, that she was writing. She held a fountain pen and wrote with bold strokes. When Ruth entered, she laid the pen down, looked up, and smiled. "Come in and have a seat, Emma."

Ruth sat, clutching her hands together in her shrinking lap.

"Are things going well for you at Sisters of Mercy?"

"Certainly. I am most appreciative of all you do for us."

"Good. Well, I have heard nothing but complimentary things about you—your willingness to help others, your friendliness to the other women, and your humble attitude in these circumstances."

The unfamiliar praise brought the sting of tears to Ruth's eyes. "Thank you."

"The success of our venture with the sewing machine has pleased everyone. Almost daily, one of the girls shows me another dress that you've remade. I believe you are aware that we have added an additional resident today. Her name is Pauline. I am assigning Pauline to Frances's cleaning crew and removing you from all cleaning duties. I believe your time will be better spent at your machine." Mother Superior held up a sack. "Here are two of my habits that I have had for a while. They need mended. Think of this as your first official duty as Sisters of Mercy's seamstress."

Relief flooded over Ruth and exploded into a smile on her

face. "I will do my best to fulfill your expectations. When will Pauline begin?"

"Tomorrow morning." Mother Superior picked up the fountain pen and Ruth left the office, carrying the sack as carefully as if it held gowns for a queen.

At supper that night, Ruth spooned beef and noodles into her mouth, listening to the conversation around her. Pearl was questioning Pauline about her previous life. "You grew up in Indianola, is that right?"

"Yes, Frances was a few years ahead of me in school." Pauline glanced down the table where Frances sat.

Frances leaned forward. "She really did live in Indianola. Unlike some of the people who say they did."

Ruth kept her eyes on her plate, concentrating on winding a noodle around her fork.

Pauline did not respond to Frances. "I would have graduated high school there in the spring. Now look where I am." She choked back a sob.

Pearl reached across the table to pat her hand. "Don't give up on your dream of graduating. Maybe you can finish next year. This isn't the end of your life. You can get through this."

Ruth touched her round belly hidden by the table. This wasn't what she had dreamed or planned either. But she didn't want to "get through this." This was her new dream.

Pauline spoke again. "Thanks. You're all so kind. Emma, where did you live in Indianola? And what did you say your last name was?"

Before Ruth could answer, Frances sputtered. "She didn't live in Indianola. That's a lie that she made up. Along with the fake dead husband."

The sudden panic that enveloped her threatened to send her noodles back up. "Excuse me. I'm going upstairs to sew." Ruth stood and carried her not-quite-empty plate to the pass-through window. Then she hurried upstairs to her machine.

Shortly after she had laid out Mother Superior's habit and began repairing the triangular tear in the skirt, Pauline knocked hesitantly at the door. "Emma?"

Ruth swiveled in the chair. "Come in, Pauline."

Pauline took a single step into the room. "I didn't mean to upset you with my questions. I don't care where you lived. I was just making conversation. Frances has always been a mean girl, even when she was in high school. I don't put any stock in what she says."

Ruth sighed. "My last name is Russo." She didn't feel like telling another person a lie that could easily be refuted.

"Nice to meet you, Emma Russo. So, is the sewing machine yours?"

Ruth told her the story of how she got the old treadle machine. "And now, Mother Superior wants me to spend my day sewing. I won't be on cleaning duty anymore."

"And Frances is mad."

"Yes, I'm sure she is. I just don't want her to get me kicked to the streets."

"Well, as far as I'm concerned, you and Mr. Russo lived on my street—Jefferson."

"Thanks, Pauline. But I don't want anyone to lie for me."

"Well, if anything comes up …" Pauline made a turning motion in front of her mouth and flipped her hand over her shoulder as if she were throwing away a key. Then she left, turning down the hall to her bedroom.

14

R uth pushed open the heavy drapes she and Doris shut at night to keep the out the cold. But the natural light made it easier to see as she sewed. Snow drifted past the panes coated with a chilly layer of frost.

Outside the window, two children dressed in winter coats, mittens, hats, and scarves waded through the fresh snow, pulling a small toboggan behind them. Ruth longed to be outside, to go for a walk, to hold out a mittened hand and catch snowflakes. Why, just because she had a baby growing inside, was she kept like a chicken in a coop?

She needed to be patient. In two days, she would have the whole day outside Sisters of Mercy. The remaining coins in her purse should be enough for streetcar fare and perhaps a sandwich for lunch. She found an old city directory in the closet and used it to obtain addresses and a map of the city.

Since being relieved of her cleaning duties, Ruth had been busier than ever with sewing. After mending Mother Superior's habits, she raised the hem on one of Sister Jean Marie's skirts, and requests came in a steady stream from the other residents to alter dresses that no longer fit. Sister Catherine asked Ruth to make several nightslips for the babies who would be born this winter, providing a worn one to use as a pattern and several yards of soft, white flannel. After she had fulfilled that request, she made simple dresses embroidered with tiny flowers for them to wear the day they went to their new families.

Ruth often sewed late at night, fashioning gowns for her own baby from the scraps she had left. She knew she would need blankets and diapers as well, but they would take more fabric—fabric that she didn't have.

She pulled out her chair and sat down to begin mending. She would start with a remake for Pauline.

When she heard someone moaning and other voices in the hall, she jumped up. She knew without checking that one of the girls was in labor. She dropped the dress on her chair and made her way to the door.

Frances leaned heavily on Pearl's arm. Margaret and Evelyn fluttered behind. All of Frances's tough demeanor was gone. "Don't let go. Ohhh, it hurts. Stay with me, Pearl."

Despite all Frances had done to make her life miserable, Ruth felt sorry for her. She asked Pearl, "Do you need help?"

Before Pearl could respond, Frances answered. "No, we don't need help. Go back to your sewing machine."

Stung, Ruth backed into her bedroom and watched as the group made their way to the stairs. In a few hours, Frances would probably give birth. And then the baby would be gone, and Frances would leave Sisters of Mercy and resume her life in Indianola.

A new worry surfaced in Ruth's mind. What if she gave birth early, before her plans were carried out? Would the nuns take her baby away and give her to someone else? She must prevent that from happening.

At supper that night, there was still no word on Frances. A few times they could hear her cry out in pain, the sound muted by the hallways and closed doors. The girls chattered over the noise, all of them no doubt thinking about their upcoming labors and deliveries.

At breakfast, none of the residents had heard anything. Ruth checked on the third floor to see if Frances was in one of the rooms, but they were all empty. She must still be in labor.

Finally, at supper, Margaret gave them the news. "Frances is on the third floor. But her baby was born dead."

There was a hush over the table as the young women pondered the news. Finally, Pearl spoke up. "Well, it's not like she was planning to be a mother anyway. She still goes back to her life. And the couple who were going to adopt the baby will probably just get the next one."

The girls relaxed. It was true that Frances had not planned on keeping the baby, and most of the girls seemed to be comforted knowing the babies they were giving up would have good homes. Ruth's heart constricted in sorrow for the tiny baby who had never taken a breath, for the adoptive parents whose arms were still empty, and for Frances.

After she ate and cleared her dishes, Ruth made her way to the third floor and knocked softly on Frances's bedroom door. When there was no answer, she opened it a crack, but Frances appeared to be sleeping. As Ruth turned to leave, Frances spoke, her voice husky with fatigue and perhaps sorrow.

"I'm awake. Who's poking their head in here?"

"It's Ruth. I just came to see if you needed anything."

Frances propped her head up on one arm. "No. I just want to sleep."

"Okay. I'll go, now. I'm sorry about your baby."

"It doesn't matter. I'm done now."

Ruth pulled the door closed and trudged down to the second floor to her bedroom.

The next morning, she was up very early. She dressed in one of Thelma's old cotton print dresses, remade twice, once to fit her last spring, and once to fit her now. She pulled on warm stockings. Pearl had loaned Ruth her coat. Although Ruth was taller and Pearl was stouter, the coat would work. It didn't exactly hide the fact that she was pregnant, but it did camouflage it somewhat. She laid the coat on her bed, put the small coin purse in her pocket, and went down for breakfast and prayers.

After breakfast, she signed out in the register in Mother Superior's office. Another lie. She was not going to a restaurant and a movie with Aunt Wanda. There was no Aunt Wanda. She filled in the name of a restaurant she'd found in the directory and hoped no one checked on it later.

Upstairs she paced a little—waiting. She didn't want to leave too early and cause suspicion. Finally, when she could stand it no longer, she put on the coat, buttoning it as far down as she could. She pulled on a wool bowler hat that Doris had loaned her and slipped her hands into a pair of heavy gloves, donations from someone who attended Saint John's.

Downstairs, she pushed open the heavy wooden doors she had walked through two months before. She took deep gulps of the fresh air. Then she walked across the porch and down to the sidewalk. According to her map, she needed to walk two blocks west to board the streetcar.

When the car stopped and the door swished open, Ruth climbed the metal steps and dropped her money in the slot. Then she sat on the slick plastic seat and clutched the edge as the streetcar lurched down the street. The car halted every block or so, adding people at each stop. By the time they reached downtown Des Moines, the car was crowded with people jostling for space.

Ruth got off the car when it stopped on Ingersoll Avenue. She only had to walk a short distance before she stood in front of a small wood frame building with a sign out front: Des Moines Employment Agency.

She took a deep breath and strode in. A young slender woman with dark red lipstick and blond curls sat at a desk. Her stockinged legs were crossed under a fashionable pencil skirt. She stood and smiled at Ruth. "May I help you?"

The confidence Ruth had felt moments before left in a rush. "I ... I need a job," she stuttered.

"Well, honey, you've come to the right place. We have an excellent rate of placement for our clients. There is a two-dollar enrollment fee, and we charge fifteen percent of your first month's wages."

Two dollars! The little coin purse didn't contain that kind of wealth. "I'm sorry. I can't pay the enrollment fee. Thanks anyway." Ruth turned to leave.

Just as she reached the door, the blond called out, "Honey, the YWCA has a free employment agency."

Ruth turned with a smile and hope rose again. "Can you tell me where the Y is?"

The blonde woman pointed. "Two blocks that direction and a block south."

"Thanks," Ruth called as she hurried outside. She walked quickly, knowing the long hours in this day were melting away.

The YWCA was an imposing three-story brick building. Ruth opened the door and walked up the short flight of stairs to a spacious lobby. A woman with bobbed hair sat at a reception desk her chair tipped back. She laid down the magazine she'd been reading. "May I help you?"

Ruth stepped forward. "I'd like to talk to someone about employment opportunities. I really need a job."

"Let me see if our employment consultant is available." The woman stood and wobbled on high heels to an office on one side of the lobby. When she returned, she smiled and said, "Mr. Jensen will see you." She waved a hand in the direction of the office.

Mr. Jensen looked up as Ruth walked in, but he didn't smile. "Sit down, please. What kind of employment are you interested in?"

He held a pencil in one hand, and while Ruth spoke his pencil tapped softly on the papers in front of him. "I'm willing to do anything. But, I have ... I mean I will have ... a child."

Mr. Jensen frowned, and the pencil paused. "Why, we don't have any jobs suitable for mothers. You need to be home with your child. Doesn't your husband have a job?"

"I don't have a husband." Ruth's voice had dropped to a whisper.

The pencil resumed its *tap, tap, tap*. "There is a home on Cottage Grove run by the Sisters of Mercy. They take in unwed mothers and place the babies for adoption. You will be safe there. Do you want the address?"

This conversation was far more difficult than Ruth had anticipated. She tried to take a breath, but it felt like something was squeezing her chest. "That's where I am living right now. I need a job, because I'm keeping my baby. I don't want her to grow up an orphan the way I did." Ruth lifted her chin slightly and waited to speak until Mr. Jensen raised his eyes and looked at her. "Please, don't you have some housekeeping jobs where I might be able to keep my baby with me?"

The frown deepened, and the pencil continued to tap as his eyes pierced her. Finally, he said, "I have the listing for housekeepers. You could apply. But you must be honest about your condition. And I must say, this goes against what I believe is the best for your baby—and for you. Those Sisters of Mercy nuns are real saints, if you ask me. And then those they take in are ungrateful." The pencil stopped and he dropped it on a typed list of names and addresses and a blank piece of paper torn from a notebook. He pushed the pile across his desk. "Copy down those addresses for which you want to apply." His wooden chair screeched as he stood and it slid across the floor.

"Thank you, sir." Ruth furiously copied names and addresses onto the paper. Surely one of these names would hire a girl who just happened to be pregnant.

15

Two hours later, Ruth stood on Grand Avenue looking up at a ornate, three-story home. She clutched her list of possible employers in one gloved hand. All but two of the names and addresses had been crossed off. Three families had already hired girls, one family had changed their mind about hiring, and four families politely said no when they learned that Ruth was expecting.

This time she didn't take a deep breath, shore up her confidence, and march to the door. Through the long afternoon, her confidence had dribbled away until she had nothing left. With her head down, she trudged to the door, and knocked.

The door opened and a girl who did not look much older than Ruth stood in the spacious entryway. She wore her blond hair in a stylish bob, perfectly waved. Her dress could have been featured in the fashion section of the *Ladies Home Journal*, but her eyes looked as if she'd not slept in a while. She cradled an infant in one arm and had a dishtowel draped over the other. "Yes?" Even her voice seemed weary.

"I'm here to apply for the housekeeping position." Ruth forced a smile.

The woman pushed the door open farther and shifted the sleeping baby to her other arm. "Come in. Did the YWCA send you?"

"Yes." Ruth followed the woman down a hall to a large sunny kitchen.

"Please, sit down. I'm Mrs. Irvine."

Ruth sat on one of the wooden chairs at a round oak table.

Mrs. Irvine shifted the baby again and sank onto a chair with a sigh. "Tell me about your experience."

Ruth lifted her chin. No more lies. She didn't have to tell everything, but what she told would be the truth. "My name is Ruth Russo. I was an orphan and came to Iowa on a train. I took care of the house for the people who took me in. Thelma was ill and died after I had been there two years, so I did the cooking, the laundry, the cleaning, as well as chores on the farm."

"Do you have experience with babies?"

Ruth's hand went unconsciously to her belly. "There were no children on the farm. But in New York, before I came, I helped a lot with the babies and younger children in the orphanage." Ruth paused. "You need to know, I'm expecting. I live at the Sisters of Mercy Home for Unwed Mothers. But I don't want my baby to be adopted. That's why I must find a job and a place for both of us to live."

It was quiet for a moment. Ruth studied the print on the skirt of her dress.

Mrs. Irvine spoke. "You mean, you would have a baby and work here?"

"Yes. But I would do all my duties. Cleaning, cooking. It might take me a little longer, but I would just work later."

Mrs. Irvine frowned. "This is a highly unusual request. I

don't know what my husband would think. Is there a telephone number where I can reach you?"

Ruth shook her head. "We're not allowed to use the phone at the Home. But this is the address." She copied the Sisters of Mercy's address on a corner of her paper, tore it off, and handed it to Mrs. Irvine.

She took the paper, then shook her head. "I'd like to help you out. And it might be fun to have a playmate for little Bobby." She looked down at the sleeping infant. "But you understand my reservations, don't you?"

"Certainly." Ruth stood. "Don't wake the baby. I'll see myself out."

As she walked down the hallway, Mrs. Irvine called, "Thank you, Ruth."

By the time Ruth took the streetcar back to Cottage Grove and walked the short distance to Sisters of Mercy, it was cold and dark outside. Supper had already been served and everyone's head turned as she walked past. She hurried upstairs to shed her hat and gloves and Pearl's coat.

Now she had to face the barrage of questions from her tablemates. Yes, she had lunch with her late husband's aunt. Yes, they saw a show at the Orpheum. She felt like she was spinning the web that would trap her again. Ruth put her fork down. "I'm really tired. It was a good day, but I am plum tuckered. Just let me eat and I will fill you in on the details later."

She could tell from a few of her friends' expressions that they felt she had rebuffed them, but she was tired of lying. Despite not having any lunch, the soup seemed tasteless. She nibbled on a saltine while the conversation resumed and swirled around her.

The next few days she waited expectantly for Mrs. Irvine to come to Sisters of Mercy and let her know she had the job.

After the long day of searching, it seemed to be her only hope. But every day went by with no sign of the woman. One day it snowed, and Ruth thought the weather might have kept her away. Another day she thought maybe the baby was fussy. Finally, she faced the realization that she had been passed over. No one wanted a housekeeper with a baby.

She buried herself in her sewing, trying to ignore the fact that every day she was closer to the time she would give birth. And she had no idea where she would go then.

The conversations around the supper table focused more and more about the upcoming holiday. Several residents were looking forward to family visits either on Christmas or the days preceding. At the Home, a special dinner would be served, and, like Sundays, the only necessary chores would be the cleanup after the meal.

But as the day approached, and the residents faced the reality that they would spend the holiday away from family, sequestered at Sisters of Mercy, more than one young woman collapsed in tears over something small or exploded in anger for a minor infraction.

Christmas morning began with a mass led by Father O'Brien. He read the story from the book of Luke. He talked about Mary, a young girl, pregnant and far from home. And he talked of her sacrifice, giving birth to a baby who would belong not to her, but a world enslaved by sin. Ruth listened carefully, her hands crossed over her abdomen, the baby inside kicking and pushing like he or she wanted to be born that very day.

Dinner consisted of several special items, many of them provided by members of the parish—a roasted turkey large enough for all of them, mashed potatoes and gravy, rolls, cranberry relish and pumpkin pies for dessert.

After they had eaten, Mother Superior brought out some games: Chinese checkers, dominoes, and checkers. Most of the girls helped clear the tables and spent a good portion of the afternoon visiting and playing games.

When Ruth finally excused herself and went upstairs, her room was still dark and quiet. Doris had met her parents in the afternoon. She'd asked them to bring Thomas but had never received an answer from them that they would.

Doris had lined up a few Christmas cards on her desk that she received in the mail and used some scraps of Ruth's fabric to cut out tiny Christmas trees, wreaths, and stars. She'd decorated their room by pinning these to their curtains.

Ruth remembered the Christmas tree that Otto had cut and brought in the farmhouse her first year there. She'd helped Thelma decorate it with strings of popcorn and some shiny tinsel from the general store in Grantsville.

Next year, she would have a child at Christmas. Would she have a tree with lights and presents underneath? Would she have a stocking to hang and later fill with fruit and maybe some candy?

Ruth pulled her suitcase out of the closet and reached inside. The black Bible and the faded picture were the only items of her mother's her aunt had given her before dropping her off at the orphanage. She kept it there, carried it on the train to Iowa, and brought it with her to Des Moines three months earlier. Ruth had never spent time reading it, but she was intrigued by the story of Mary.

She thumbed through the rustling, tissue-thin pages until she found the book of Luke. She didn't have to read far before she found the passage. She read with joy and sorrow the ancient story, how an unwed mother gave birth to a Savior.

16

Two weeks after Christmas, Ruth woke with a mild backache. She must have spent too many hours sitting at the sewing machine yesterday. Her belly was getting so large that it was difficult to find a comfortable position to run the treadle and move fabric through the feed.

She glanced at the empty bed across the room. Doris had given birth December thirtieth, and her parents had whisked her away the day after. Ruth had caught a glimpse out the window of Doris's baby leaving with his new parents. He was wrapped in a blanket from fabric that had been donated at Christmastime. And she guessed he wore one of the dresses she'd made—maybe the one with yellow flowers embroidered on the bodice. It gave her a warm feeling to know she'd done something for a tiny baby who'd lost one mother but found another.

Ruth picked at the plate of scrambled eggs served for breakfast. Her ravenous appetite had dissipated overnight. She wondered if she was coming down with something. Several of the residents had colds.

She finally picked up her plate and took it to the window. Upstairs, she had difficulty focusing on her sewing. She emptied her closet and rearranged her clothes, keeping Doris's side empty. Another pregnant girl could arrive at Sisters of Mercy at any time.

Ruth opened her dresser drawer and straightened it. Her back still ached. The residents weren't supposed to lie on their beds or be inactive during daytime hours, but maybe she could close her door and stretch out just a little.

Within a few minutes she was asleep, dreaming she was back on the farm. A knock on her door startled her awake. "Come in." She stood and smoothed her hair and dress.

Sister Jean Marie opened the door slowly, a black skirt draped over one arm. "Emma? Are you okay?"

Ruth followed her new policy of telling the truth. "My back has been hurting. I thought if I lay down for a few minutes it would get better."

"Has it gotten better?"

"No. It seems to be worse. I don't know what I did."

"Honey, maybe you're in labor."

"But it's too early. Dr. Osborne said the end of January."

"Dr. Osborne doesn't decide when the babies come. He can only predict. The babies themselves decide. Your baby may think it's time."

"What if she isn't developed enough? Will she be premature?" Ruth's worries overshadowed the pain in her back.

"You're only two weeks ahead of schedule. Your baby should be fine."

Ruth's voice trembled a little. "What should I do?"

Sister Jean Marie patted her arm. "I give you permission to lie down if you want. It doesn't hurt you to walk around a little either. When you start having contractions, time them and see how far apart they are. And when you need to, you may come downstairs to the birthing wing."

"Okay." Ruth sank back down on her bed. Another worry rose, like some dark shadow pressing her down. "Sister?"

"Yes?"

"You know I plan on keeping my baby?"

The tiniest of sighs slipped from Sister Jean Marie. "Mother Superior and I are still hoping you change your mind, dear. I'll be back to check on you every hour." She slipped from the room, pulling the door shut behind her.

Ruth tried to sleep but couldn't. She rollercoastered from excitement over finally meeting her baby to worry and back to excitement. She walked the hall a few times, but after meeting Margaret and telling her she was in labor, other girls kept popping their heads in. "How are you, now?"

Just before lunch she had an actual contraction. The strength of her body's tensing and the pain that seared her abdomen surprised her. She tried to count the seconds until the next one, but lost track. Soon the contractions seemed to be coming one after another. The time had come to move downstairs. She was midway on the stairs when another contraction hit. She clutched the bannister and hoped she wouldn't collapse on the stairs.

Sister Jean Marie was passing through the dining room when she saw Ruth. She rushed to her side, and when the contraction was over, they moved together to the birthing unit.

In the tiny white room was a bed with rails on both sides that could be raised. The nun helped Ruth out of her clothes and into a hospital gown and then into the bed. The contractions were coming very close now, and Ruth gasped and clutched the bed rail. "Don't leave me, Sister," she called as the wave of pain abated.

Sister Jean Marie wiped her forehead with a cool cloth. "I'm right here, dear. I'll be with you."

Sometime later, Ruth was aware of Doctor Osborne's presence in the room. He and Sister Jean Marie were talking in hushed tones. Then he stood by her bed. "I'm going to give you something to sleep now. When you wake up, your baby will be gone."

The haze of pain-induced confusion lifted. Ruth sat up. "No! Don't take my baby away. She's going to stay with me." She grabbed the bedrail and struggled as if to get out of the bed.

Sister Jean Marie held her shoulders. "Ruth, calm down. Doctor Osborne means you will no longer be pregnant."

Doctor Osborne held a needle, and Ruth was suddenly frightened, not of the needle, but what might happen if she went to sleep. She struggled harder. "No. Please, don't. I don't want to go to sleep." Then another contraction hit, and she could only grasp the rail and moan. At the height of the contraction, she felt the sting of the needle in her arm.

She fell back on the pillow and, in a very brief time, drifted into a deep sleep.

17

Ruth's eyelids felt as if a heavy hand held them shut. She wanted to roll over, but her body wouldn't respond. She groaned. She needed to wake up for some reason. *What was it?*

She forced her eyes open. Bright lights glared in her face. Her midsection tightened, and a recently familiar pain gripped her. She looked down at her belly. Her baby! Where was her baby?

She tried to raise her arms, but they were fastened at her side. "Help," she croaked.

No one answered. She thrashed from side to side, but she couldn't break either her arms or legs loose. "Help me! Where's my baby?" Her voice gained strength and she shouted.

She relaxed slightly when she heard the click of footsteps on the linoleum. The door swung open, and Sister Jean Marie was there. "I'm sorry, Emma. I stepped out for a moment. You were sleeping so soundly. Here, let me unfasten your restraints."

"Where is my baby?" Even to her ears, her voice sounded frantic.

Sister Jean Marie kept her hand on Ruth's arm. "Please lie still. You mustn't get worked up. You just gave birth."

Tears ran down Ruth's face. "Where is she? Where is my baby?"

"The baby is being taken care of. Don't worry. You must sleep so you will heal." Sister Jean Marie spoke soothingly, but her words brought no comfort.

The door swished open, and Doctor Osborne stood beside her bed. "Let's move her to the cot in the recovery room. We may need this bed later tonight."

Ruth wondered who else was about to give birth. Doctor Osborne and Sister Jean Marie slid their arms under her and helped her to a cot in a small room adjoining the birthing room. The nun bustled around her, covering her with a blanket, fluffing her pillow, and patting her shoulder.

Doctor Osborne appeared at her side holding a needle. "This will help you sleep."

Ruth tried to sit up. "I don't want to sleep. Please, let me see my baby." She tried to push him away, but Sister Jean Marie held her right hand, and the doctor held her left arm firmly. And although she struggled, the fog crept over her and pressed her to sleep.

When she woke again, she was cold. Her blanket had slipped to the floor. She had the feeling that it was very late, but she couldn't tell for sure. There were no clocks or even a window in the room to judge the time. Both the birthing room and the recovery room were dark, but a sliver of light showed under the door that led to the long hall.

Ruth leaned over, grabbed the blanket and clutched it around her. Still, she shivered. Was it from the chill in the air, or from the feeling of dread that washed over her? She lay quietly for a few minutes, then pushed the blanket off and sat up, her bare feet on the cold floor shocking her awake.

She stood and took a few tentative steps. Grasping the furniture, she made her way across both rooms and opened the door. Sister Jean Marie sat in a small rocker in the hallway, her head lopsided and her eyes closed.

Ruth wondered if she could tiptoe past and find her baby. But her first step hit a creaky board, and the nun's eyes flew open.

"Emma," she gasped. "What are you doing out of bed?" She bounced out of the chair and over to Ruth.

Ruth let herself be led back to the cot. She sat down but refused to lie back. "Sister, when can I see my baby? Where is she? I'm awake now. She must need to be fed. Please, bring her to me."

Sister Jean Marie didn't answer as she tucked the blanket under the thin cot mattress. When she finally looked up, Ruth thought she saw tears in her eyes. Her voice was thick. "She's gone, Emma. She went with her new family, wearing one of the beautiful dresses you made."

Grief clutched Ruth's heart. "No! She's my baby. You can't do that." Tears streamed down her face, and she threw off the blanket the nun had tucked around her legs. Her voice rose as she wailed. "I never gave permission for my baby to be adopted. Let me go. I have to get her. She's not an orphan."

Sister Jean Marie gently took Ruth by the shoulders. "You did give permission. You signed the papers just after the baby was born. And she's gone now. It's best for everyone. Please lie back and get some sleep. It isn't good for you to be so worked up."

Sobbing, Ruth fell onto her pillow. She cried until the flood of tears had dried up and there was only an emptiness that reached to her very core.

PART TWO

18

R uth set her suitcase down and looked up at the house on Grand Avenue. A window with open drapes gave a peek into a downstairs room, most likely a parlor. The curtained upstairs windows showed no light. Snow, heaped in messy piles, lined both sides of the sidewalk leading to the massive front door. She bit her lip and walked up the steps.

Mrs. Irvine answered her knock on the door.

"I'm Ruth Russo. I applied for the job of housekeeper, and I wondered if the position was still available. My circumstances have changed." Ruth looked down at her scuffed and worn hand-me-down shoes and swallowed. This wasn't the time to lose control of her emotions. "My baby has been adopted."

Mrs. Irvine's eyebrows rose. "Come in, Ruth. Let's not let in the cold air."

Ruth stepped gratefully into the warmth of the hallway and closed the door behind her. The thin cries of an infant shattered the quiet home.

"Excuse me, it sounds like Bobby is awake." Mrs. Irvine hurried away, and Ruth stood awkwardly in the entryway clutching her battered suitcase. If the position had been filled, she wouldn't have invited her in, would she?

After several minutes, Mrs. Irvine returned, holding a red-faced baby. "We came by the Home for Unwed Mothers and asked for Ruth, but they said they had no residents named Ruth."

Like a dip in the icy snow, the truth registered. She'd been caught in her own lies. Ruth struggled to breathe. It was impossible to speak. She'd sabotaged her own escape plan, and now it was all too late. Too late to save her baby. She tried to keep the shock of the revelation from registering on her face. Finally she gasped, "I lived there, but the nuns try to keep everything very private. That must be what happened."

Mrs. Irvine continued. "When we couldn't hire you, we found someone else, but she quit yesterday, so yes, the position is open. When can you start? I really need someone."

Ruth lifted the suitcase slightly. "I can start now. I've left the Home and have no need to return."

"Swell." Mrs. Irvine blew a breath of relief and shifted the baby to her other shoulder. "Your room will be in the attic. Let me get a bottle fixed for Bobby, and I'll show you around."

Ruth set the suitcase down and shrugged out of the too-tight coat Sister Jean Marie had given her from donations. She surveyed the spacious entryway which could have held the entire apartment in New York where she had lived as a child. To her right was the parlor, with stiff velveteen couches. To her left, pocket doors closed off a room. A library, maybe? The staircase rose in front of her, curving to the second floor. And a third floor beyond that. Ruth had never even been in a house so grand, and now she would live here. As a servant, she reminded herself, but she couldn't stop the almost giddy feeling of excitement rising above her sorrow.

Mrs. Irvine and Bobby came down the hall, Bobby

squirming and fussing. Ruth's new employer plunked the baby into her arms and handed her a warm glass bottle of milk. "Here, take him in the kitchen and feed him. Maybe then he will be quiet while I show you your duties."

Ruth's heart constricted as she looked down on the now wailing infant. When she poked the nipple in, Bobby immediately closed his mouth and gulped the warm milk.

"You know about burping him, right?"

Ruth had only a vague notion, but she nodded. "Of course." She and Bobby would figure it out.

She settled into one of the wooden kitchen chairs. As Bobby drank, a thin line of milk dribbled from his mouth. Ruth wiped it away with a clean diaper tucked around his neck. When the bottle was half-gone, she set it down and lifted him to her shoulder. After a few tentative soft pats, she used a little more force. Bobby rewarded her with a loud, milky belch. She wiped his chin and reinserted the bottle.

When he finished, she burped him again, then laid him in her lap and spoke to him. "I'm Ruth. I will be living here at your house, and I think you will be one of my duties. So I hope you like me."

Bobby waved his fists and smiled up at her. Ruth fought back tears and refused to think about the baby girl whom she missed with every fiber of her being.

Mrs. Irvine, who had disappeared after Ruth began feeding Bobby, came into the kitchen. "Oh, good, he's finished. You can put him in his bassinet and come with me." A small wicker bassinet stood at one side of the kitchen. Ruth laid Bobby in it and draped the burp cloth over the side. Then she picked up her coat and suitcase and followed Mrs. Irvine up the stairs.

"You can put your belongings up in your room." Mrs. Irvine opened a doorway in the hall and motioned to a narrow staircase.

Upstairs, a long hallway led to four rooms with sloping ceilings. Ruth opened the first door, but that room was full of boxes and trunks. The second room stored dusty furniture piled in a haphazard way. The third one was mostly empty. The last room she entered had a metal bed and a tall chest of drawers. A small, curtained window looked out over the side yard. Ruth set her suitcase on the worn floorboards and laid her coat across the bed. Then she went back downstairs.

Mrs. Irvine showed her the rooms on the second floor—the nursery, the Irvines' bedroom, a guest bedroom, and a bathroom. She described Ruth's cleaning duties for each one. A tall built-in closet held cleaning supplies. Back on the main floor, they circled through the parlor, a formal dining room, and a library. Ruth was amazed by the sheer number of rooms in this fancy house.

In the kitchen, Mrs. Irvine opened the door to a real electric refrigerator and pointed to a package wrapped in butcher paper. "I have ground beef for meatloaf. You do know how to cook, don't you?"

"Yes, ma'am." Ruth nodded as she looked around at the tall cabinets. This kitchen was larger than the one at Sisters of Mercy. She itched to see what was stashed behind the doors.

Bobby had been making noises since they came downstairs, and now, he erupted in cries—high-pitched, screeching cries.

"Will you get him?" Mrs. Irvine asked. "I have a headache, and I need to lie down."

"Certainly." Ruth hurried to the bassinet and lifted the shrieking baby to her shoulder. His cries continued as Ruth patted and jostled him. Nearly an hour later, Bobby fell asleep after Ruth had walked what seemed like several miles through the downstairs rooms. Carefully, she placed him in the bassinet and covered him with a blanket. Did her baby's new mother cover her with one of the blankets that Ruth had made? She swallowed hard and walked into the kitchen. She opened the refrigerator and noted that another bottle had been prepared.

She removed the ground beef and an egg, found some bread in a box on the counter and a bowl in a cupboard. As she stirred the ingredients together and shaped the loaf for baking, she fell into the familiar rhythms of preparing food and nurturing others. After she'd placed the meatloaf into the oven, she mixed up a batch of biscuits, then peeled and boiled potatoes for mashing. She heard Bobby stirring and making noises in his bassinet as she poured chocolate cake batter into a pan.

She filled another pan with water and set the bottle in it to warm. When the baby's sounds became cries, she went to the bed. "Hello, Bobby. It's me, Ruth, again. I have your bottle ready." She lifted him to her shoulder. "I think we'd better find out where your mom keeps the dry diapers."

Upstairs, she found a stack of clean diapers in the nursery. Using the changing table, she laid Bobby down, and despite his protests, she got the wet diaper off, powdered his bottom, and put on a dry one. When fastening one of the pins, she pricked her finger. At least she hadn't hurt the baby. She hoisted him to her shoulder, checked the bottle's temperature, then sat in a rocker in the parlor and fed him.

By the time she laid Bobby back in the bassinet, the edges of the meatloaf were brown and crisp. She pulled it out of the oven and slid the cake in. She had just finished setting dishes on the table when Mrs. Irvine walked in. She had changed her dress, and her lips were painted a bright red.

Mrs. Irvine looked at the table set for three. "Oh, we sit at the dining room table for dinner. And these are not the dishes we use. We use the china for dinner. Just leave your plate here,

Ruth. You may eat in the kitchen after you serve Mr. Irvine and me."

Ruth's cheeks flamed as she removed two of the place settings from the kitchen table and set the dining table for two, using china from the cabinet Mrs. Irvine indicated. Shortly after she'd finished, Mr. Irvine arrived home.

Mrs. Irvine rushed down the hall to greet him, while Ruth checked to make sure things were ready. She poured iced tea into two glasses for their table. How different this was from meals on the farm, or even in the big dining room at Sisters of Mercy.

A tall man with a full head of dark hair swept off his forehead entered the room. Mrs. Irvine followed behind him. "This is Ruth, dear. We have dinner all fixed. Let me take your coat and hat."

Mr. Irvine nodded toward Ruth. "I hope you'll stay with us longer than the last girl did." He handed his coat and hat to his wife then bent over the bassinet. "How's my little pal tonight?" He held out one long-fingered hand for the baby to grasp.

When both the husband and wife were seated, Ruth served the meat loaf, biscuits, and mashed potatoes. Then she cleared some of her cooking dishes, piling them by the sink to be washed. The cake was done, and she cut generous portions for the Irvines.

When they were finished with their meal, Mrs. Irvine opened the door. "You may clear the dishes, now, Ruth."

Ruth took the food back to the kitchen and fixed a plate for herself. Then she put the Irvine's dishes to soak in the sink. She'd just sat down when a wail came from the bassinet. Bobby needed to be fed again.

19

Life at the Irvines left little time to grieve. Cleaning the huge house, cooking meals, and caring for little Bobby kept Ruth's mind and hands busy. Although she'd prepared all the meals on the farm, cooking for the Irvines was quite different. Mrs. Irvine wanted vegetables with her meals, and she wanted Ruth to try all sorts of new recipes that she found in her women's magazines.

"I want you to make these biscuits for supper." Mrs. Irvine pulled a small cardboard box out of her shopping bag.

How could biscuits come in a box? But it was a mix, and you simply added water. Ruth dutifully prepared them for dinner, but Mr. Irvine informed his wife that she was not to purchase the boxed mix again. He much preferred Ruth's homemade biscuits.

The Irvines often went out in the evenings—to dinner, a show, or to visit friends. Then Ruth had time she could call her own. She would feed and put Bobby to bed, then sit in the rocker in the spare bedroom next to the nursery and read. Those were the nights she remembered the card games in

Pearl's bedroom or reading *Black Beauty* with Doris. Ruth wished she had addresses for the girls so she could write to them. But it seemed when the door of Sisters of Mercy swung shut behind them, the whole experience, even the baby they'd given birth to, was forever closed.

Sometimes the Irvines came home slightly inebriated, laughing and leaning on each other as they climbed to the second story. Ruth would go to her chilly bedroom on the third floor feel under the mattress for the wool sock, pull it out, and count the coins—money saved to find her baby. Then, she crawled beneath her quilt, and, longing for all she had lost, cried herself to sleep.

The first Saturday, she cleaned the house from top to bottom, taking care of Bobby's needs in between the dusting and mopping. When the Irvines returned from their shopping trip, Mrs. Irvine hurried upstairs with her bulging sacks from Younkers and J.C. Penney's.

Mr. Irvine lifted Bobby from the bassinet and held him on his lap. "Now, when you get just a little bit older, we'll take you shopping with us, son. And I might even spring for a Green River from Woolworths." Bobby cooed back at him, wiggling with pleasure.

Ruth smiled at them. "He loves his daddy."

Mr. Irvine glanced up. He always seemed surprised to see her. "I guess he does."

Ruth shook out the dishtowel she'd been using and hung it up. "Will you and Mrs. Irvine be attending Mass in the morning?"

Mr. Irvine stared at her. "No, of course we won't. For one thing, we're not Catholic, we're Presbyterian. But most Sundays we sleep in. You can plan breakfast for nine tomorrow."

By the time the Irvines came downstairs the next morning,

Ruth had fed, dressed, and put Bobby down for a nap, prepared bacon, eggs and biscuits, and set the table in the dining room.

As she sat down to her breakfast in the kitchen, she thought about her friends, gathered in St. John's for Mass. Ruth wasn't Catholic, she couldn't partake in Holy Communion or the other Sacraments. Was she Presbyterian now? What did that look like? And how did she talk to God if she didn't know what she was? Would God even listen to someone like her?

She looked down at the plate of food before her and then she bowed her head. "God, it's me, Ruth. I don't know if You can hear me or even if I should talk to You. But I am grateful for a job and good food." She paused a moment before whispering, "Amen."

The rest of the day, she was too busy tending to Bobby's needs and the Irvines' requests to miss the solemn rhythms of Mass she had grown to enjoy.

Mondays were wash days. Ruth carried the heavy baskets of laundry downstairs to the basement. In one of the dingy corners stood a gas-powered machine with a hand wringer. She loaded the machine and watched while the clothes tossed back and forth in the soapy water. Then she fed the clothes through the wringer, filled the tub with clean water for a rinse cycle, wrung them out again, and carried the baskets to the back yard, where she pinned the wet clothes on the clothesline. On snowy or rainy days, she draped the laundry on a cotton rope strung from the basement rafters.

This particular Monday felt unseasonably warm for February. Ruth lugged the first basket of clean wet clothes upstairs, put on her coat, and carried the laundry to the yard. The clothespins hung on the line in a bag, and she clipped the stiff wet clothes to the heavy wire. As she added items, the line sank lower and lower.

She stopped to rub her fingers, numb from the wet and cold. A screen door slammed at the house next door. She looked up to see a brown-skinned girl, about Ruth's age, her hair covered with a bright scarf. She carried a basket out to the clothesline in her yard and began pinning the clothes on the line. Ruth gave what she hoped was a friendly wave and then stooped to lift more soggy clothes from the basket. As she clipped the last of Mr. Irvine's T-shirts to the end of the clothesline, she heard a voice.

"Hello. Are you the Irvines' new girl?"

Rubbing her hands together, Ruth walked to the fence that stretched between the two yards. "Yes. I've been here two weeks."

The girl giggled. "That's a lot longer than most of them stick it out."

Ruth glanced over her shoulder to make sure Mrs. Irvine wasn't popping out of the house with something else for her to do. "They treat me okay. There's just a lot to do."

"I know what you mean. When's your day off?"

Ruth paused to think. "I don't know. They've never mentioned a day off. Is it usual for housekeepers to have one?"

"Well, yes. I have Sundays off. So, I can go to my church, and then I go home for dinner at my mom's."

"If I had a Sunday off, could I go to your church?"

The girl looked at Ruth in surprise. "Why, I guess so." She cocked her head and added. "You'd be the only white girl there."

"Oh." Ruth thought about how most of her life something had made her different—being an orphan, being pregnant, being a housekeeper. "That wouldn't bother me, but maybe you would rather I not come."

"It would be fine with me. By the way, my name's Donna."

"I'm Ruth." She shifted the empty basket to her hip. "I'd better get back inside. Wash days are the longest."

"I know what you mean. Nice meeting you, Ruth." Donna smiled and waved before picking up her own empty basket.

That night, the Irvines went out for dinner. Ruth fixed her supper as Bobby watched from his playpen. He was beginning to roll, so the bassinet had been moved out, and Mr. Irvine had come home with a large cardboard box. He spent most of one evening setting up the new contraption.

When she'd finished her ham salad sandwich, Bobby started to fuss. She put a bottle to warm in a pan on the stove and then picked him up. "Hey, little buddy. You'll be eating sandwiches before we know it." She jostled him on her hip. "But maybe we should start with cereal." She kissed the downy top of his head and wondered if someone held her baby girl on their hip and kissed the top of her head.

She carried Bobby into the parlor where she sat in the rocker and fed him. He clutched the bottle and drank hungrily. It seemed Bobby grew or changed some every day. And with each new accomplishment, she imagined what her baby was doing. She wiped a tear off his forehead, but he didn't seem to mind.

When he finished, Ruth burped him, carried him upstairs, and dressed him in a warm flannel nightgown and a dry diaper. She rocked and sang to him, and when his eyes drooped, she laid him in the crib, covered him with a blanket, and tiptoed from the room.

Mrs. Irvine received a new *Ladies Home Journal* in the mail, and Ruth leafed through the pages, finally settling in to read a short story, "The Shopkeeper's Dilemma."

A few hours later, Mr. Irvine's voice startled her awake. The magazine slid to the floor, and she picked it up hurriedly and smoothed the cover.

"How was Bobby?" Mrs. Irvine stood at the door of the guest bedroom.

Ruth laid the magazine on the rocker. "He was fine. He rolled over twice in the playpen. He's always trying something new." She stepped into the hall. "When is my day off?"

Mrs. Irvine's eyebrows shot up. "I didn't know you required a day off. Do you have some place to go, or something to do?"

Ruth took a deep breath. "I'd like to go to church."

"Well, yes. I guess Sunday would be a good day for you to have off. Mr. Irvine will be home to help me with Bobby if I need it. We won't be able to pay you for that day."

"I understand. Thanks, Mrs. Irvine." Ruth climbed the stairs to her bedroom, wondering if Donna's church really would welcome an unmarried white girl who had given birth to a baby who was no longer hers.

20

R uth poured a cup of coffee and set it before Mrs. Irvine. "When do you plan to start Bobby on some cereal? Sometimes he acts as if he's still hungry."

Mrs. Irvine leaned over to watch Bobby trying to roll to his tummy in the playpen. "Look in the pantry. I think I bought a container of Pablum last shopping day."

Ruth handed a plate of bright-yellow scrambled eggs and buttered toast to Mrs. Irvine and then went to look for the Pablum. She found the container behind some Cream of Wheat cereal and read the instructions on the side of the box. There was still hot water in the teakettle, and she mixed a few spoonfuls with the powdered cereal. Then she put Bobby on her lap.

Mrs. Irvine brought her a small silver spoon with a curved handle. At the first taste of the unfamiliar food, Bobby's face grew quizzical. He rolled the cereal in his mouth, then pushed it out with his tongue. The gooey, gray mass dribbled down his chin.

Ruth patiently wiped it off his chin and tried another

spoonful. This one he swallowed. By the time the bowl was empty, his mouth was eagerly flying open for the next bite. Mrs. Irvine had finished her breakfast, and she held out her arms for her son.

Her voice took on the high-pitched baby-talk she always used with Bobby. "Does my little snookums like his cereal? Mommy bought it just for you."

Turning away from his waving fists, Mrs. Irvine told Ruth, "I want to get the house cleaned top to bottom in the next few weeks. My mother is coming for a visit and will stay through Easter. Let's start by cleaning upstairs. You can move the bassinet to the attic. I don't plan on using it anytime soon." She chuckled slightly, twirling a curl around one index finger.

"Sure. Do you want me to start with the guest bedroom?"

"Yes. It will be warm enough today for you to take the rugs out and beat them, maybe even wash windows."

"I'll start right after breakfast." Ruth picked up Mrs. Irvine's dirty dishes and moved them to the kitchen sink.

After eating breakfast and lingering a minute or two over a cup of strong coffee, Ruth hurried upstairs. She folded the bassinet legs and hoisted it ahead of her up the stairs to the third floor. After unlatching and pushing open the door of the storage room, she searched in the jumbled mess to find room for the wicker bed. She shoved a trunk and a floor lamp aside and was about to slide the bassinet in next to a chest of drawers when something caught her eye. Hidden beneath a pile of clothes was a sewing machine. The hand crank was dusty and draped with cobwebs but at a tentative push, the needle moved up and down.

Ruth slid the bassinet farther back against the large, dark-stained chest. Then holding the knowledge of the sewing machine like a secret hope, she hurried down to the guest bedroom. Much later, after the rugs were beaten, the floors scrubbed, the furniture polished, and the bed remade with fresh bedding, Ruth approached Mrs. Irvine in the parlor where she was reading the *Ladies Home Journal*.

"The guest bedroom is clean. I can start on your bedroom tomorrow."

"Great. My mother expects a clean house when she visits."

"I put the bassinet in the storage room."

"Like I said, I hope I don't need it for a while. Not that I don't love little Bobby." Mrs. Irvine glanced toward the playpen where Bobby chewed on the leg of his teddy bear.

Ruth shifted from one foot to the other. "While I was in there, I saw a sewing machine."

"Oh, yes. My mother-in-law gave me that old thing as a wedding present. I've never used it." Mrs. Irvine glanced down at her magazine, as if she wished Ruth would go.

"If you'd let me bring it into my room, I know how to sew. I could do your mending and make clothes for Bobby."

Mrs. Irvine frowned. "Why, I guess that would be okay. Just don't be up there sewing when I need you in the kitchen."

"No, ma'am." Ruth felt like skipping as she went to the kitchen to prepare dinner.

That night, she moved the machine into her already crowded bedroom and cleaned off the dust and the cobwebs. Then she took in the seams on one of her dresses. She had lost the weight gained during her pregnancy, and most of her clothes bagged around her petite frame.

The rest of the week, Ruth worked every night remaking her dresses. She brought the clothes she'd made for her baby down from the closet and thought about remaking them for Bobby, but he was a big boy, and she didn't have enough material. She held them close for a moment before returning them to the high shelf. She mended some of Mr. Irvine's shirts.

At this rate, it wouldn't be long before she used up the rest of her thread.

On Saturday, Mr. and Mrs. Irvine left to do some shopping downtown. Ruth hadn't seen Donna outside to tell her she planned on accompanying her to church, so after she put Bobby down for his morning nap, she crossed the yard and knocked on the neighbor's back door. Donna opened the door. "Ruth. What can I do for you?"

"I'd like to go to church with you tomorrow, but I don't know what time."

A grin blossomed over Donna's face. "Did you get Sunday off? Keen. Meet me outside at 9:30. We can take the streetcar."

Ruth looked down at her scuffed brown shoes. "I don't have church clothes."

"Anything you wear will be fine."

Donna stood at the door and waved as Ruth made her way back to the Irvine's.

The next morning, Ruth put on her least-faded dress, a hat, gloves, and the dark green coat Sister Jean Marie had given her. She picked up her purse and walked halfway down the stairs before remembering the purpose of this outing. She returned to her room and opened the bottom drawer of the small chest. Underneath her underwear lay her mother's Bible. She hadn't opened it since Christmas, when she read the story of Mary giving birth. The memories of being pregnant washed over her and tears flooded her eyes. Ruth brushed them away with one gloved hand, tucked the Bible under her arm, and marched downstairs.

She heard Bobby crying in his playpen, but she took a deep breath, opened the front door and stepped out into the chilly air.

Donna stood on the sidewalk and gave a little wave as Ruth

crossed the yard. "I'm so glad you got the day off. Are you ready for a morning of worship?"

Ruth smiled. "I think so." She brushed at a worn spot on the hand-me-down coat. "Do I look okay?"

Donna's laugh was hearty. "Do you think God cares what you wear to His house? And the people who attend my church don't care either. But you look real nice, Ruth. That color looks good on you."

The two young women walked toward the streetcar stop. Once there, they only had to wait a few minutes before the car rumbled into view. It stopped with a squealing protest from the wheels. They boarded and dropped the coins in the receptacle, then moved to the middle of the car where a seat was empty.

Ruth and Donna chatted as the streetcar swayed down the tracks, sharing information about their respective jobs and employers.

Donna asked, "Where did you live before you took this job?"

Ruth paused, not wanting to lie anymore, yet not wanting to share the painful details of her life.

Mercifully, the streetcar screeched to a stop. Donna grabbed at the bar on the back of the seat in front of them and stood. "Oh, this is our stop. I almost missed it."

Ruth followed her out of the car. This neighborhood was quite different from where the Irvines lived. Small frame houses clustered close to the street. The smell of cooking fires filled the air. Couples in their Sunday best walked down the wooden sidewalks, many of them with children marching behind.

Donna's church was a white wooden building with a tall steeple and a wooden cross at the top. A bell pealed out, announcing worship time. At the door, a gentleman in a suit greeted Donna warmly. "Sister Donna, it's so good to see you this morning."

Donna, her hand still engulfed in the man's large one, turned to smile at Ruth. "Elder Ron, this is my friend, Miss Russo."

The man's smile was warm and welcoming, and he released Donna's hand to shake Ruth's. "We're glad to have you join us for worship this morning, Miss Russo."

As they moved into the church, Ruth glanced over her shoulder. Elder Ron watched them enter with a slightly puzzled expression on his face.

Donna leaned close and whispered, "I bet that's the first time he's welcomed a white girl into our church." Both of them giggled softly.

Ruth followed Donna to a pew near the front. Men, women and children continued to file in. A soft buzz of conversation was punctuated with occasional raised voices: "Halleluja! We been praying for that." "Well, ain't that the truth." "Do tell, Sister Lisbeth."

A family slid into the pew next to Ruth. Three stair-step girls were dressed in crisp cotton dresses. Their hair was pulled into neat braids, and they each wore bright-colored hair bows. Ruth smiled at the children, but they eyed her suspiciously and scooted closer to their parents.

A woman in a red-flowered dress and an elaborate hat walked to a piano at the front of the church. She played a few bars of music, and the talking ceased. Everyone stood, and a hum began softly, then swelled until it seemed that the church burst into song with one voice. Then, song after song ebbed and flowed through the sanctuary. The people swayed with the music, sometimes shouting, sometimes clapping.

Ruth watched wide-eyed, feeling slightly uncomfortable. She glanced around, but no one stared at her—they were focused on worship. Ruth sang a few simple lyrics and even swayed stiffly with the music.

A short man climbed the two steps to the stage of the small church. The singing faded, and the people sank to their seats. The man wiped his nearly bald head with a handkerchief before speaking. "That was some mighty good singing."

From nearly every pew there was a chorus of "amen," "praise Jesus," and "uh, huh." Then, the pastor asked everyone to stand as he read from the Bible. Ruth tried to find the page in her Bible but gave up and listened intently, memorizing the scripture reference so she could look it up when she got home. He read from the book of Luke, a story Jesus told about a shepherd looking for a lost sheep.

Everyone sat again, accompanied by pews creaking, clothes rustling, and whispers of small children accompanied by hushes from parents. The pastor began speaking, and for nearly an hour, he paced the front of the stage, his voice rising and falling. Occasionally, he paused to wipe his face with the handkerchief.

Throughout the sermon, the congregation encouraged him. "Amen! Preach it brother. Hallelujah. Thank you, Jesus." He finally wound down and asked the congregation to bow their heads for prayer. The prayer was lengthy, and the response from the people in the pews continued, softer and quieter: "Ummm, hmmm. Yes, God. That's right."

When the pastor spoke the final, "Amen," the church exploded with noise as people greeted one another. Donna introduced Ruth to several people as they made their way out of the church.

Donna went home with an aunt for dinner, so Ruth returned to the streetcar stop and rode back to the Irvines alone.

The house was empty when she arrived. A note on the table

from Mrs. Irvine told her that they had gone out for the day. Ruth changed her clothes and found some cold meat in the refrigerator for lunch. Then she went up to her room to sew.

As she mended a nightslip of Bobby's, torn in the wringer on the washing machine, she thought about the sermon. Ruth knew she was like the shepherd. No matter how many children she cared for, she would never stop looking for the one who was lost.

21

M r. and Mrs. Irvine didn't return until nearly ten. Ruth heard their footsteps on the stairs, and then Mrs. Irvine poked her head into the little attic room. "We're home."

Ruth scooted her chair away from the sewing machine. "Do you want me to put Bobby to bed?"

"No, he fell asleep in the car on the way home, so I just removed his jacket and put him in the crib. He can sleep in his clothes tonight." She pulled Ruth's door shut, and her footsteps echoed down the steps.

Ruth turned back to the sewing machine, and a wave of loneliness washed over her.

The next morning, Bobby woke as the first rays of sun poked through Ruth's window. She dressed quickly, then lifted him from his crib and changed his soaked diaper, dropping it in the diaper pail. Then she chose a clean white dress embroidered with little yellow ducks, slipped it on him, and carried him downstairs. He mouthed a rattle in the playpen while Ruth went to the cupboard for his cereal.

Bobby had quickly accepted this new food and opened his

mouth for every spoonful, screeching when the spoon didn't come fast enough. After Ruth scraped the last bite from the bowl, Mrs. Irvine came downstairs and lifted Bobby from her arms.

"And how's my little baby this morning?" she cooed.

Ruth fixed Bobby's bottle and handed it to his mother before pulling out items for the Irvine's breakfast.

As she fried eggs and leftover slices of ham, Mrs. Irvine set down the bottle Bobby had drained and laid him in his playpen. He promptly rolled to his tummy and grabbed at the wooden slats.

Ruth smiled at him. "He's going to be crawling before we know it."

Mrs. Irvine sipped her cup of coffee and nodded. "Yes, I suppose so."

Mr. Irvine strode into the room and bent over the playpen. "Good morning, Buster." Bobby gurgled back at him, but Mr. Irvine had already taken a seat in the dining room and unfolded the newspaper Ruth had fetched from the front porch. He sipped a cup of coffee laced with cream and sugar and studied the front page.

Ruth arranged the eggs, ham, and slices of toast onto plates and placed them on the table in front of them.

Mrs. Irvine laid a napkin on her lap. "Ruth ..."

"Yes?" Ruth stopped mid-stride on her way back to the kitchen, her chest tightening with anxiety.

"We understand you went to church with the Halstead's girl?" Mrs. Irvine lifted her fork but held it above the plate as if unsure what to stab first.

"Yes, Donna asked me."

"We would prefer you not spend your time off with the Negroes. It just doesn't look right." Her fork stabbed a piece of ham. Mr. Irvine had not raised his eyes from his plate.

Ruth nodded. "Yes, ma'am." Images of the warm and welcoming church members surfaced and faded in a cloud of disappointment. What would she do on her day off now? And how would she learn more about the shepherd?

She fled to the kitchen and had just finished her breakfast and washed the dishes when Bobby squawked. She lifted him out of the playpen and carried him upstairs for a diaper change and his morning nap.

While Bobby napped, Ruth carried clothes down to the basement and started the washing while Mrs. Irvine readied herself for her after-lunch bridge club meeting.

Ruth hung the first load of clothes, pinning them carefully with the clothespins from a striped bag. A row of clothes already hung out to dry at the Halstead's house. She'd missed her opportunity to chat with Donna, but how would she explain the Irvine's request? As she pinned the last shirt, Mrs. Irvine called from the back door. "Ruth, Bobby is awake. Would you mind taking him? I need to finish waving my hair."

Ruth changed Bobby's diaper and settled him in his playpen with a rubber ball and a cloth book before hurrying back downstairs to start another load of laundry. She was just feeding a pair of Mr. Irvine's pants through the wringer when she heard the screams.

She raced up the steps and nearly collided with Mrs. Irvine in the kitchen. Bobby had one chubby leg poking through the slats of the wooden playpen. It appeared that he tried to roll over and his leg had twisted. Mrs. Irvine reached him first. She gently maneuvered his leg through the slats and picked up the sobbing baby.

"Why weren't you watching him?" She glared at Ruth.

Ruth tried to pat Bobby's back, but his mother moved him away from her.

"I'm so sorry. I was downstairs with the laundry."

Mrs. Irvine sat down and examined Bobby's leg carefully as Ruth watched helplessly from across the kitchen. Finally, she looked up and nodded. "I think he's okay. I'll stay here in the kitchen with him. Just go finish the laundry."

Ruth trudged back downstairs. She fed the rest of the clothes through the wringer, feeling like she had been wrung out as well. She quickly hung the wet clothes outside, glad for the sunshine that would dry them despite the chilly temperatures.

When she came back in, Bobby was in his playpen again. Mrs. Irvine must have gone back upstairs to get ready. Ruth lifted him out and held him close. There was a small red mark on his leg where it had been caught between the rails. Ruth hoped it would fade before she had to explain anything to Mr. Irvine.

She gave Bobby a kiss and put him back down while she warmed up leftover ham and potatoes for lunch. Mrs. Irvine came downstairs dressed in a new polka dot dress. She ate in the kitchen, while Ruth held Bobby and fed him some mashed banana.

"Here. Let him try these potatoes." Mrs. Irvine held out her spoon.

Bobby mouthed the strange new food before swallowing and opening his mouth like a small bird, waiting for the next bite.

Ruth and Mrs. Irvine laughed at his eager expression. Ruth asked, "Do you want to hold him, or should I put him back in his playpen?"

"Oh, I don't want to muss my dress." Mrs. Irvine brushed at the skirt.

Ruth laid Bobby on his tummy in the playpen. He wobbled for a moment, then toppled to his back and grinned up at her. Ruth cleared away her employer's dishes and cleaned up the kitchen. She still had another load to put in the washing machine, dinner to prepare before Mr. Irvine arrived home, and, of course, she would take care of Bobby.

Much later, after the Irvines were both home and dinner had been served, Ruth laid Bobby in his crib, tucked a blanket around him, and slipped outside for a walk. The temperature had dropped, but something in the air hinted at spring. She took her time, looking at each home as she passed. Most of them were large with two or three stories, spacious lawns, and stately entrances. Lamplight spilled softly from curtained windows, and Ruth imagined the families gathered within—playing games, reading, discussing events of the day. A few houses had wide porches, and occasionally a woman or child would wave as she passed by.

Ruth quieted her inner longings with a pragmatic shake of her head. She would never be a part of a family. That dream had been stripped from her, along with her innocence.

As she circled the block and returned to the Irvines', she passed the Halstead residence. A surge of sorrow rose when she thought of Donna. Her past denied her a family, and now a friendship had been denied as well. Ruth kept the tears in until she shut her bedroom door.

22

One of Bobby's small hands grasped Ruth's blouse, the other rested on his chin, his tiny thumb secure in his mouth. His eyes blinked and fluttered shut. She rocked him a while longer, softly singing some of the lullabies she remembered Mama singing, "Hush Little Baby, Don't Say a Word" and "Baa, Baa, Black Sheep."

Finally, she stood and laid him in the crib. For a moment she stayed, patting his back and wondering. Did anyone rock her baby to sleep and sing to her? With a sigh, she turned and went downstairs. She needed to finish the dishes she'd left soaking when Bobby had started fussing.

When the kitchen was clean again, she folded the dishtowel and hung it up, planning to hurry upstairs to sew. Then she remembered—she'd run out of thread while mending Mrs. Irvine's green dress.

Mr. and Mrs. Irvine were in the parlor reading.

Ruth cleared her throat. "I'm sorry to bother you."

Mrs. Irvine looked up from her book of poetry. "What do you need, Ruth?"

"I was sewing up the seam of your green dress and ran out of thread. I thought maybe I could take Saturday off this week instead of Sunday and go downtown to purchase thread and some other items I need."

Mr. Irvine set his copy of *Life Magazine* down. "Evelyn, your mother is coming in Tuesday. We could take her out for dinner on Saturday night."

Mrs. Irvine pressed her lips together. "Yes, that would work." She nodded at Ruth. "Go ahead and take Saturday off. Then you will be here on Sunday, is that correct?"

"Yes, ma'am. Good night."

The Irvines chorused, "Good night," as they returned to their reading. Ruth climbed both flights of stairs to her bedroom and made a list of things she wanted to buy during her trip downtown.

The next few days were a flurry of preparations before Mrs. Irvine's mother came. The entire house needed to be recleaned, even the areas Ruth had scrubbed only days before.

Bobby fussed more than usual, and sometimes Ruth had to leave him fussing in his playpen or crib to get the work finished. Mrs. Irvine seemed able to ignore him more than Ruth, concentrating on lists of meals she wanted Ruth to fix and serve. Many of them were new recipes she'd clipped from her women's magazines.

Mr. Irvine picked up Mrs. Nelson from the train station. When Mrs. Irvine introduced her to Ruth, the tiny gray-haired woman eyed Ruth over her spectacles with steel-blue eyes. "I hope you are providing a stimulating and nourishing environment for my grandson."

Ruth smiled. "I certainly try, Mrs. Nelson."

After their first conversation, Mrs. Nelson took no more notice of Ruth, unless she wanted her to fix Bobby's bottle or refill her iced tea.

Bobby no longer spent time in his play pen. He sat on his grandmother's lap or rolled around on a blanket at her feet. She insisted that he accompany them when they went out, even when it was naptime.

"Oh, he can sleep in the car on my lap," she told her daughter and son-in-law.

In the morning, Ruth listened for Bobby's cry, only to find him downstairs with his grandmother. Her daily chores had lessened, but she missed caring for the baby.

Saturday, she woke early with a rush of excitement as she thought about her trip downtown. Pushing aside fears of getting lost, Ruth dressed in the clothes she'd worn to church with Donna. She avoided going to the kitchen, because she knew she would end up fixing a breakfast, feeding Bobby, or tending to a chore. She pulled on her gloves, made certain that her hat was straight, picked up her pocketbook, and marched out the front door.

Her day off seemed like a treasure, and she felt like skipping down the sidewalk.

However, the bright sunshine was deceptive, and Ruth shivered in the cool morning breeze as she waited for the streetcar. She hopped from one foot to the other. No chill in the air would spoil her day off.

The streetcar came, and Ruth got on, dropping her fare in the container. The car was crowded with people, so she grasped a pole and stood, swaying as they moved. Minutes later, the driver stopped the car and opened the doors. "Walnut Avenue," he announced.

Ruth stepped down into a mass of people who all seemed in a rush to get somewhere. The noise was overwhelming—cars honking, newsboys shouting on the corners, and the continuous hum and clank of the street cars. For a moment, she stood and watched. Then with a grin, she straightened her hat and joined the crowd. She took her time, looking in each window and deciding what she would buy if her little purse held hundreds of dollars rather than a few coins.

At Madison's Dress Shop, she stood for several moments in front of the window admiring the dresses and hats.

The door swung open and a small man with a gigantic mustache smiled at her. "Good morning, Madam. Would you like to come in and try on a dress? Perhaps the yellow polka-dotted one? It would look lovely on you."

"No, thank you." Ruth moved back from the window. "I'm just looking." She walked on down the street, trying now to refrain from pausing too long in front of the windows. Instead, she watched the stream of people and when her eyes lit on an infant, she studied the face intently, hoping she could somehow recognize a baby girl she'd never seen.

When she passed a cafeteria, her stomach rumbled, and she remembered she'd missed breakfast. Ruth was tempted to go inside and buy a pastry and a cup of coffee, but after mentally counting the coins in her purse, she kept walking.

At Woolworths Five and Dime, she picked out her thread, a yard of material to make new nightslips for Bobby, and a pair of stockings. She eyed the silk stockings and wished she could buy the luxury item instead of the thick cotton socks.

She browsed through the aisles, looking at the other items on display. Then she paid for her purchases, left the store, and started down the sidewalk again. She stopped in front of a hardware store with gardening items in the window. Would Mrs. Irvine would let her put a garden in the back yard? They could eat fresh vegetables all summer, and maybe she could even put up some for winter. And, maybe there would be more than they could use, and she could sell a few vegetables and add to the meager amount in her hidden sock.

"Ruth. Hey, Ruth Schmidt."

Ruth dropped the sack holding the stockings as fear washed over her in waves. She bent to pick it up, but she couldn't control her trembling hands.

A tall, broad-shouldered young man slid to a stop, panting. "What are you doing in Des Moines?"

She turned her head away. "My name's not Ruth Schmidt."

Jack Maher. Her classmate in Grantsville when she was permitted to attend. He cocked his head at her and a lock of hair slipped from his carefully combed wave and drooped over his forehead. "What? Are you married now?"

Ruth shook her head, allowing herself a glimpse into Jack's blue eyes before looking down at the sidewalk again. Jack had been one of the few young people in Grantsville who had treated her kindly, not as if being an orphan was a disease one might catch. Once he even carried her books and walked her home, even though he lived in the opposite direction.

Ruth whispered as if someone passing by might be listening. "Jack, forget you saw me here. And please don't tell anyone."

She started to walk away, stumbling on legs that felt numb. Suddenly, Jack was at her side. He grasped her elbow.

"Ruth, I've thought about you for three years. The least you owe me is an explanation." He continued to hold her arm. His hand was warm and gentle. "Rizzo's is about a block away. They have a Saturday special—usually spaghetti. What do you say? May I buy you lunch?"

Ruth pulled her arm away, trying to calm her racing heart as waves of panic washed over her. But what would it hurt to have one meal with Jack? She was nineteen now, and no one could force her to return to Grantsville. And her shameful secret had been wrenched from her arms.

She clutched her pocketbook. "I don't have enough to buy a meal."

Jack's smile was broad and sincere. "This is my treat. Come on." He took her arm again, and they strolled down the sidewalk.

Rizzo's was a small Italian restaurant with aromas that transported Ruth back to her childhood in New York. Before her mother became ill, she spent hours in the kitchen stirring up spicy marinara sauce and rolling out dough for homemade noodles. Ruth stood on a chair and begged to help. She smiled at the memory.

When the hostess showed them to a small table, Jack pulled out her chair. Then he sat across from her. "So, what are you doing in Des Moines?"

"I work for the Irvines. They have a baby boy who's almost five months old. What are you doing here?"

"I'm going to law school at Drake University."

Ruth was genuinely pleased for him. "Wonderful, Jack. A lawyer. I knew you would do something big. You were always so smart."

Jack laughed. "No smarter than the girl who always bested me in the spelling and geography bees."

The waiter appeared at their table, and Jack ordered the spaghetti special for both of them. "You do like spaghetti, don't you?"

Ruth smiled. "My last name, the one my real parents gave me, is Russo. I'm one hundred per cent Italian. So, yes, I love pasta."

"The Schmidts didn't adopt you?"

Ruth's body tensed. "They provided a home because I was an orphan. But, no, they didn't adopt me. I was fifteen when I came to Iowa. They needed someone to help Thelma, not a child to raise."

Jack leaned over the table, listening to her. "Taking care of

Thelma—is that what you did after you stopped coming to school?"

"Yes. I could only come if she was feeling well. And when she got really sick ..." Ruth's voice trailed off and she looked away.

"I missed you when you weren't at school. I had no competition for the spelling bees and essays."

"Oh, I never gave you any real competition. Tell me about law school. Is it really difficult?"

Jack talked about life at the university and Ruth relaxed. Their plates of spaghetti came along with a basket of warm, homemade Italian bread. As they ate, they talked about their lives in Des Moines, Jack shared snippets of classes he enjoyed, Ruth recounted funny stories about Bobby.

When their plates were empty, the waitress cleared them away and brought Jack the bill.

Ruth gathered her bag and gloves. "Thanks for the lunch. It was fabulous."

Jack stood and helped Ruth slide her arms into her jacket. "Can I see you again? Do you have a number where I can ring you up? Or an address where I can write to you?"

Tears filled Ruth's eyes as she looked up at him. "Today has been a gift I never expected. Please try to understand, Jack. You must not contact me. I can't see you again." Before he could respond, she ran from the restaurant and down the sidewalk, losing herself in the Saturday crowd.

23

Ruth woke and stretched. She listened for the sounds of Bobby stirring in his room below hers. Then with a surge of joy, she remembered it was Saturday—her fourth one off. She threw back the quilt and hummed a bar or two of "Dinah" as she washed up at the tiny washstand by her bed.

She glanced at her current sewing project, a stuffed bunny she was making for Bobby from a soft, worn blanket Mrs. Irvine had given her. She hoped to have it finished by Easter next week but needed some embroidery thread for the face.

Since Mrs. Nelson arrived, it seemed Ruth's life became even busier. The Irvines expected three large meals a day. And, although Mrs. Nelson loved to coo over Bobby, she was quick to hand him over to Ruth if he fussed, or needed a diaper change, or a bath. But today, Ruth had the day off, and she was headed downtown.

Thirty minutes later, as she walked toward the front door, she heard Bobby wailing in the kitchen. "Ruth!" Mrs. Irvine called.

With a sigh, Ruth turned and went down the hall. Mrs.

Irvine held the baby out toward her. "I can't get him to stop crying, and I'm trying to fix breakfast for my mother. Please, will you feed him before you go?"

"I can do that." Ruth took Bobby and held him close until his sobs turned to hiccups. She sat him on her hip as she warmed milk, fixed cereal and mashed a banana. Then she spooned the gray gooey mixture into his eager mouth. After he finished eating, she wiped his chin and a spot on her dress where his little fingers went from his mouth to her skirt. She laid him in his playpen, and he rolled to reach his cloth book. At last, Ruth slipped out the door.

When the streetcar doors swished open and the driver announced, "Walnut Avenue," Ruth wished she'd spooned a few bites of the cereal into her own mouth. The smells of pastries and bread from the nearby bakery made her stomach rumble. But those were luxuries she couldn't afford. She marched down the sidewalk toward Woolworths.

A young man leaned against the building, holding a paper-wrapped pastry. Ruth was so focused on his doughnut, she didn't look at his face until he reached for her arm. "Ruth. I can't believe I found you again. That Saturday at Rizzo's—I paid for our meal, turned around, and you were gone. I've been standing outside Woolworths every Saturday this month, hoping you'd come by."

Ruth pulled her arm from his grasp. "Why, Jack? I told you not to contact me."

Jack shook his head. "I can't do that." He sang a few bars of "The Very Thought of You." "Please, Ruth. This must be your day off. Spend it with me. We can go to Union Park, take a boat ride, go to Rizzo's again, whatever you want. And if you give me a good reason, I promise it will be the last time. I won't stalk you at Woolworths on Saturday mornings. I'll leave you alone."

The pleading in his blue eyes melted something inside her, and she pushed her fear to the back. "I need to do some shopping. If you want to wait, I'll give you an answer when I return."

"I'll be here." Jack's smile followed Ruth into the store. She stood in front of the embroidery thread, looking for the perfect shade of pink for a bunny's nose, and trying to decide if she could risk spending a day with Jack. She glanced toward the back of the store, hoping to see a rear entrance, but there didn't appear to be one. She wasn't sure if she was relieved or disappointed.

She finally picked a bright shade of pink and some black for whiskers and carried them to the front. As she dug the coins out of her purse, she could see Jack's form through the front door. Her heart hammered as the clerk said, "Thank you," and handed her a small paper sack. She glanced again toward the back and then strode to the front door and Jack.

He held out his arm, and Ruth slipped her hand through. "One day, Jack. I will spend one day with you."

"Then I will make this day as special as I can." He bowed slightly, sweeping his spare arm in front of him. "What does the lady desire? Will it be the park? The movies? A drive in the country?"

Ruth stopped abruptly. "A drive?"

Jack's smile was brighter than the morning sunshine bathing the street. "I have a Ford. Not brand new, but she's clean and runs well. A man who is working at the law offices of Martin and Brown needs transportation."

"Where's your car?"

"Parked over on Locust Avenue."

Ruth resumed walking. "I've never been in a motorcar."

Jack tucked her arm close and grinned. "Well, we must remedy that situation at once. A road trip it is!"

Ruth practically skipped to keep up with Jack's long-legged strides. She tipped her head up to let the warm spring sunshine bathe her face, and the heavy packages of worry, shame, and fear slid temporarily to the ground.

"Here's my tin can." Jack's flourish indicated a green Model A Ford parked at the curb. He opened the passenger door and held Ruth's hand lightly as she settled herself in the seat. Jack slid into the driver's side and looked at Ruth with a grin, "Are you ready for this?"

Ruth laughed in reply. Jack flipped a lever on the steering wheel, maneuvered a knob on the floor between them, turned a key, and the motor sputtered to life. Jack steered the car into the downtown traffic. He turned at the corner and went around the block, heading east on Grand.

Ruth watched through her window as the town rolled swiftly by. Her nose bumped the glass.

"You can put your window down," Jack shouted over the noise of the motor. "Just turn that handle."

Ruth cranked the handle around and the glass slid down. The wind blew against her face and threatened to blow her hat off. She held it on with one hand and leaned out, waving to the people on the sidewalk.

A huge building topped with a golden dome loomed in the distance.

Ruth gasped. "The capitol?"

"Yes. That's our state capitol. I thought you lived in Des Moines."

Ruth stared until she could no longer see it. "I've never been here, though." She thought of the months she was sequestered at Sisters of Mercy. And how little she'd done and seen since being employed by the Irvines. But not today. Today, she was off to see the world.

They made one stop at a small Italian grocery for their deli sandwiches—salami, cheese, and a generous sprinkling of pepperoncini slices. Jack lifted two Cokes out of the cooler and paid for the sandwiches and the drinks.

Jack turned the Model A north, and within a short time they were out of the city. The fields—vast stretches of dirt with cornstalks poking up like broken springs through bedding—waited for the seed that would turn them into the farmer's garden. Red barns stood with doors gaping open to welcome herds of dairy cows or large, shaggy horses grazing nearby.

Ruth hungrily gazed at the scenery flowing past.

"Does it make you miss Grantsville?"

Jack's voice startled Ruth out of her reverie. She shuddered. "Not in the least."

In the quiet that followed her outburst, Jack frowned, his forehead wrinkling. "You don't miss anything?"

Ruth's breathing quickened and she felt sweat prickling under her arms, despite the cool breeze through the still-open window. "Maybe the animals, especially the kittens." A memory surfaced. Ruth had rescued a tiny orange kitten whose mother rejected it and she brought into the house. She remembered the softness of his fur and his barn-sweet odor. Then she heard the thunder of Otto's voice when he came inside that night, and his scowl as he scooped up the kitten and threw it to the ground outside. She found the tiny lifeless body the next morning and buried it in the orchard.

Tears made the passing farms blur, and she blinked and looked down at her hands clutching the seat.

Suddenly Jack's warm hand covered hers. "I don't know what happened, but I'm sorry. I'm sorry I even mentioned it. Let me tell you about where I'm taking you."

Ruth turned to him and smiled. "Okay."

"We're going to Ames first. That's where Iowa State College is."

Ruth thought about Pearl, the rest of the girls, and their little lost babies. Did Pearl ever return to Iowa State?

"But that's not where we're going. We'll breeze through Ames and then go west. There's a state park called The Ledges. We can have our picnic there and see the canyons. The park has some keen rock formations and a little stream that runs through it. How about it?"

"Sounds perfect."

Jack talked on, telling her about the hiking trails in several state parks. Ruth had never been to a park unless you counted the square in Grantsville. The grassy block held a stone bandstand where they held concerts in the summertime. The first year she had been with the Schmidts, before Thelma had been bed-ridden, they'd gone to the Fourth of July celebration. The town band gave a concert of patriotic songs.

"Do you remember the first year I was in Grantsville? The Fourth of July?"

Jack's forehead wrinkled. "Was that the time the band played, and I asked you to dance?"

Ruth giggled.

"You turned me down." Jack sounded indignant.

"Only because I didn't know how to dance."

By now they were both laughing.

The city of Ames rolled into view and they both grew quiet watching the buildings. They left the main road for a few blocks and drove by Iowa State College. Ruth leaned close to the window and looked for Pearl, but she didn't see any familiar faces.

A short time later, they turned into Ledges State Park. Jack pulled an old blanket from the trunk and they spread it out on the grass for their picnic. After eating, they climbed the steep trail to Table Rock, a gigantic flat rock overlooking the canyon. They slipped and slid their way back down, and Jack removed his socks and shoes to wade in the chilly creek by the road. Ruth sat on a rock and giggled when he gasped at the cold. When the sun began slipping behind the tree covered bluffs, they returned to the car for the long drive home.

Jack stopped the car in front of the Irvine's house. By the time he set the brake and made his way around the car, Ruth had already opened her door and stepped out. Jack reached for her hand, but she held it in front of her. "One day, Jack. But it was the most wonderful day ever. Thank you for today. Please don't walk me to the door.." She hurried up the walk without looking back, but she knew he stood and watched until she entered.

Bobby was already in his crib for the night and Mrs. Nelson and the Irvines were listening to the radio. Ruth went quietly up to her room. Then she lay on her bed and recalled the details of her wonderful day, treasuring each one like a precious gem in a jewelry collection, until she drifted off to sleep.

24

The warm breeze tickled Ruth's hair as she carried the basket outside. She shook out a clean, wet diaper and fastened it on the clothesline with a pin. She knew she didn't deserve Jack's friendship. She couldn't let it continue. If he knew the secret she held, her shameful months at Sisters of Mercy, and her deep wounds of grief for the baby girl who haunted her dreams, he would turn from her in disgust. She'd had the one day, but there would be no more.

She shook out another diaper and pinned it up, each one sharing clothespins, like a line of children holding hands for Red Rover. She gazed into the blue sky. Jack was simply an old school chum, a pal from her childhood. She could spend one day with him and it wouldn't mean a thing.

The Halstead's back screen-door banged open and shut and Donna appeared, lugging a basket of wet laundry. She waved and smiled at Ruth.

Ruth pinned up the last diaper and with a guilty look back toward the Irvine's, skipped over to the fence to say hi.

"Easter's this Sunday. Want to come to church with me

again?" Donna asked, never breaking the rhythm of her clothes-pinning.

Ruth shook her head. "The Irvines want me to take my day off on Saturday since Mrs. Irvine's mother is here. On Sunday, they go to church in the morning while I stay home and get the dinner ready so they can eat when they get home."

"Oh, too bad. Don't you miss church?"

"Not so much. It's nice to have Saturday off so I can shop and do things downtown. Last Saturday, I went with a friend to Ledges State Park."

"Keen. Tell me all about it." Donna talked around a clothespin she held in her mouth.

With another glance towards the house, Ruth gave her friend a quick rundown of the day, omitting only the frantic beating of her heart when Jack put his hand over hers. Then she grabbed the empty clothes basket and went inside to pick up another load of wet clothes.

Two days later, Ruth was dusting the furniture in the parlor when the mailman dropped a handful of envelopes through the slot in the front door. Mrs. Nelson came by and scooped them up. She rifled through the envelopes, then held out a small white one. "Ruth, there appears to be mail for you."

Ruth shook her head. "I don't think so. Who would be writing to me?"

"I'm sure I have no idea. But it has your name on it."

Ruth took the card and held it. "It does have my name. And the address." She ran her fingers lightly over the writing. The return address had no name and wasn't familiar. "Who sent it to me?"

Mrs. Nelson sniffed. "You'll have to open it to find out." She laid the other mail on the coffee table, then sat in an overstuffed chair. She picked up a book of poetry she'd been reading last night.

Ruth tucked the envelope under her apron and into the pocket of her dress. All day long the sharp corners poked her leg, a constant reminder that someone knew her, and where she lived. As she cared for Bobby, she wondered if it was an invitation to a party or a dance. As she stirred the spaghetti sauce for dinner, she wondered if it bore bad news—a threat to her, or the report of someone's death.

When she washed the last dish from dinner and hung up the towel, she flew up the stairs, stopping briefly in front of the nursery to make sure little Bobby was sleeping soundly. Then she took the attic stairs two at a time, closed the door to her room, and breathlessly sank to her bed, holding the card in her hands. Trembling, she pried the envelope open and lifted out a plain ivory card.

Ruth, Meet me in front of Woolworths at 9 am on Saturday. Just one more day.

Yours, Jack

She leaned back against her pillow and read it a second time, then a third. What should she do? Follow her heart or listen to reason? She had two days to make a decision.

Saturday morning, Ruth woke early. As she dressed, she heard Bobby in his crib. At first, he made happy little babbles. By the time she'd dressed and used the bathroom, his babbling had increased in volume, and the tone had become less contented. When she entered the nursery, his whimpering stopped immediately. He gave her a huge smile and held up both his arms.

Ruth lifted him out, changed him, and carried him downstairs. Mr. Irvine sat in the dining room with a cup of coffee and the newspaper. Mrs. Irvine was in the kitchen heating a bottle.

"Oh, there you are. Do you have time to make breakfast before you go?" Mrs. Irvine always looked confused in the kitchen. Ruth handed Bobby to his mother, and he eagerly reached for his bottle.

Ruth took out a mixing bowl and stirred up a batch of pancakes. After serving the Irvines, she made a small dish of cereal for Bobby and fed him. Then, she changed him from his nightslip to overalls and put him down for his morning nap.

Finally, she ran a comb through her hair, grabbed her purse and left for the streetcar.

Jack leaned against the brick wall of the Woolworths building. He watched her exit the streetcar and strode across the sidewalk to meet her. "I'm glad you came. Shall we take another adventure?"

Suddenly, the sun shone brighter, the smell of flowers filled the air, and Ruth felt like dancing down the sidewalk. "I'm glad I came too."

Jack smiled broadly and offered his arm. They strolled all the way up Grand to the capitol, and then back down again on the opposite side of the street, talking about the window displays and laughing about nothing.

They stopped at Rizzo's for spaghetti and lingered over cups of coffee and tiramisu. Then Jack drove the motor car to Union Park, where they walked along the river front and watched the boats. A weeping willow tree was just leafing out, the leaves unfurling on the stems. Jack held the branches aside, and they stepped in next to the tree's trunk, their own private room by the river.

Jack reached for her hand. "These last two Saturdays have been wonderful, Ruth. The best I've ever had."

"I've enjoyed them too." Ruth's heart filled with strange

new feelings, and she wished the day would never end—that she and Jack could just stay in their willow room.

"Can we meet next Saturday?"

Ruth tried to calm her fluttering heart. "Mrs. Nelson will be leaving on Monday. I'm not sure if the Irvines want me to take my day off on Saturday or not."

"I'll be in front of Woolworths waiting. Ruth, I'd wait forever for you." Then Jack lowered his head until their lips met. The kiss was sweet and tender, full of promise. Still holding her hand, he led her out from under the tree.

They stopped to watch a family of ducks paddling in a lake made by the backflow of the river. The mother and father ducks tried frantically to stay between the onlookers and the newly hatched ducklings. Ruth thought of her little girl, and how she could never shield her from danger.

"Maybe I should get back to the house. I have an Easter gift to give Bobby. Just a little handmade rabbit, but I want to give it to him before bedtime."

"Sure. You're pretty attached to that little boy, aren't you?"

Ruth shrugged. "I spend more time with him than anyone else. His parents are always busy."

Jack frowned. "When I have kids, I want to take them places, show them things, teach them."

"You'll be a good daddy." For a second, she imagined Jack and her with a child, bringing him here to Union Park, but she quickly pushed the thought away. It could never, ever happen. When they reached Jack's car, Ruth realized the lateness of the hour. "Does the streetcar go out on Grand this late?"

"No problem." Jack helped her into the passenger seat. "It will be as easy for me to take you home as to take you downtown."

It took only a few minutes to drive to the Irvine's residence.

As the car pulled to a stop at the curb, Ruth thought she saw the curtains on the parlor window move.

Jack stepped around the car and opened the door for her. She placed one hand on his arm and he walked her to the door. "I'll see you next Saturday?"

"I hope so. Have a happy Easter."

"You too."

Ruth stood at the door until Jack returned to his car. She waved as the Model A pulled from the curb and chugged down the street. When she opened the door, Mrs. Nelson stood there with Bobby in her arms.

"Who was that young man you were with?" she demanded.

"His ... his name is Jack. Is something wrong?"

"What is his last name?" she hissed. Bobby began to fuss and to reach for Ruth.

"It's Meyer. He's an old school friend." Warning bells rang in Ruth's mind.

"I knew it. Jack Meyer is my nephew. My sister's oldest child. Does he know you had a child by another man?"

Ruth's legs wobbled and threatened to give way. She shook her head. "No. He knows nothing of my time in Des Moines."

"You must never see him again, Ruth. Never. He's a smart boy from a good family. He deserves better than you."

Bobby's fussing escalated to wailing. Mrs. Nelson turned and carried him into the parlor. Ruth fled upstairs to her room wishing she could wail like Bobby.

25

R uth woke with swollen eyes and a heavy heart. In the gray predawn hours, she could see her clothes in a rumpled pile on the chair where she'd dropped them before crawling into bed last night. Then she'd cried for hours.

After she washed and dressed, she shook out the worst of the wrinkles and hung up her clothes. Bobby was singing in his crib, so she quickly straightened her sheets and spread the quilt overtop. She pulled the finished rabbit out of the closet and held the stuffed toy behind her as she entered the nursery.

"Good morning, little buddy. I missed seeing you yesterday."

Bobby peered at her through the wooden slats of the crib. He chortled with delight and waved his chubby arms. Ruth held the rabbit out and his eyes widened as he studied the strange creature.

"It's a bunny. He's come to keep you company."

Bobby reached for the rabbit, and when she gave it to him, he hugged it close. While Ruth lifted him from the crib, he held the toy tightly by one fuzzy leg.

She changed and dressed him easily as he was occupied with his new rabbit. Mrs. Irvine had bought Bobby a new sailor suit with a white shirt, knickers, and blue tie. He looked adorable in it with his blond hair and bright blue eyes.

Ruth carried Bobby downstairs where Mr. and Mrs. Irvine and Mrs. Nelson were all drinking coffee in the dining room. Ruth handed the baby to his mother and fixed Bobby's breakfast before starting the adults' meal. She served scrambled eggs, muffins, and canned peaches while Bobby played with his rabbit in his playpen. Then she cleaned up as the Irvines and Mrs. Nelson left for church, Bobby still clutching his rabbit.

All day Easter Sunday, Ruth kept busy. She served dinner when everyone returned home. Bobby was fussy because he had missed his morning nap. When he finally fell asleep, Ruth spent the afternoon cleaning up from the meal. Everyone just ate leftovers in the evening, so when Mrs. Nelson offered to put Bobby to bed, Ruth gratefully handed him over and hurried up the steps to her room.

She pulled out a pile of the Irvines' clothes that needed mending. The hum of the sewing machine and the rhythms of feeding the material under the needle soothed her spirit. The memories of the Saturdays with Jack kept returning, no matter how she tried to focus entirely on her sewing. But the possibility of Mrs. Nelson exposing her shameful secret to Jack was more than she could bear. She finished the last torn shirt and folded it.

She searched in a pile of papers until she found the envelope Jack's note had come in. She copied the return address onto a new envelope and wrote a brief note.

Dear Jack,

I am unable to meet you this Saturday. Please do not contact me again.

Ruth

Then she sobbed herself to sleep for the second night.

The next morning, as Mr. Irvine was leaving to take Mrs. Nelson to the train station, Ruth handed Mr. Irvine the envelope. "Would you be able to mail this for me?"

Mr. Irvine took it with a nod. "Certainly."

Mrs. Nelson eyed the envelope curiously, and Ruth hoped the snoopy old lady would open it and, knowing Ruth had ended her relationship with Jack, never share what she knew.

As the week passed, Ruth found herself longing more and more for her little girl. As Bobby passed each developmental level she wondered: *Is my little girl rolling over? Has she sat up by herself yet? Does she love mashed bananas and cereal?* And most of all: *Do her parents love her as much as I do?*

With Mrs. Nelson gone, the household resumed a routine. Most of Bobby's care fell to Ruth, and she delighted in the affectionate little boy. He refused to go to sleep without his Easter rabbit's ear clutched in one hand and the thumb of his other hand in his mouth.

When Saturday rolled around, Ruth took the streetcar to Union Park for a walk, thinking the spring flowers would cheer her. But the memories of the day spent there with Jack brought a surge of pain, and she returned to the Irvine's house and spent the afternoon sewing. Mrs. Irvine had given her a sack of clothes she was discarding, and Ruth altered them to fit. She had a new and fashionable wardrobe, just no place to wear it.

On Monday, Donna was at her clothesline when Ruth

carried out her first basket. Donna waved cheerily and walked over to the fence.

"Have you been to the Ledges again?"

Ruth braced herself for the wave of emotions. "No, we were busy with Easter."

That was the perfect diversion. Donna chatted on about her church's service and Easter with her family.

Ruth moved toward the clothesline. "I better get these hung out. My little Bobby goes through so many clothes, now that he's eating real food and trying to crawl."

Donna gave a little wave. "Thanks for visiting. Oh, before you go, how's your friend that you went to the Ledges with?"

The wave swept over Ruth and tugged her toward the depths. She managed a weak smile. "Oh, we're not seeing each other anymore."

A puzzled look swept over Donna's face. "That's too bad. What happened?"

Ruth shrugged, pretending not to care. "There were things in my past ... he's going to be a lawyer." She shook her head. It was too complicated, and as kind as Donna was, she didn't feel she could share any of it. "I'd really rather not talk about it."

Donna's look turned to one of compassion. "I understand. You take care now." She lifted her basket and walked toward the house. Just before she went in, she called over her shoulder. "You know Jesus said, 'The truth shall set you free.'"

26

All week, Ruth puzzled over Donna's comment, "The truth shall set you free." How could telling any of her ugly past set her free? Her secrets weighed on her like boulders at The Ledges, and she was certain there was no escape. The truth could not set her free.

It felt safer to stay at the Irvines rather than risk meeting Jack downtown, or to go elsewhere by herself. So Saturdays were spent as her other days, cooking and taking care of Bobby. On Sunday afternoons, she would retrieve the sock from under her mattress and add a portion of her wages from the Irvines. Then, she would count the coins, wishing there were more.

The second Saturday after Easter, she approached the Irvines about planting a garden. They had no objections if she prepared, planted, weeded and harvested it herself. She chose a sunny spot at the back of the yard and found an old, rusted spade in the shed to turn over the dirt. Mr. Irvine brought home a hoe one day and she worked the dirt until it was fine and free of weeds and grass. Donna loaned her the Halstead's seed catalogue, and a few days later she had a handful of colorful packages promising a back yard full of tasty vegetables.

"These are beets." Ruth showed Bobby the package. "They're round and red. And these are beans. Long and green." Bobby squealed and reached for packets. Ruth laughed and put them up out of his reach. "I hope you're as excited for the real thing as you are the seeds."

The following Saturday was warm and sunny. The Irvines were visiting friends and had taken Bobby with them. Ruth put on the faded dress she'd worn when she left the farm in Grantsville. Less than a year had passed, but it felt like a lifetime ago. She was a different person now. She lifted her chin and went outside to the garden.

Two hours later, she stopped to rub her aching back and to view her accomplishments. She'd planted two rows of lettuce, one row of beets, and three rows of beans. The tomato seeds she'd started inside were sprouting. They would be transplanted to the garden later. Now for the onion sets, the round bulbs that would be green onions soon, and would mature into large, yellow onions if left until fall.

She pushed her hair from her face and knew she'd left a dirty smear. It sounded like a car stopped in front of the house, but she couldn't see because the shrubbery hid the back yard. She turned back to the garden.

Ruth used the edge of the hoe to drag a furrow in the dirt, then leaned the hoe against the shed and reached for the sack of onion sets. She had just finished patting the dirt back over the tiny yellow bulbs when she saw a figure walking through the shrubbery into the back yard.

She straightened and wiped the sweat from her eyes. Jack stood in front of her in sharply pressed blue pants and a crisp, spotless white shirt. Ruth looked down at her faded, dirt-stained dress and wanted to cry.

"Hello, Ruth."

"Jack." Ruth wanted to shout at him, to cry, and to hug him all at the same time.

"What's going on? Why did you tell me not to contact you? I think I deserve an explanation."

At that moment the screen door next door opened. Donna stood on the back steps, and when Ruth glanced at her, she waved slightly. Ruth heard Donna's words in her mind, "the truth shall set you free." That's what Ruth wanted, wasn't it, to be set free?

She took a deep breath. "Yes, Jack, you deserve an explanation. Can you give me fifteen minutes to clean up?"

"I told you I'd wait forever for you, and I meant it."

"Then I'll meet you at your car." Ruth raced into the house and upstairs. There wasn't time for a bath, but she sponged off with a washcloth. She pulled out of the closet one of the dresses that had belonged to Mrs. Irvine. The dark blue skirt hugged her hips, and she was glad she had lost the weight from her pregnancy. The bodice was blue as well, but a white collar framed her face. She used her fingers to comb through her dark curls that tumbled to her shoulders. She put on a touch of lipstick, grabbed a handbag, and, with a deep breath, walked downstairs and out the front door.

Jack was leaning against the fender of the car. When he saw her, he stood and walked to the passenger door and opened it. He whistled through his teeth. "You look amazing."

"Thank you." Ruth settled into the seat, hoping she would not lose her courage. "Can we find a quiet place to talk? Not a restaurant."

"Sure. How about Union Park?" Jack turned the key and the Model A roared to life. A short time later, he turned into the park. Daffodils and tulips bloomed cheerily at the entrance, and the huge oak and elm trees were sprouting green leaves.

The gazebo was empty. Jack pulled off the road and held the door open for Ruth.

The shaded bench inside was cool, and Ruth shivered.

"Want my jacket? It's in the car. I can get it for you."

"No, I'm fine." Ruth glanced sideways at Jack and watched his hands resting on his leg, waiting. The chill was not from the breeze off the river, it was from the memories flooding over her. Jack reached for her hand, but she shook her head.

"I need to tell you some things. They'll change the way you see me. But I want you to know, the past few weeks have been the best of my life. You have been a kind friend to me." Jack leaned forward as if to speak, but she lay a finger against her lips.

"Mrs. Irvine's mother, Mrs. Nelson, is your aunt, your mother's sister."

Jack's brow furrowed. "Aunt Nancy? And the Mrs. Irvine you've been talking about, that would be my cousin, Mildred? Mother told me she'd married, but if I ever knew her married name, I forgot it. And when I moved to Des Moines, Mother gave me her address, but I never looked her up."

Ruth nodded. "So, what I'm about to tell you, what she knows, you would have probably found out eventually. I just want to be the one to tell you, not her."

Jack's frowned deepened, but he remained silent.

"I came to Des Moines almost a year ago. I lived for five months at the Sisters of Mercy Home for Unwed Mothers." Tears trickled down her cheeks and dripped off her chin.

Jack reached over, offering her his spotless white handkerchief. She took it and wiped her face. When he spoke, his voice was low and threatening. "Who was the cad that did that to you and then left you?"

Ruth didn't answer, struggling to breathe.

Jack suddenly sucked in his breath. "It was Otto, wasn't it?

Oh, Lord, what did he do to you? He raped you, didn't he, Ruth? That's why you were so frightened when I spotted you in Des Moines."

Ruth sat frozen, unable to respond, even if she knew what to say.

"And you came to Des Moines by yourself. And had the baby."

Ruth could no longer stem the flood. She doubled over, her face in her hands and sobbed. "She was a baby girl. I wanted to keep her, but the sisters ... they took her ... they gave her away." Jack's arms went around her, and Ruth turned into his shoulder and cried.

After a long time, when the only sound was her ragged weeping, Jack gently lifted her chin. "You know, none of this is your fault. You have nothing to be ashamed of."

Ruth's voice was the tiniest whisper. "But I had a baby. And I wasn't married."

Jack's strong arms pulled her close again. His voice was hoarse, but tender. "Oh, darling, it doesn't matter. You did nothing wrong."

Ruth sat in the comfort of Jack's arms until slowly, her tears subsided. She sat up and blew her nose on his handkerchief, then held up the limp, wet cloth. "I promise I'll wash this and get it back to you."

"Does that mean I get to see you again? You won't keep sending me notes saying not to contact you?"

Ruth shook her head. "You say my having a baby doesn't matter. But your aunt and your cousin know about her. They'll tell your parents, and your parents won't want you to be friends with someone like me. Jack, it will be best if we don't see each other. I just felt like you deserved to know why."

Jack put a hand on each of her arms. "Listen. My parents

aren't like that. If they ask me, I'll tell them the truth. You had a baby, and she was adopted. They won't hold it against you."

"You don't know. They will see me as ... as tainted." Her voice quivered.

"They will see you as I do, a wonderful girl who had something terrible happen to her."

Jack wasn't going to budge. Ruth sighed. "Okay. We'll be friends. Just friends. But you must promise me that if your parents object to you spending time with me, we'll end it. I could never forgive myself if I came between you and your family."

"Deal. Now come and walk with me by the river." Jack reached for her hand and pulled her to her feet.

Darkness shrouded the house on Grand when Ruth slipped inside and upstairs to her room. As she passed the nursery, she paused a moment to whisper, "Sweet dreams, little buddy." She could barely make out Bobby's form, but she could see one bunny ear drooping through the crib slats, and she was certain the other ear was clenched in Bobby's fist.

27

On Tuesday, Mr. Irvine picked up his wife after work, and they went out with friends for dinner. Ruth was glad she could finish the ironing without interruption. When they returned, Mr. Irvine carried a large box into the house.

"It's a Taylor Tot Baby Stroller." Mrs. Irvine clapped her hands as Mr. Irvine pulled the stroller from the box. "Now that the weather is nice, we can take walks with Bobby in the evening. Or I can take him in the morning. My doctor said sunlight is beneficial to babies' health."

Although Mrs. Irvine talked about how she could walk and push Bobby, Ruth ended up being the one who used the stroller the most. From the first time she stuffed his chubby legs through the holes and wheeled him down the sidewalk, Bobby loved going for walks. He usually fell asleep, and Ruth could carry him inside and lay him in his crib without waking him. The stroller also proved handy as a place where he could sit and watch while she worked in the garden. Ruth checked on the garden daily, pulling a weed here and there, pinching off a yellowed leaf.

Saturday morning, Ruth met Jack in front of Woolworths. His appreciative whistle made her happy she had worn one of Mrs. Irvine's remade dresses, finger-waved her hair, and put on some lipstick. He held out his arm for her, she slipped her hand through and they window shopped, exclaiming at the new products in the windows. They ate sandwiches at Woolworths, then went to the Paramount Theatre for the matinee showing of *Chance at Heaven*. Ruth was breathless with delight in seeing Ginger Rogers on the big screen. Jack was the perfect gentleman and never even reached for her hand in the darkness of the theater.

After the movie, they stopped for an ice cream sundae and sat talking until the drugstore closed.

Ruth spent three glorious Saturdays with Jack. They had picnics, took a boat ride on the river, flew a kite, and took drives in the Model A. So, when Mrs. Irvine called her into the parlor on a Sunday afternoon, she was not prepared for what her employer had to say.

"We were under the impression that you were no longer seeing my cousin, Jack Meyer."

Ruth drew in her breath. Someone must have been watching out the window when Jack brought her home last night. "We're just friends. We drove to Carlisle yesterday to see Watt's Hill where the haystack murder took place. That's all. Is something wrong?"

Mrs. Irvine didn't look at her as she spoke. "My mother called yesterday. She told me if you continue to see Jack, I should let you go, and that I shouldn't have someone with your moral character taking care of Bobby, anyway. She's coming for a visit the first of June." Mrs. Irvine twisted her hands in her lap and grimaced as though she had a stomachache.

Mr. Irvine laid down the paper. "You know that Jack is

graduating from Drake University and is apprenticed to Martin and Brown law firm?"

Tears pricked at Ruth's eyes, but she kept her head up and her voice calm. "Yes. I do know that."

"My question is, why would an up-and-coming young lawyer want to spend time with a girl who is damaged goods?"

The question wrapped itself around her like a cloud of poisonous gas, sucking her breath, rendering her unable to speak.

The look on Mr. Irvine's face was one of utter disgust. "You must be providing him with some interesting diversion, but if you have any notions of him marrying you, he won't. A lawyer needs someone from his level of society, someone who will be an asset to his career."

Ruth felt bile rise in her mouth. She swallowed and stuttered. "Can I have a week to find another place?"

Mrs. Irvine looked bewildered. "Oh, we don't want you to leave, we just want you to stop seeing Jack."

Ruth looked out the window at the lengthening shadows and wished she could leave immediately. But she had nowhere to go. She turned back to Mrs. Irvine. "I think it would be best for everyone if I resigned."

Mrs. Irvine looked at her husband and held out her hand as if pleading for help. He nodded his head. "Certainly. You may have a week. We will need time to find a replacement for you as well."

A yowl from the nursery signaled the end of Bobby's nap.

Ruth shifted on her chair. "Do you want me to get Bobby?'

Mrs. Irvine stood. "Yes. We're going to get the stroller out and take him for a walk. It's such a lovely day."

Ruth lifted Bobby from his crib and held him close, her tears falling on his head. How could she stand not holding and caring for this little boy who had been such a part of her life for the past four months? Bobby squirmed and raised one chubby hand to pat her cheek. "Okay, let's get your diaper changed. Mommy and Daddy are going to take you for a stroller ride."

As soon as the Irvines closed the front door behind them, Ruth raced to the Des Moines *Sunday Register* discarded beside Mr. Irvine's chair and thumbed through the job listings. There were several she thought she might qualify for, so she got a pencil and piece of paper and carefully copied the contact information.

The listings included an ad for a housekeeper, two waitressing jobs, and one for a seamstress in a glove factory.

Ruth also turned to the section listing apartments and rooms for rent. Most of them rented for far more than she was currently earning, and she was unsure of the salary at any of the jobs she had chosen as possibilities. She used the same paper and copied the contact information for several rooms.

Then she went out to the kitchen to prepare supper for the Irvines.

Hours later, she finally fled upstairs, shut her door tightly, and threw herself across her bed. She slept little, cried a lot, and tossed and turned with her memories.

The next morning, she rose early, washed her face, and went to the basement to start the weekly washing. She had one load washed and hung outside before she fixed breakfast. When Mrs. Irvine came downstairs, Ruth asked permission to use the telephone to call prospective employers, and to switch her day off to Tuesday or Wednesday so she could interview.

"I have a luncheon on Tuesday, but I suppose I could spare you a while on Wednesday. Could you still make dinner that day?"

"Certainly." Ruth replied, chafing inwardly at the restrictions. She hoped she could squeeze in interviews. If she could get one.

She fed and dressed Bobby, put him in his playpen, and made her calls. After being told three times the position had been filled, or she didn't have the necessary qualifications, Ruth dialed her last prospect, the glove factory. She talked to two different women, then a Mr. Lewis came on the line. "This is Mr. Lewis. I understand you want to apply for a position at our factory."

"Yes. My current job is ending, and I need to find another."

"Do you have experience in commercial sewing?"

"Not commercial. But I do a lot of sewing at home—making my own clothes and doing alterations for others."

"Hmmm." Ruth pictured him taking notes. She held her breath and hoped. "Miss, can you come by the factory today for an interview?"

Her heart sank. "No, that isn't possible. I can come on Wednesday, though."

There was another "hmmm" and a lengthy pause. "Okay. Wednesday it is. I can visit with you at 10 a.m. Do you know where we're located?"

Ruth readied her pencil to write.

"The factory is at 309 Court Avenue, downtown. I'll see you at 10:00 Wednesday morning. I can't promise you anything but an interview."

"Thank you very much, Mr. Lewis." Ruth felt like skipping and dancing. But she went to the basement to start the laundry in the wringer washer.

While she was hanging the second load of laundry, Donna came out of the Halstead's house with her load. Ruth slipped over to the fence.

"I've been let go, so I won't see you anymore."

Donna's face registered astonishment. "But the Irvines love you. Mrs. Halstead is always talking about how Mrs. Irvine was lucky to find you."

Ruth sighed and shifted the basket on her hip. "They aren't happy that Jack and I spend time together."

Donna's astonishment turned to confusion. "Your boyfriend that took you to the Ledges? Are you seeing him again? Why would they care if you're with him? He isn't secretly involved in the Mafia or something, is he?" She giggled slightly.

Ruth shook her head. "It's kind of complicated. He's not a boyfriend, he's just a friend. But Jack and Mrs. Irvine are cousins, and Mrs. Irvine and her mother don't think I'm good enough for him." With a glance toward the house, she added, "I have things in my past."

Donna shrugged. "Don't we all? Past or present. Let him who is without sin throw the first stone."

Donna certainly had some strange sayings. Ruth turned to go. "Thank you for being kind to me. I always looked forward to Mondays."

Donna's smile spread across her face. "I'll miss you. You have been a friend to me as well."

They each carried their baskets, Donna to the clothesline, and Ruth into the Irvine's house.

Sometime between the second and third basket of laundry, Ruth realized that Jack would be waiting to meet her on Saturday. Although, she'd said they could just be friends, she knew in her heart it wouldn't work. He needed friends without a past. He needed someone who would "be an asset to his career."

Previously, she'd written Jack and told him not to contact her. But he always found her somehow. That must not happen now. She would take flight and disappear. Des Moines was a large city. Surely there was a small spot she could hide.

While the laundry dried in the spring sunshine, she put Bobby in the Taylor Tot and worked for a while in the garden.

When the garden was weed-free, she stood for a moment looking at the sturdy vegetables and wondering who would take care of her fledgling plants. She sighed and brushed the dirt off her hands before lifting Bobby from his stroller and twirling with him in the grass, leaving her breathless and him giggling. She held him close for a moment and whispered, "I'm going to miss you so much, Bobby."

He squirmed at being held so tightly. Ruth pulled the stroller, leaving it behind on the porch when she went inside.

When she went to bed that night, she found her paper and envelopes.

Dear Jack,

My position at the Irvines has been terminated. I do not know where I am going yet. You have been a good friend.

Sincerely yours,
Ruth

Maybe someday, when she had a good job, she could look Jack up and they could laugh at the things the Irvines and Mrs. Nelson said. Maybe.

All day Monday and Tuesday, Mrs. Irvine asked Ruth to do lots of extra jobs, mostly cleaning things that could have waited until fall. Ruth replied to each request with a smile and "Certainly," but it was late each night when she climbed the stairs to her bed. Then, lying in the darkness, she felt each aching muscle. But even more, she felt the ache of loss—her mother, her baby girl, and now sweet Bobby. And Jack. She remembered Donna's comment about casting stones. She certainly felt like throwing rocks at someone, but her sin was the largest of all.

28

Ruth woke Wednesday with a sense of purpose. Orphaned at eleven, sent to Iowa at fifteen, she'd learned to take care of herself. She couldn't stop now. She made sure her dress, hat and gloves were spotless and straight. Then, clutching her handbag, she marched down the stairs and out the front door.

The sidewalk was still damp from the morning rain, but the sun shone brightly, and in every yard spring flowers displayed their colors. Ruth inhaled the fragrance of the lilac blooms as she strode to the streetcar stop.

After a short ride, Ruth dismounted and gazed up at the tall brick building. *Hulling Garment Industries* was written on the side in large black letters. Some of the confidence she'd felt earlier vanished as if whisked away by the gust of wind tugging at her.

She took a deep breath and opened the heavy door. Inside, the hum and clack of machines rang in her ears and a smell—part oil, part fabric, part dust—assailed her nose. A wooden door with a glass window was to her left. A sign on the door said *Office,* so Ruth pushed it open and entered.

A round little woman with gray curls and tiny glasses smiled up at her. "How can I help you?"

"I have an interview with Mr. Lewis at ten." Ruth smiled briefly.

"And what's your name?"

"Ruth Russo."

The secretary pushed a button on a black box. A thin crackly voice responded. "Yes, Miss Young?"

She pushed the button a second time. "Ruth Russo is here for her interview."

"Send her in." The box hummed and then was silent.

Miss Young pushed her tiny glasses up. "Mr. Lewis will see you now. Right through that door." She smiled as if she were giving Ruth a gift and indicated a door.

Ruth opened the door and walked into a slightly larger room. Several messy piles of paper, assorted fabric scraps, finished gloves, and coffee cups lay strewn across a large desk. A tall, broad-shouldered man pushed his chair back and stood, offering a hand.

"Welcome to Hulling Industries, Miss Russo." After they shook hands, he nodded toward a wooden chair with a stack of fabric. "Please sit down."

When Ruth hesitated, he made his way around the desk, lifted the pile of fabric and set it atop a heap on another chair.

"Thank you," Ruth murmured as she sat and smoothed her skirt.

Mr. Lewis settled in his chair behind the desk, leaned forward and folded his hands. "Tell me a little about yourself. What schooling, jobs you've held, and why a pretty woman like you isn't married."

Ruth fleetingly thought of Donna's remark on truth. How

much of her very personal story was necessary to share with a prospective employer? She skimmed over her childhood and gave no reason for her move to Des Moines. Trying to be discreet, she told him, "At the first place I lived when I came to Des Moines, there were a lot of girls, and I altered and mended our clothes. That kind of turned into a fulltime job. So, I am quite familiar with the process of making garments. Although, I've never made gloves."

"And why did you leave that job?" Mr. Lewis's question hung in the air like a black thundercloud. Ruth could almost hear an ominous rumble of thunder.

"I thought, umm, I needed to ..." Ruth's eyes dropped to her hands tightening in her lap. Would she never be able to run from this shame? She took a deep breath and lifted her head. "It wasn't a real job. I was at the Sisters of Mercy Home for Unwed Mothers."

Now Mr. Lewis looked uncomfortable. "Oh, I see." He suddenly seemed interested in one of the messy piles of paper. Finally, he looked at her again. "Where have you been since that time?"

"I've been with a family on Grand Avenue. I do the housework and help with their child. I found an old sewing machine in the attic, and I have been making and altering clothes there as well. My position has ended, not because I didn't do what was required of me, but because of their objections to some of my friends." Ruth tilted her chin up slightly.

"Hmmm." Mr. Lewis's fingers drummed quietly on his desk. "I'd like to help you out, Miss Russo, I really would. You seem to know your way around a sewing machine, and that is helpful here. But I interviewed two men on Monday, and my priority is to hire men who are supporting a family. Perhaps you could return to the farm you mentioned?"

A cold shiver ran through Ruth's body. "No, that is not possible."

"I will keep your name on file, in case something opens up." Mr. Lewis stood. "I enjoyed visiting with you. You might try the YWCA. Sometimes they have job listings. I wish you luck."

Ruth nodded. "Thank you." She made her way out of his office, past Miss Young, and outside. She stood, breathing in great gulps of the fresh air and refusing to give way to tears. Then, she plodded to the streetcar stop and, rather than sitting, paced on the grass. What could she do now?

The streetcar swayed into view and, with a few screeches, came to a halt. Ruth climbed the steps and sank gratefully into an empty seat near the back. While the streetcar bounced along, she considered his advice to go to the YWCA. Even though the counselor had objected to her keeping her baby, he had been kind and helpful. And she had plenty of time before the last streetcar. A little hope crowded out her fears. She tipped back her head and closed her eyes.

When the streetcar stopped, Ruth hurried down the steps. She looked up and down the street she had walked so many times with Jack. Shaking off the memories, Ruth walked the three blocks to the YWCA. When she entered the brick building, she recognized the well-dressed receptionist, but the woman didn't seem to remember her.

"May I help you?" she asked.

"I need to speak to the employment counselor. I need a job."

"Just a minute. I'll see if he's busy." The woman stood slowly and walked to the office door marked *Employment*. After a pause, she disappeared inside.

Ruth waited, trying to imagine another placement, another family, another baby.

"Mr. Jensen will see you now." The receptionist lowered herself back into her chair at the desk with a sigh and began to write in a spiral book.

Ruth opened Mr. Jensen's office door.

"Come in. Sit down. Tell me your situation." His voice was brusque, and he seemed very much in a hurry to get her out of his office.

"I came here last November and got a job from your listing. A housekeeping job. That job is ending, and I need employment again."

Mr. Jensen studied her intently. "Are you the woman who was, ahem, in a family way?"

"Yes." Ruth's eyes dropped to her lap. "But my baby was adopted, so that isn't an issue now."

"Well, I'm glad you made the right choice for the child. This will make it easier for you to find employment."

Ruth looked up and leaned forward. "I'm willing to do anything. I had an interview this morning at the glove factory, but they told me they give priority to men with families. I don't have a family I support, but I have no place to go if I don't find a position."

"You don't have any relatives you could stay with?"

"No sir, I'm an orphan." Ruth had never felt so alone.

"Well, here is a listing of housekeeping positions open. Unfortunately, we have no other listings that you would qualify for at this time. These are hard times. Everyone gives priority to men with families." Mr. Jensen slid a sheet of paper across to the desk to Ruth. "And if you need a bed for a time, the Salvation Army has a shelter for women here." He laid a brochure on top of the list of possible employers. His index finger tapped the address.

Ruth picked up both papers and stood. "Thank you, sir. You've been very helpful."

"Good luck to you," he responded as she closed the door behind her. The receptionist was still busy typing at her desk and didn't speak as Ruth left.

At the streetcar stop, Ruth studied the list. Many of the addresses were close to the Irvines. She got a pencil from her handbag and jotted down the addresses in order so she would not spend time going back and forth.

Two hours later, Ruth had visited all six listings. Either the position had been filled, or they wanted someone with a driver's license, or they just didn't want her. She sat down on a bench near the streetcar stop and wished she could cry. She used her handkerchief and blew her nose. Then she remembered the other paper, the brochure that Mr. Jensen had given her, pulled it out of her pocket where she had stuffed it, and smoothed out the creases.

The address of the Salvation Army was not far from where she sat. She walked the few blocks.

A sign on the brick building said *Salvation Army, Preaching the Gospel and Meeting the Needs of the Community.* Wide steps led up to a set of double doors. Several people entered and exited the building. One man in ragged clothes sat on the steps smoking a cigarette. He tipped his hat as Ruth walked past. "Howdy, ma'am."

She nodded politely at him without responding. Inside the building more people pushed past her, but no one who seemed to be in charge. She didn't know where she should go, or who she should talk to. She smelled food cooking somewhere, and there was a line of people in the hallway. She spotted a woman about her age clutching the hand of a little boy and holding a baby to her shoulder.

Ruth approached her. "I need to speak to someone about staying here. Do you know where I should go?"

The woman shifted the sleeping baby to her other

shoulder. "You need to find Major Harrison. He's an older man with white hair. He's around somewhere. Check down that hall." She pointed in the direction Ruth had come from.

"Thanks." Ruth turned and went back up the hallway. A man who matched the woman's description came out of a room as she walked past.

"Major Harrison?" Ruth asked.

"That's me. What can I do for you, young lady?"

Ruth suddenly felt the weight of the day's burdens overtake her. Her hands covered her face, and her shoulders shook as the tears spilled out.

"Here, here," Major Harrison spoke in a soothing voice. "Why don't you tell me your situation? I'm certain we'll be able to help in some way."

Ruth took a handkerchief from her pocket and wiped her face. "I've lost my job and I have no place to stay. The man at the YWCA gave me this brochure. He said you had a shelter here." She took a deep breath and held it.

"Yes, we do have a shelter. How about you get in line for the evening meal, and after we eat, you and I will visit?"

Ruth suddenly remembered she'd promised to make dinner for the Irvines. And it was getting late.

"Can I come Saturday? My job lasts until Friday, and I need to get back there now and make dinner."

"Of course. Come by Saturday morning, and we'll talk then." Major Harrison turned to a poorly dressed man who had been standing at his elbow, obviously needing to speak to the Major.

Ruth walked to the streetcar stop, feeling a tiny bit less burdened. If she qualified, she'd at least have a place to live.

29

When Mrs. Irvine came in the kitchen, Ruth served her bacon and eggs on the everyday plates. "My last day will be Friday," she announced as she poured a cup of coffee.

"But I haven't found another girl yet," she sputtered. "My mother can help with Bobby, but who will cook dinner? And clean the house?"

Ruth stuffed the surge of guilt deep inside and reminded her employer. "You had no one before I showed up on your doorstep. I am certain you will be able to find someone soon. I will try to get some meals made ahead so you only have to heat them up."

Mrs. Irvine threw up her hands. "I can't think about this now. I have a tennis lesson this morning. And my mother comes tomorrow."

Ruth heard the clatter of her footsteps as she went upstairs to get ready. She would be up there for an hour or more, washing, choosing an outfit, and putting on makeup. Ruth picked up the washcloth and wiped Bobby's face and hands. She lifted him from the highchair and plopped him on his bottom in the playpen. "There you go little buddy. It looks like it's just you and me today. Maybe we can take a walk before your nap." Bobby's grin, showing off his two new teeth, wrenched her heart. What would it be like to not see his little face in the mornings?

Friday morning, the Irvines announced they were leaving early in the day so they could do some shopping before picking up Mrs. Nelson from the train station. They would not be taking Bobby, as Mrs. Irvine wanted him to take a good nap. "Would you fix that beef roast for dinner, and clean the parlor and dining room?" Mrs. Irvine asked before they left.

"Certainly," Ruth replied as she headed up the stairs to the nursery.

But the day did not go as planned. Bobby fussed almost continually, and if she ignored his whimpering, it quickly escalated to all-out wails. Ruth was rocking him in the parlor when the Irvines returned with Mrs. Nelson. The roast hadn't been put in the oven, the dining room floor still needed mopping and Bobby refused to nap. When Mrs. Nelson entered the parlor, she headed straight for Bobby, who took one look at his grandmother, shrieked, and locked his arms around Ruth's neck.

"What's this? My own grandson won't come to me?" Mrs. Nelson whined.

"Oh mother, he's been teething. He's just fussy. Give him a little bit and he'll warm up to you."

Ruth pried Bobby's arms off her neck and handed him to Mrs. Irvine. "I'll go finish up dinner."

On the way out of the room, she could hear Mrs. Nelson saying, "I thought you'd gotten rid of that girl."

Ruth made as much noise as possible in the kitchen, banging the roaster on the counter and slamming cupboard doors. She didn't want to hear one more word from that cantankerous woman's mouth. She prepared the roast, made a jello salad, and baked a chocolate cake that Mr. Irvine was particularly fond of. And, only fifteen minutes late, dinner was ready to serve.

While the Irvines were eating, Ruth took Bobby upstairs for bed. She changed his diaper and dressed him in a soft yellow nightslip she'd sewn. Then she rocked him, singing the lullabies he loved. At last, his eyelids fluttered shut and his beloved bunny slipped to the floor. Still Ruth rocked, knowing it would be the last time she would hold Bobby. When she heard the Irvines moving from the dining room to the parlor, she laid him in his crib and tucked the bunny in beside him.

Then she went to get her supper and clean the kitchen. As soon as everything was put away and the kitchen was spotless, she hurried back upstairs. She could hear the murmur of voices in the parlor and wondered what was being said about her.

Safe inside her room, she pulled out her old plaid suitcase and pulled items from her drawers and lay them inside.

A knock on the door interrupted her as she folded dresses from her closet. "Come in," she called.

Mrs. Irvine pushed the door open, came inside, and pulled the door shut behind her. "Please, Ruth, can you stay? I mean, I understand if you want to go somewhere for a few weeks while my mother is here, but then won't you come back? I can't do all this by myself, and I don't think we'll find someone like you. You're so good with Bobby, and he is very attached to you." To Ruth's consternation, Mrs. Irvine's lower lip trembled and her blue eyes, so like Bobby's, filled with tears.

Her heart wavered for a minute. But then she shook her head. "No. I've already made arrangements elsewhere." She didn't mention that elsewhere meant a bed at the Salvation Army. "It will be for the best. And I'm sure you will find someone else, and she will love Bobby too. He is a sweet little boy."

"Is there nothing I can do to change your mind?"

"No, nothing. I will leave early tomorrow."

As Mrs. Irvine turned to go, Ruth saw the sewing machine sitting by the closet. "Do you want me to put the sewing machine back in the storage room?"

Mrs. Irvine paused, her hand on the doorknob. "No. I don't want it. Take it with you."

Ruth couldn't believe it. "Are you sure?"

"Yes, think of it as a gift from me to you."

"Thank you. That's very generous. And thanks, too, for providing me employment at a time I really needed it."

Mrs. Irvine only nodded as she pulled the door shut behind her.

Later, Ruth turned the quilt down and crawled into bed. Her closet was empty. Her dress for tomorrow was draped across the chair. And her suitcase and sewing machine sat by the door.

She was ready for another flight.

PART THREE

30

Friday morning, Ruth woke from a restless sleep. Outside her window, darkness still shrouded the houses. She caught herself listening for sounds from the nursery, but she was no longer employed by the Irvines. With a sigh, she washed and dressed, then folded her nightgown and laid it on top of her other clothes and fastened the suitcase shut.

She stripped the sheets from the bed and carried them down to the basement, putting them in a basket beside the wringer washer. Back upstairs, she paused outside the nursery. Bobby was making the singing noises that would certainly lead to louder cries if someone didn't get him soon. She longed to hold him one more time, but she mustn't.

Ruth hurried up to her room and glanced around, making sure she had everything. Then she picked up her suitcase in one hand, the sewing machine in the other, and walked out of the Irvine's house.

When the streetcar squealed to a stop, Ruth hefted her luggage up the steps and sank into the first empty seat, grateful to put her possessions on the floor. She watched as the large homes on Grand slid past. Most of these homes had families who hired at least one or two people to help. Surely, she would find another position soon. The shaded street's spacious lawns gave way to businesses and taller brick buildings. The capitol's golden dome gleamed brightly in the distance.

Ruth's buoyant mood dissipated with each roll of the streetcar's wheels. She had walked away from her residence of four months and now was not only without a job, but homeless. She wasn't even sure that the Salvation Army would take her in. When the streetcar stopped, she lifted the suitcase and sewing machine and trudged down the steps.

In the short distance from the streetcar stop to the Salvation Army, the weight of Ruth's two burdens grew heavier and heavier. Her arms ached, and sharp pains stabbed her back. She stopped, set her luggage down, and stared up the wide stairs at the front doors. She felt the same mix of terror and anticipation as when she stood on the stage at the operahouse, waiting to see if a family might choose her. Would she find a refuge here?

A well-dressed middle-aged woman glanced at her curiously as she hurried by on the sidewalk. Ruth took a deep breath, picked up her possessions and climbed the steps. Inside, people jostled past her, most of them headed down the hallway toward the sounds and smells of food cooking.

Ruth waited in the foyer, wondering where she should go and feeling slightly lost. A round-faced woman with frizzy gray curls strode by, then stopped and came back. "Could I help you?"

Ruth set the sewing machine down again. "I'm looking for Major Harrison."

"Oh, he won't be here for a while." The woman glanced at the suitcase. "Are you a new resident?"

"I hope to be. But I haven't been approved yet."

The woman smiled, making the tiny spectacles on her nose bob. "Well, have you had breakfast?"

Ruth's stomach rumbled. "No, I left early this morning. I don't want to take something that was meant for others, though."

"There will be plenty. Let's get you something to eat while you wait. By the way, my name is Edna." She held out a hand lined with large, blue veins.

Ruth shook her hand, then picked up the sewing machine. "I'm Ruth." She followed Edna down the hall to a large dining area. Most of the people were seated and eating.

Edna stepped to the counter. "Could we have a breakfast for this young lady?"

A man in a white apron held out a tray with a large bowl of oatmeal, a small bottle of milk and a piece of buttered toast. Edna placed a spoon on the tray and carried it across the room to a table where only a few people were seated.

Ruth set down her luggage and pulled a metal folding chair out. "Thank you so much." She smiled at Edna.

"You're welcome, dear. If you'd like a cup of coffee, there's a pot in that corner." Edna pointed. "When I see Major Harrison, I'll tell him you're here."

Ruth served herself a cup of coffee and sat on the flimsy chair. The man across the table looked up and nodded at her but did not speak.

Ruth murmured, "Hello," before turning her attention to the food. The bland oatmeal tasted wonderful, maybe just because someone else had fixed it. She took her time, sipping coffee and eating, occasionally glancing around at her fellow diners. Most of them ate hurriedly, without talking, wasting nothing, before returning their trays to the kitchen and rushing out.

Ruth finished her toast and oatmeal and was just wondering if she could help herself to a second cup of coffee, when she spotted Major Harrison weaving between the tables. He stopped and greeted each person, putting a friendly hand on one man's shoulder, squatting down to talk to a child, and laughing at a woman's comment.

Ruth stood, stacked her dishes on the tray, and brushed the crumbs from her skirt.

Major Harrison smiled, his eyes crinkling under bushy white eyebrows. "I see you found your way back."

"Yes, sir. I'm ready for the interview whenever you are."

"Why don't you take your dishes up and then follow me to my office? I have a few minutes, and it looks like you have time as well." His eyes glanced over her luggage.

Ruth took her tray to the counter and thanked the young girl who came to pick it up. Then she walked across the room to where Major Harrison waited.

The Major's office was a tiny room with bookshelves, a large wooden desk, and two chairs, one on each side. Every available space in the room held piles of papers, books, and newspapers. The floor was cluttered with sacks of clothes and other items Ruth assumed were donations for the needy. Of whom she was now one, she reminded herself.

Major Harrison scooped a pile of papers off the chair. "Please, have a seat."

Ruth sat, her feet tucked between the suitcase and sewing machine.

Major Harrison walked around his desk and sat opposite her. He leaned forward, clasping his large hands on a pile of papers. "Now, tell me your name and your story, dear."

The use of the endearment was almost too much for Ruth. She felt tears pricking her eyelids, but she held them back. "My name is Ruth Russo. I was born in New York City ... " For several long minutes, she told him of her train ride to Iowa and her work on the farm, her flight to Des Moines and, remembering Donna's advice on truth, the reason for it. She skimmed over her months at Sisters of Mercy and the baby girl she still longed to hold. She told him about her job at the Irvine residence and what her duties had been.

"And why are you no longer working for them?" Major Harrison's voice didn't hold a crumb of judgement.

Ruth looked down at her hands, clutched in her lap. "It's complicated. Mrs. Irvine has a cousin who I knew back in Grantsville. We were school chums. He lives in Des Moines now, and we became reacquainted. Mrs. Irvine and her mother, his aunt, felt I shouldn't spend time with him on my days off. You know, because I'd had a baby. They told me I couldn't work for them if I continued to see Jack." Tears quivered at the edge of her eyes.

"Mmm-hmm. I see. And is your relationship with Jack a romantic one?"

Ruth, her head still bowed, shook it. "No, we are only friends." She thought about how her heart beat when Jack held her, and the time he kissed her under the willow tree at Union Park. She repeated, "Only friends. And he no longer knows where I am."

"And after you left the Irvines, there is nowhere else you could go? How about the family you lived with in Grantsville? The family that took you in."

Ruth's head lifted, her eyes widening, her heart pounding. "Oh, no. I must not go back. Thelma is dead and Otto ... Otto doesn't treat me right. Please, don't contact him."

Major Harrison paused a moment before answering, his voice kind and gentle. "We won't contact him. I promise you. We have a bed for you here, Ruth. And we will work with you to find suitable employment. Now, a few house rules."

He continued with the orientation, telling her the rules of the shelter. She listened carefully, but most of what he said was about being polite, sharing, and respecting others.

Then he asked, "Are you a woman of faith?"

Ruth hesitated, not sure how to answer. "I go to church when I can."

"That's a start. We do require anyone who is a resident here to attend at least one of our weekly services. We have one Sunday morning, Sunday evening, and Wednesday evening."

Ruth nodded. "I'll be there."

"Until you find employment, you will work here at the citadel full time. Several of our residents work in the kitchen. Every day, the number of people to whom we serve dinner increases. For some, it's their only meal of the day. And when someone tucks an extra roll in their pocket, I imagine they are sharing with someone too frightened or too proud to come in. Now, I've done a lot of talking. I'll stop, but I have one more question. What's the story on that?" The Major pointed to the sewing machine. "We've had a lot of people come here carrying some unusual things, but I don't think anyone has ever brought a sewing machine."

Ruth chuckled. "I love to sew. My previous employer gifted it to me when I left their home. I make clothes, alterations, mending—I can do pretty much anything with this machine."

"That's good to know. I will be sure to keep that in mind as we look for employment. Now, what questions do you have?"

Ruth shook her head and smiled. "None. You've explained everything quite well. Would you like me to work in the kitchen right now?"

Major Harrison gave her a broad smile. "I appreciate your eagerness to begin. Let's get you settled in first. I'll have Edna show you where your bed will be and let you stow your belongings. We start preparing for the evening meal at two p.m."

He stood, leaning heavily on his desk as he did. He held out one large hand to her. "I think you will be just fine, Ruth. It will be a pleasure to work alongside you. I don't think you'll need our services for long."

"Thank you." Ruth's cheeks warmed at his kind words. She lifted her suitcase and sewing machine then followed Major Harrison down the hall. Edna was wiping the tables in the dining room.

"Edna, I believe you have met Ruth. Would you have time now to take her upstairs and show her where she can put her things?"

Edna took one last swipe at the table, catching some stray toast crumbs. "You bet. Let me just put this towel back in the kitchen." She hurried toward the kitchen, and Major Harrison strode off in the other direction. Ruth waited, holding her luggage, until Edna returned.

"You're gonna stay with us awhile, huh?"

"Not too long, I hope. Only while I'm in between positions. I want to find another job soon." Ruth followed Edna upstairs and down a hall. A door opened into a room lined with beds. Beside each bed was a small chest. One wall had a long row of hooks. Most of the hooks had a dress or coat hung from it.

Edna patted a bed near the door. "This bed will be yours. And the chest on that side. You may use any empty hook on that wall over there, but we ask that you only use one. I'll get you some sheets." Ruth set the suitcase and sewing machine down with a grateful sigh.

In a few minutes, Edna was back with a set of threadbare sheets, a thin blanket that had been mended, and a small coarse towel. "The bathroom is through those doors. Of course, you will share it with everyone in this room. Is there anything else I can get for you? We're rather shorthanded in the kitchen."

"No, no. This will be fine." Ruth lifted her suitcase onto the bed and began filling the drawers of the chest.

Edna placed a hand on her arm. "If you need anything, just ask me."

"Thank you." Ruth looked around the room. It wouldn't be much different than Sisters of Mercy or the orphanage, would it?

She finished putting her clothes away, hung two dresses on one of the hooks, and slid the suitcase under her bed. Then she made her bed with the sheets and blanket Edna had brought her, thankful the winter weather was over. The thin blanket wouldn't keep anyone very warm. Everything but the sewing machine was put away. It was too high to fit under the bed. She moved the chest over a few inches and slid the machine in beside her bed. Then, for a few minutes, she sat.

She wondered what was going on at the Irvine's house, who had given Bobby his breakfast, and if they remembered to give him his rabbit at naptime. She thought about Jack. What would he think if he knew where she was now?

Then Ruth stood, smoothed out the blanket, and went downstairs to help in the kitchen.

31

Ruth turned in a circle so she could view all of the huge kitchen. An older man stood at a sink methodically washing dishes. A thin woman with carrot-red hair peeled potatoes. And Edna carried a stack of clean trays to the serving counter.

When she saw Ruth, a look of relief spread over her face. She set down her trays and hurried over. "I'm glad you're here. One of our workers didn't show up and left us short-handed. Can you peel potatoes while Leigh makes meatloaves?"

"Sure." Ruth took the knife the woman handed her and picked up a potato.

An hour later, her hand ached from clutching the knife, her back ached from leaning over the bucket, and her feet ached from standing in one spot. Potato peelings stuck to her skirt and one elbow.

Leigh tucked the last meatloaf into the oven and came to look at the mound of peeled potatoes. "Let's get them cooking." She hoisted a huge pot to the counter and dropped the potatoes in, a few at a time. "We'll use two or three pots." She pointed to where they sat, so Ruth filled another one. Leigh added water, set them on the stove, and turned the fire on under them. Then Ruth helped her empty large cans of green beans into a separate pot to warm.

"While the meatloaves are cooking, I'll show you how we serve." Leigh explained the process of getting people through the line as efficiently as possible.

"How many people do we feed?" Ruth helped carry stacks of clean plates to the serving station.

"Some nights, as many as one hundred. Not only residents here, but anyone from the neighborhood who needs a meal as well."

The man, whom Leigh called Enos, took his cloth and a towel and wiped down all the tables and serving counters. He worked without speaking, but when Leigh thanked him for cleaning the area where she'd made the meatloaves, he smiled at her, showing a mostly toothless mouth.

The two women put out silverware and poured glasses of water. Leigh made coffee in the big pot. By four o'clock a line began forming in the hallway. The crowd waited patiently, someone occasionally hushing a crying child or sputtering an exclamation in a conversation. "You don't say!"

Edna and Major Harrison opened the door at five. Major Harrison prayed, asking God to bless the food, and the people gathered to partake. They filed in eagerly, gaunt faces lit by smiles as they anticipated the meal.

Leigh, Ruth, and Enos worked without stopping for the next two hours. When the last diner brought his dishes to the counter, Leigh gave it to Enos to wash and handed Ruth a tray. "It's our turn to eat."

The green beans were gone, and the only meat loaf left was

a dark crust from the edge of the pan. But there were still potatoes. Ruth filled her plate, got a glass of water, and sat across the table from Leigh.

"What about Enos?" Ruth asked as she took a bite of the potatoes.

Leigh shook her head. "He won't eat until he's done all the dishes. He'll wash ours, then he'll take his food to go. I think he shares with someone else."

"Where does he live? I thought he was a resident here."

Leigh took a drink of her water. "No. I think he might live in Hooverville. I don't know for sure. He doesn't talk much to anyone. But he's here every day. He helps out wherever Major Harrison needs him."

"Do you live here?" Ruth hoped she'd found a friend in this new place.

"I do." Leigh's smile lit up her face. "But not for long. I got a job working for a family in Ames. I think the father is a professor at Iowa State College. They're picking me up in their motorcar Monday morning."

"Wonderful." Ruth felt a pang of disappointment.

Leigh chattered on while Ruth finished her meal. "This job is an answer to prayer. Major Harrison told me how God cared for me, and now I see."

Ruth put her fork down and drank the rest of her water. She reached for Leigh's tray and stacked it on top of hers. "I'll take our trays to Enos. Are we finished in the kitchen, or is there more to do?"

"No, we can go upstairs now."

The dormitory upstairs buzzed with women's chatter. Ruth waited in line to wash her face and brush her teeth. A few others in line greeted her and welcomed her to the shelter, but mostly she was alone with her thoughts.

She'd had a baby and lost her. How could God care for someone like that?

Sleep came slowly. After the last woman turned out the lights and crawled onto her bed, the unfamiliar noises of eleven roommates, the scratchy blanket that provided little warmth, and the worries over what was next consumed her.

When at last her eyes closed, it seemed only a short time later they flew open as the women lined up for the bathroom. Leigh stood at the foot of her bed. "Aren't you the sleepyhead? Better get moving. I don't think you want to be late for services your first Sunday here."

Ruth had forgotten it was Sunday morning. She dressed in a hurry, bumping into the woman whose bed was closest. She ran a comb through her curls, wishing she'd had time to do some finger waves, then followed the other stragglers downstairs. A few things lay out on the counter for breakfast— bread for toasting, canned fruit, and leftover oatmeal. The women talked quietly while they ate and, after finishing, they did their own dishes or wiped up crumbs with a cloth.

The chapel was a large room downstairs. The furnishings were simple—rows of scratched wooden pews, a raised stage with a plain wooden pulpit, and a picture of Jesus at the front. Ruth followed the women as they entered. Several people were already seated. She looked for Leigh, but she sat in a pew with people on either side of her. Ruth spotted Enos by himself in one of the pews near the front.

"May I sit with you?" she asked.

Enos blinked up at her. "Okay, if you want." He scooted sideways to make more room.

Ruth settled into the pew and noticed the small Bible in Enos's hands. He leaned toward her. "Have you heard Major Harrison preach before?"

"No, I haven't."

"Well, Miss Ruth, you are in for a treat. He's going to knock your socks off."

"I hope not." She giggled. "My toes will get cold."

Enos chuckled. "The Major knows his Good Book."

Ruth started to ask what good book, then realized Enos meant the Bible. She wished she'd remembered to bring her mother's Bible. She never seemed to be prepared for church.

One woman Ruth recognized from the dormitory began playing the piano. Major Harrison stepped onto the stage and lifted his arms. "Let's stand and sing, 'Onward Christian Soldiers.'"

Ruth stood and tried to sing along, although she did not know the words very well. But she felt that an army surrounded her, jubilant voices pouring out words of hope.

They sang several songs, the last one a slow, sweet melody, almost like one of the lullabies she'd sung to Bobby.

Major Harrison waited until everyone had settled in the pews again before he began speaking. As he talked, Ruth's mind wandered. She glanced around at the people and knew many of them would not be here next week or the week after. Across the aisle from her a woman her age held a baby on her lap. A toddler, maybe two, leaned against her side with his thumb tucked in his mouth. Beside the boy sat a man in tattered overalls. His hands were clasped in his lap as he listened to the Major. The woman turned and looked at him and they exchanged a smile over the heads of the children.

Ruth blinked back tears as she yearned for something she knew she could not have. Something she did not deserve.

Major Harrison's voice rose and fell. He talked about Jesus —dying for our sins, rising to forgive people. But Ruth knew He could never forgive her. She would never have a family to love and hold.

They stood and sang a final song, "Blest be the Tie That

Binds." Enos picked up his Bible and thumbed through the frayed pages. "This always fills my heart with hope. Jesus is our hope."

Ruth smiled at him, but she knew her hope was in her own hands.

32

Shortly after the morning service, Ruth returned to the kitchen. They prepared a noontime meal for the community on Sundays. Another church service would be held in the evening. After dinner, Ruth lay on her bed for a nap and slept until nearly time for the evening service. Groggy and feeling rumpled, she sat in a chair at the back by herself.

When Ruth returned to the dormitory, most of the women were already there. Some sat on their beds and wrote or read, some lined up to use the bathroom, and others had blankets pulled up and already slept. On the bed next to hers sat a tall, broad shouldered woman with long stringy hair streaked with gray. "Your chest is too close to my bed." She spoke in a sour tone.

"I'm sorry. I pushed it over because I needed space for my sewing machine."

"Well, I want it moved. Put your sewing machine somewhere else. Who brings a sewing machine to a shelter anyway?"

Ruth looked around the crowded room. "I don't have another place. It won't fit under my bed."

The woman's voice grew louder. "I don't care. It's in my space, and I want it moved."

Several women were now watching the conflict. One of them moved over beside the beds. "Nellie, it's okay. That space wasn't being used."

"Yes, it was. I put my book there." Nellie stared at Ruth with narrowed eyes.

A sliver of fear ran through Ruth. "I didn't mean to cause trouble. I'll ask Edna if there's somewhere else I can put it." She pulled the sewing machine out and moved the chest back over. Then she tucked her feet up and tugged the machine close to her bed.

Nellie stood and stretched, looking down at Ruth. "I sure hope it isn't in the way when I get up to pee tonight. I'd hate to stumble and damage it." Then she left and joined the line for the restroom.

While she was gone, Ruth changed into her nightgown. Then, foregoing washing her face and brushing her teeth, she crawled up on the bed and slid between the sheets. When Nellie returned from the restroom, Ruth kept her eyes closed and pretended sleep.

The next morning, some of the women commented on how unreasonable Nellie had been. But no one had a good suggestion for storing the sewing machine.

The woman who had to tried to soothe Nellie told Ruth, "She just gets like that sometimes. I don't think she's quite right here." She tapped her head. "And I do think she could be dangerous. So just be careful."

Ruth shivered, despite the warmth of the kitchen where they were baking biscuits.

When Edna arrived, Ruth asked her if there was another

spot she could store the machine.

"Oh, Ruth, I just can't think of a good place right now. Mondays are busy days. Give me some time to think, and I'll try to find one." She bustled off to the next thing that needed her oversight, and Ruth returned to her job—rolling and cutting out biscuits and placing them on large sheets to bake.

That evening, there was a meeting in the dining room for the twelve women at the shelter. Major Harrison reminded all of them there was a fifty-cent rental fee due the first of June. Ruth knew she had that much left in her little coin purse, but she must have a job after that. He asked them to continue following the rules. Edna read the work schedule for the week and told them it would be posted in the dining room. Then Major Harrison prayed at length for all of them.

Some of the women continued to sit in the dining room visiting, but Ruth hurried upstairs. She wanted to be able to get to the bathroom and get ready for bed before the line got long. Only one woman was upstairs. Ruth remembered Leigh had introduced her as Sarah. She was sitting on her bed in a nightgown reading. Ruth wove through the maze of beds to hers.

The sewing machine lay on its side and the pin that held the spool of thread in place was bent to one side. The handle that cranked the wheel was broken and lay a short distance away.

Ruth's gasp brought Sarah over to survey the damage as more women entered. Ruth knelt and righted the machine and picked up the broken handle.

"Who would do this?" Tears rolled down her cheeks and she angrily wiped them away. "Now, I can't even sew."

Sarah spoke up. "I bet Nellie did this. I heard you two arguing last night. She's a mean woman. You don't want to cross her."

Ruth bit her lip, and her hands clenched. She would never have the money to repair the machine.

Other women gathered around, offering expressions of sympathy and comfort. Most agreed it had probably been Nellie.

"I didn't see her at the meeting tonight," one of them said.

"I don't see why Major Harrison doesn't kick her out," another chimed in.

The group suddenly grew quiet as Nellie and another woman walked into the room. No one said anything as they made their way across the room.

"Why's everyone standing around and blocking the walkway?" Nellie's voice was harsh and loud.

Some of the women walked away towards their own beds, but Sarah spoke up. "We're looking at what you did to Ruth's sewing machine."

A scornful sneer spread across Nellie's face. "I didn't do nothin' to her precious sewing machine. I should have, though, since it was sticking out in my space." She peered down at the broken machine. "Ha! You ain't gonna be sewing on that for awhile."

Ruth couldn't keep quiet any longer. "You need to pay to have it repaired."

Nellie laughed. "I didn't do it. And you can't prove nothing. So, don't hold your breath waiting for me to get that fixed." She dropped her jacket on her bed and walked toward the bathroom.

Ruth placed the broken handle on the base of the machine and scooted the whole thing over next to her bed. Then she slipped into her nightgown. When she closed her eyes and waited for sleep, she let one hand dangle over the side to touch the machine.

33

Monday morning, Ruth asked Edna again if there was a place to store the machine. Sarah was passing by with clean trays and asked, "Did you tell her what happened last night?"

Ruth didn't respond, but Edna probed. "What happened?"

"I went upstairs after the meeting and found my sewing machine tipped over and damaged."

"Oh, I'm sorry." Edna's hands clasped at her chest; her eyes laced with concern. "Do you have any idea how it happened?"

Ruth sighed. "Sunday night, I had an argument with one of the other women. I put the machine between my chest and bed and that pushed the chest over in her area. She was upset, but I didn't think she'd break it."

"Do you have proof that it was her?"

"No." Ruth shook her head and wished she were someplace else.

Edna glanced at the line forming for breakfast. "Tell me the name of the resident you were arguing with so I can speak to her."

"Please, I don't want to cause further trouble. I just need someplace else to store the machine. And, somewhere I can take it to get it repaired."

"After breakfast, bring it down and put it in Major Harrison's office. This will just be temporary, you understand. We'll talk more later about who might have done the damage."

"Certainly. Thanks so much." Ruth hurried back to help Sarah put out the trays and breakfast utensils. They served breakfast to a long line and ran out of eggs. But no one complained when they were only given a piece of toast. Ruth and Sarah ate theirs together after everyone had been served.

Sarah nibbled her toast slowly and washed it down with a small glass of water. "Do you have any job prospects yet?"

"No." Ruth wrapped her fingers around the coffee cup, relishing the time and conversation with another woman her age. "I meet with Major Harrison tomorrow. I hope he has some good suggestions."

"I go to the canning factory today at two." She grinned at Ruth. "You'll have to do the dinner preparations without me."

"It won't be the same. And Leigh is gone too."

Sarah nodded. "I hope she has a good home in Ames."

"A professor and his wife? Sounds pretty good to me." Ruth tipped her cup and drank the rest of her coffee. "Thanks for eating breakfast with me. It's nice to have someone to talk to."

The next hour was spent cleaning the kitchen. Ruth checked to make sure that Major Harrison was in his office before she carried the machine down. She tapped on the door.

"Come in." Major Harrison's voice, cheerful as always, boomed through the door.

Ruth pushed the door open. "Edna told me I was to bring my sewing machine to your office."

"Yes, put it down over there. And sit down and tell me what happened."

Ruth checked to make sure the chair was empty before sitting. Without mentioning Nellie's name, she told him about the argument and then finding the sewing machine broken.

Major Harrison's bushy eyebrows drew together, and for several moments he was quiet. "I'm sorry this happened, Ruth. These are difficult times, and we all handle things differently. I don't want to wrongfully accuse anyone. We'll bring it up at our next house meeting, but the fact is, we may never know the truth. In the meantime, the machine can stay here."

"Thank you, sir." Ruth rose to go.

Later, Ruth stood in the kitchen wondering how to start. Edna wasn't around, Leigh had moved to Ames, and Sarah was at her job interview. Even Enos was missing. Ruth went to the pantry and pulled out a large sack of potatoes. She could peel them. They served potatoes every night.

She had almost finished the sack of potatoes when Sarah rushed in. Her cheeks were flushed, and her eyes were bright. "I guess it's just you and me, chum. I saw Edna in the hall, and she said she had to take care of a 'situation.' I hope she's kicking Nellie out for what she did to your sewing machine."

Ruth stood up, wiping her hands on her apron. "We don't know that Nellie did it," she cautioned. "Do you know what the menu is?"

"Chicken. We better get it started." She headed toward the fridge and pulled out bags of chickens. She looked at them in confusion. "Do you know how to cut these up?"

Ruth nodded and picked up a large knife from the holder. She laid the chicken on the cutting board and sliced off a wing. "How was your interview?"

Sarah turned with a gigantic grin spreading across her face. "I got the job. One of their secretaries just quit because she's in a family way. And I walked in."

"When do you start?"

"Next Monday. The other woman is finishing out the week."

Ruth smiled, truly happy for the bubbly young woman. "Good for you. You won't have to be in the shelter long. Why don't you start the potatoes, and I'll get these birds cut up?"

When the potatoes were in the pots, they floured the chicken and started warming the skillets. Suddenly they heard a loud hiss and sizzle. The potato water had boiled over. Ruth rushed over and turned down the heat. There would be a gooey mess to clean up later.

They turned back to the skillets and added the chicken to the hot, melted fat. When Sarah laid a large chicken breast in, the grease spattered onto her arm. "Ouch!" She grabbed her arm and dumped the plate with the flour onto the floor, shattering the plate and coating both them and the linoleum with a cloud of flour.

At that moment, Edna arrived. She stood in the kitchen surveying the chaos.

"I burned my arm," Sarah offered as an excuse.

"Run it under cold water," she told Sarah. Then turning, she spoke to Ruth. "Get the broom and sweep up this mess." Edna went to the skillet and turned some well-browned pieces over.

Ruth and Sarah rushed to do what Edna had ordered. In a matter of minutes, the chaos in the kitchen changed to efficiency. Enos arrived, and in a short time, they were all busy serving. Much later, after Edna had left and they were cleaning, the girls collapsed in giggles.

"You had flour in your hair." Ruth chortled.

"Did you see Edna's face? She couldn't believe we had made such a mess of things."

"Good thing Enos arrived. He just cleaned up our messes without saying a thing. He didn't even ask how it happened."

They giggled again as they hung up their towels and went upstairs to the dormitory.

When Ruth crawled into bed, her heart still overflowed with joy. It had been a long time since she'd laughed with a girlfriend.

34

As Ruth stirred the oatmeal the next morning, she warned Sarah, "Don't distract me. If we burn this, there won't be anything to serve."

Sarah giggled as she lifted a stack of bowls to the serving counter. "I won't, I promise." She came over to the stove to peer into one of the big pots. "It's a good thing I got a job as a secretary, not a cook."

Ruth laughed. "Oh, I think you could learn."

"Maybe." Sarah looked thoughtful. "I've been thinking. If you get a job, too, we could share a room somewhere."

Ruth paused in her stirring. "That would be keen."

"And every weekend, we'll go to a shindig and dance till the sun comes up." Sarah smiled as she returned to setting out serving dishes.

Enos arrived and set out bottles of milk as Sarah and Ruth served the oatmeal and pieces of toast. As the last of the diners straggled past, Sarah spoke to Ruth. "I need to find some clothes to wear to work next week. I have two dresses, and yesterday I tore one of them on that cabinet door." She pointed to a nail poking from a corner cupboard.

Ruth plopped another spoonful of oatmeal into a bowl and handed it to an elderly man who gave her a toothless smile of thanks. She turned to Sarah. "If my sewing machine hadn't been damaged, I could fix you right up. Let's see what we can do by hand."

Enos cleared his throat. "Don't mean to be eavesdropping, ladies. Do you have a broken sewing machine?"

Ruth sighed, and, unwilling to repeat the story again, just answered, "Yes."

"Would you like me to take a look at it?"

Ruth looked at him in astonishment. "Well, I guess you could."

"I know a lot about machines. Maybe I could fix it for you."

Ruth handed another bowl to a little girl. "I have nothing to pay you."

Enos smiled at her. "How about if I get it fixed, you repair my Sunday shirt for me?"

Ruth smiled. "That's a deal."

When breakfast was over and they had cleaned the kitchen, Ruth walked with Enos to Major Harrison's office. She knocked and waited for his hearty, "Come in."

Enos followed her in, and she explained. "Enos has offered to look at my sewing machine."

Major Harrison and Ruth watched as Enos lifted the machine to the desk. His fingers gently manipulated the broken spool holder. He bent over to examine the part where the wheel should fit. Finally, he stood, his hand resting on the machine.

"I think I could get this running for you. I have some parts at home. I used to have a little business ..." his voice trailed off.

"Now Major Harrison's giving me the help I need to get back on my feet. Care if I take this with me?"

Ruth shook her head. "Certainly. It's of no use to me now. Keep it as long as you need."

Enos picked up the machine, holding the broken wheel in his other hand. "We need to get it running so you can fix those clothes for Sarah." He nodded to Major Harrison and left.

"Sit down for a minute, Ruth. Let's visit," Major Harrison requested.

Ruth lifted a stack of baby clothes from the chair, her heart bumping in her chest. Did a "visit" mean she'd broken a rule?

"Just put them over there." The major waved his hand toward a group of sacks that held donated items. Ruth laid them down and settled into the chair. "Thank you for allowing me to store my sewing machine in here."

"You're welcome. I hope Mr. Phillips can get it running for you."

Phillips must be Enos's last name. Ruth had never heard him called anything but Enos.

Major Harrison leaned forward. "I've heard good things about you these last few days. Edna says she appreciates your help in the kitchen. But I know you don't want to work here forever." He reached across the desk and handed her a paper. "This is a list of some job prospects you can visit."

Ruth breathed a sigh of relief and glanced down at the short list of names and addresses. She looked up with a smile. "Thanks, Major Harrison. I will contact them." She waited a moment then asked, "Is there anything else?'

"No, no. That's all. Thank you, Ruth."

There was only a short time between cleanup from breakfast and preparation for the evening meal. Ruth flew upstairs and ran a comb through her hair, grabbed her hat and gloves, and left for the job search.

Two hours later, Ruth trudged back into the citadel and out to the kitchen, pulling off her hat and gloves and tossing them on one of the chairs in the dining room. Sarah stood by the stove in the kitchen.

"I'm sorry," Ruth apologized. "I was checking out the list of possible jobs that Major Harrison gave me. The bus ran a little behind schedule, but I got here as fast as I could."

"You're fine." Sarah pulled two sheet cakes out of the oven. "Look what I whipped up all by myself."

"Those look terrific. What do I need to do?" Ruth looked around for Edna, but she wasn't in the kitchen.

"I hate to ask, but can you do the potatoes again?"

"Sure." Ruth pulled the sack of potatoes over to a stool. She intended to sit down for this task today.

"How was the job search? Any possibilities?"

Ruth attacked the potato with the knife, slicing off the peeling and letting it drop in the waste bucket. "Every single listing had already been filled, or they weren't interested in a young woman. At one of the housekeeping positions, the employer asked if I was Italian. When I told her that I was, she said she could never hire an Italian." She punctuated her words with a toss of the potato into the deep pot where it landed with a thunk.

Sarah shook her head, her mouth pursed. "As if you were less of a person because of where your parents came from."

Ruth picked up another potato, and nearly sliced into her finger. She took a deep breath and slowed down. Both women worked silently for a while, concentrating on their tasks.

When Edna arrived, flitting through the kitchen as always, she paused at the cakes. "Look at these. Our guests will love having a dessert. You two have been working hard." She opened the pantry door and moved a few items around, perhaps inventorying the contents.

When Enos came, instead of going immediately to wash dishes, he came to where Ruth stood, mashing the potatoes in the big stock pan in which they'd been cooked. "Your sewing machine is ready and working. I left it in the Major's office."

Ruth paused, the masher held up like a trophy. "That is wonderful. Enos, thank you so much. I wish I could repay you."

"I left my torn shirt on top of the machine. You fix it up as best you can, and we'll be even." He grinned at her before turning to the dirty dishes in the sink.

The line for dinner was already forming in the hall. From the kitchen, you couldn't see the people, but you could hear a low murmur. As serving time neared, the volume of the voices increased.

Edna glanced around the kitchen and asked, "Are we ready?"

Sarah nodded. "Sure. Let them in."

When the door opened, the hum of voices quieted, and Ruth heard only the shuffling of feet as people moved toward the kitchen. She stepped to her serving station, plopping generous helpings of mashed potatoes on each plate, while her mind wrestled with the frustration of not having employment. Would she end up like the women in the line, their weary faces creased with discouragement, hands held out for the food that kept them alive?

After everyone else had been served, Sarah and Ruth got a tray and filled plates for themselves. Enos wrapped his dinner in paper and tucked it into a lunch pail he carried with him.

Ruth sat at the table nearest the kitchen. A woman and her two children were seated across from them. The boy looked about three or four years old. He scooted off his chair and whispered in his mother's ear.

"Can you wait?" she asked him.

He shook his head emphatically and began to wiggle and

dance. His mother stood, hoisting her baby on her hip and grabbing for his hand with the other.

"There's a privy outside in back of the citadel. Would you like me to hold your baby while you take him?" Ruth held out her arms.

"Would you? Thanks." The woman handed the infant to Ruth, then hurried off with the toddler.

Ruth settled the baby on her lap, holding her cheek against the fuzz of the little girl's downy hair for a moment. The round blue eyes staring at her reminded her of Bobby. As Ruth talked to her, she relaxed, and reached for Ruth's plate. "Are you hungry?" Ruth fed her a few spoonfuls of mashed potatoes, and she ate eagerly. She wiped the baby's mouth with her apron and was rewarded with a wide grin showing two tiny new teeth. Ruth's heart wrenched. *Did her baby girl have teeth yet? Had she sampled mashed potatoes? Did someone love her as much as she did?*

The mother returned. "Thanks so much. It's hard with the two of them."

Ruth reluctantly lifted the little girl back to her mother's arms. Sarah, seated next to her, chattered on about what she was going to do when she started her new job next week. Ruth listened without responding. When the mother and son finished their meals and left, her arms still ached.

35

Ruth shoved the last of the clean bowls onto the shelf and hung up the dishtowel. She missed Sarah. Her friend left early in the morning for her job at the canning factory. They still saw each other, but now she was handing Sarah her dinner, not giggling together over some mishap in the kitchen.

"That's good, Helen. We're done here." Ruth spoke to the large, older woman wiping the counters. The new resident slowly rinsed out the cloth and left without a word. Helen's husband, a rail car loader, had been killed in an accident, and she seemed wrapped in a shroud of shock and grief. She worked methodically as they prepared meals, and didn't interact with residents or community members, speaking to them only when necessary.

As Ruth was leaving the kitchen, Edna entered with a woman Ruth hadn't met, but noticed in the dining room.

Edna gave a small flourish of her hand as if she were presenting Ruth with a gift. "Ruth, this is Daisy. And Daisy, this is our best kitchen helper, Ruth."

Daisy's blonde hair didn't look authentic, and despite her thick layer of makeup, wrinkles gave evidence of her age. But she gave Ruth a bright, cheerful smile.

"Welcome to the Salvation Army, Daisy." Ruth wondered why Edna introduced her.

Edna didn't let her wonder long. "Starting with breakfast, I'd like you to train Daisy. When she is fully trained, let her take over your kitchen duties, and you will be free to spend your days looking for employment."

"I will be glad to train her." Ruth gave what she hoped was an encouraging smile and felt a small burden lifted from her shoulders. Surely, with more time to look, she would find a job.

The next morning, Ruth began training. Daisy seemed eager to help and learn. She kept her positive attitude and showed up early for the evening meal preparation. As soon as they finished serving, Helen approached Ruth. Her face looked pale and gaunt. "Do you mind finishing up, since you have Daisy to help? I have a headache."

"Not at all," Ruth spoke gently. "Go right now and lie down. We'll clean up."

After Enos left for the night, Daisy stacked the clean trays. Then she stepped close to Ruth and whispered, "I know where you can get steady employment."

Eyebrows raised, Ruth turned to look at her. "Where?"

"Downtown. There's a place for good-looking girls to stay. You work with gentlemen clients at night ..." her voice trailed off as Edna walked in.

Edna checked the kitchen, running her hands over the counters looking for sticky spots and opening cupboard doors to make sure everything was in its place. She spoke to Ruth. "I'd like you to work through breakfast tomorrow with Daisy. If you feel she has adequate knowledge to take over, you may use your day for a job search. I hate to lose you You're a good worker in the kitchen."

Ruth's cheeks warmed to the praise. Then she remembered the conversation with Daisy. She waited until she heard Edna's footsteps fade down the hall. Then she asked, "Gentlemen clients? You don't mean—be a—a lady of the evening, do you?"

Daisy put her finger to her lips. "Shush, girl. You want the Major to come in here preaching? Yeah. It's not all bad. It's a job, you have a place to live, and you make enough for some keen clothes."

Ruth's mind whirled back to her years on the farm after Thelma died. She thought she might be sick as her stomach twisted and bile rose into her mouth. "No. I couldn't do that. Not ever."

Daisy shrugged. "Suit yourself. I'm just suggesting a way out for you. Me, I got too old for what the men want. But you're young and pretty."

Ruth didn't feel young. She felt as if she'd lived a hundred years already. She wiped off the last counter. "I think we're done, Daisy. I'm going to get out my sewing machine and do some alterations."

Hours later, she put the sewing machine back in Major Harrison's office and climbed the stairs to the dormitory. Most of the women were already asleep, sprawled across their beds to catch any breezes from the open windows. Two women stood smoking on the fire escape, and the smell of the cigarette smoke drifted over the room. One of them laughed and quickly muffled it with her hand.

The next morning Ruth went to get one of her nicer dresses, the polka-dotted one that Mrs. Irvine had given her, from its hook on the wall. The hook was bare. Had she mistakenly put it on another hook? Ruth walked back and forth, checking the entire wall of hooks. No sign of that dress or the dark blue one that she was certain she'd hung underneath. She scanned the room. No one was wearing one of her dresses. Returning to the empty hook, she spoke up over the sounds of the women getting ready for the day. "Has anyone seen a green, polka-dotted dress, or a navy-blue one? They seem to be missing from my hook."

Most of the women ignored her question. A few looked up, shook their heads, or called out, "No."

A woman who'd arrived a few nights earlier looked up from her bed where she'd propped herself up on one elbow. "You're a seamstress. Just make yourself another one."

Making a new dress was impossible. She had no fabric or even a dress she could remake. She tugged the faded old dress from the farm over her head and tried to smooth out the threadbare skirt. It would have to do. At least she still had a hat and gloves.

She carried them downstairs with her. After guiding Daisy through breakfast preparations, she left her and Enos to serve, and joined the line for breakfast. The meal this morning was oatmeal and toast. Ruth wasn't hungry, but she knew she would be after she'd walked through downtown, searching for a sign in the window, or some employer willing to take on an unmarried woman from the shelter. So, she spooned the bland cereal in and washed it down with the weak coffee.

She stacked her bowl, spoon, and cup to hand them off to Daisy, when Major Harrison walked in. His eyes searched the room, and when they lit on her table, he walked straight over.

"Good morning, Ruth. Would you please come into my office when you're finished?"

Her heart began to race. "Yes, of course. I'll be there in a few minutes." She carried the dishes to the kitchen and then walked on trembling legs to the office. The room held the usual disarray. Ruth lifted a pile of folders and sat down, holding them on her lap.

Major Harrison stood and reached across his desk. "I'll take those folders. Things just seem to multiply in here."

With a guilty look at the sewing machine taking valuable space, Ruth handed the stack to him.

The Major reached behind him and pulled out a pair of men's pants. "I have a job for you, if you're interested. I've lost a little weight lately and my wife thinks these need to be taken in. Could you do that?"

Ruth couldn't stifle the sigh that escaped her lips. She took the dark dress pants and questioned him about how much needed to be taken in. When she was sure she could alter them accurately, she folded them on her lap and asked, "Is that all, sir?"

"Oh, no. I have some other news for you. There's a little Italian grocery store on the southside. They're looking for a woman to help make sausage in preparation for their summer festival. I thought of you because you're our only Italian resident. The job only lasts until the end of June, but who knows, if they like you, they may make the job permanent. Are you interested?"

"Yes, of course." Ruth jumped to her feet. She felt like dancing around the office. Thankfully, there was no room. "Where do I go to apply?"

Major Harrison's grin was almost as wide as Ruth's. He handed her a small piece of paper. "Here's the address and the person you need to contact."

Ruth read the address and the man's name: Louis Sartori. "Can I go there now?"

The Major made a shooing motion with his hand. "Go. And God be with you."

During the short streetcar ride, Ruth's emotions wavered

back and forth more than the swaying vehicle. She remembered with sweet longing the Saturday she and Jack had picked up sandwiches from Sartori's. Then she thought of how important this interview would be, and her stomach tightened into knots of nervousness.

Ruth walked three blocks from the streetcar stop and paused before she crossed the street. She gazed up at the two-story, red brick building with the prominent sign above the door, *Satori's*. Then she smoothed out her faded skirt, straightened her hat, and marched inside. When she opened the door, a bell tinkled announcing her arrival. Her footsteps echoed softly on worn wood floors. The aromas of freshly baked bread, meats, and Italian spices surrounded her, and Ruth inhaled deeply. A man stood behind a counter slicing meat with a large, shiny knife. When Ruth paused, he looked up and asked, "May I help you?"

She swallowed the surge of nervousness and smiled. "My name is Ruth Russo, and I'm here to apply for the part-time job. Major Harrison from the Salvation Army sent me."

"*Splendido*." He smiled back at her and spoke in heavily accented English. "Let me finish slicing this salami, and I will be right with you."

Ruth walked the width of the store peering down the aisles and inhaling the lovely smells. For a moment, she was transported back to her mother's kitchen and the warmth and love that had surrounded her. Then she turned and walked back to the meat counter. Her mother's kitchen existed lifetimes ago.

Mr. Sartori laid down the knife and wiped his hands on his apron. Then he beckoned her behind the counter and into a dimly lit back room. He motioned to a wooden kitchen chair. "Please, sit down." He lifted a pencil from behind his ear, pulled a miniscule pad of paper from his apron pocket, and gave her a smile that turned the ends of his mustache up. "Your name?"

"Ruth Russo."

"You are Italian?"

When Ruth affirmed that she was, Mr. Sartori threw up his hands and let loose a string of his melodic native language.

Ruth couldn't help but grin. "I'm sorry, Mr. Sartori. My mother emigrated from Italy before I was born. I only remember a few words of Italian."

His smile faded and his mustache drooped. He spoke in English again. "Oh, what a shame. Well, tell me your job experiences."

Ruth skimmed quickly over the last few years, focusing on her work in the kitchen for the Irvines and the Salvation Army. When she finished her litany, she looked up at Mr. Sartori. The pencil and pad of paper lay in his lap.

"So, no experience in a grocery store or making sausage?"

Ruth shook her head. "No."

"Are you capable of learning?"

A sliver of hope poked Ruth and she raised her head. "Why, yes, I feel I learn quickly."

"You understand this position is only for a short time. I need assistance in making the extra sausage we will sell during our festival."

"Yes, that is what Major Harrison told me."

"Well, I like you, Ruth Russo, and if you feel you could work with an old Italian grocer like me, you're hired."

"Thank you, thank you, sir." Ruth shook Mr. Sartori's hand, hope spreading over her like butter on warm-from-the-oven bread.

"When can you start?" he asked.

"Right now, if you want."

"*Splendido*." Within a matter of minutes, Ruth, attired in a white apron, began weighing and wrapping sausage.

PART FOUR

36

Ruth's stomach knotted with nervousness as she opened the door. She'd worked the specified two weeks, the festival was over, and business was returning to normal. She fully expected that she would be told today her services were no longer needed. She stepped into the back room and Mr. Sartori greeted her. "*Buongiorno*, Miss Russo."

Ruth slipped the apron over her head. "Good morning, Mr. Sartori." She stepped toward the bakery area but stopped as he cleared his throat.

Mr. Sartori spoke carefully in English. "You have been great help these last two weeks. I did not think I'd need you after today. But I just learned my niece is going to be married. She and her husband are moving to Chicago. Would you be interested in a permanent job? Do you think you could learn to bake the Italian breads?"

Ruth didn't hesitate. "Yes!" She loved the small bakery in the back of the store. A fulltime job would allow her to find a room somewhere—and move out of the shelter. She'd been learning some Italian—enough to understand the customers if they asked for something. And she felt at home in the little store that smelled of herbs and sausage and fresh baked bread. Ruth nodded emphatically. "Yes, I'm sure I will be able to do it."

"*Splendido,*" Mr. Satori exclaimed.

Splendido indeed. Ruth could not contain her smile as she returned to her duties.

Ruth told Sarah her good news that evening as they ate together. Sarah jumped up from her chair, almost sending it toppling, rounded the table, and hugged Ruth. "I knew you could do it. We're both employed. Now, we can rent a room together and we'll never need the shelter again." She gave a little twirly dance. "Do we want a room near downtown or on the south side? Maybe we can find a place in between."

Ruth laughed. "I don't care where it is. I can walk or take the streetcar to work. How will we go about finding a room?"

"I've been watching the listings in the *Des Moines Tribune*, but haven't contacted anyone. They may want a month's rent in advance."

The two girls took their empty dishes to the kitchen, then scooched their chairs close and began making plans. When they looked up, the dining room was empty, and there was only the distant clinking of dishes in the kitchen.

That night, as Ruth lay in the warm upstairs dormitory, she fell asleep with a hope as bright as the moon light shining through the window.

———

One week later, Sarah's search for a place to live had found nothing suitable. Rooms were either too expensive, or too far from the streetcar, or already rented. "We'll never find anything. We'll be living in this shelter forever." She stirred her bowl of oatmeal vigorously, as if it were to blame.

"Something will come up. I know it will. We just have to be patient." Ruth patted Sarah's shoulder before carrying her dishes to the kitchen, then hurried out to catch the streetcar.

Later that morning, two women came into Sartori's. They stood nearby as Ruth filled the bakery shelf with fragrant rounds of focaccia bread and long golden ciabatta loaves. Ruth listened closely as the women spoke, their hands elaborating their conversation. She caught the words *la camera*. That meant a room. She finished stocking the shelf as quietly as she could, striving to both hear and understand the conversation. The women stopped talking and moved closer.

"May I help you?" Ruth asked politely, wishing she could trust her limited Italian.

One of the women spoke in English. "Were these baked this morning?"

"*Certo*. I baked them myself."

Both women selected a loaf of ciabatta and turned to leave.

"Excuse me." Only her desperation made Ruth bold enough to speak. "Did I hear you say you had a room to rent?"

The customers conversed in rapid-fire Italian for a moment. Then the younger one of the women, the one who spoke English, turned to Ruth. "*Sì*. She has a room upstairs in her house."

Ruth wished she could speak fluent Italian. She gestured to herself. "My friend and I," she held up two fingers, "we're looking for a room. Would you rent to us?"

Again, the women spoke between themselves in Italian. Then the younger woman nodded. "*Sì*. She would rent to you."

"*Splendido!*" Ruth could hardly contain her excitement. "How much?"

The older woman held up two gnarled fingers, and the

younger woman explained. "Two dollars a week. The room rents for two dollars."

Ruth did the math in her head. She would be able to pay rent, buy food, and even save some. She could fund a search for her baby girl.

The younger woman held out one hand, "I am Viola Gallo. And this is my mother, Beatrice Gallo."

Ruth introduced herself. "May I come look at the room after we close today?"

"*Certamente.*" Viola said. She reached into her handbag and pulled out a small notebook and a pencil, wrote an address on the paper, and handed it to Ruth. "We will hold the room for you."

"*Grazie.*" Ruth couldn't keep her feet from dancing as she hurried back to the bakery.

When Mr. Sartori propped the closed sign in the window, Ruth had already cleaned up her station and prepped for the next day's baking. She pushed her hat over her curls and skipped out the door. Mr. Sartori followed her out, fumbling for the key in his pocket.

"Where can I find this street?" Ruth held out the paper Viola had given her.

Mr. Sartori looked up and pointed. "Just a block in that direction."

"Thank you," Ruth called over her shoulder as she hurried off.

When she got to the street, she turned to the left. The house was three blocks down, just south of the downtown. Convenient for both her and Sarah. The houses in this area were not as large or lavish as those south of Grand where the Irvines lived, but the one matching the address Viola had given her was a neat two-story with a large porch. Hoping she would be able to accurately decipher what Beatrice said,

Ruth knocked on the door and was relieved to see Viola inside.

Viola lifted a small hook that kept the screen door closed and let herself out. "Follow me." She walked around the corner of the house and climbed a staircase to the second floor. She used a large skeleton key to open a door that swung open to a large room with high ceilings. Light poured into the room from tall windows. Worn but clean quilts covered the two beds. A large chest and a washstand with a pitcher completed the furnishings.

Viola opened an inside door and pointed down the hall. "You may use the bathroom or the kitchen downstairs when you need. You are welcome to eat with the family, but that will cost one dollar a week more."

Ruth clasped her hands to her chest. "It will be perfect. We'll take it."

She followed Viola down to the kitchen where Viola pointed out a shelf where the two girls could store food. Then, with a promise to return the next day with the first week's rent, Ruth left through the kitchen door.

All the way to the streetcar stop, Ruth floated on clouds of joy. When she walked up the steps to the Salvation Army Citadel, her elation kept building. The supper line for serving had dwindled. Ruth squeezed past the stragglers and scanned the dining room for Sarah. When she spotted her, she waved and hurried to her table.

"We have a room," Ruth blurted out.

Sarah's fork clattered to her plate. "A room? Where? How much? How did you manage that? I thought you were working at the store today."

Ruth pointed to an empty chair at the table. "Save me a place. Let me get supper before they stop serving. It's perfect—it even has two beds. I'll join you and tell you all about it."

The girls hardly took time to eat as they talked and planned. They would move in on Saturday when Sarah did not have work.

37

Ruth pulled the battered suitcase from under the bed, trying to make as little noise as possible. The snores of sleeping women surrounded her as she pulled items out of her chest-of-drawers. She tiptoed to the hooks and removed her remaining dress, folded it, then laid it on top of the suitcase. Across the room, she could see Sarah sitting up and rubbing her eyes. Ruth gave her a smile and wave as she carried her belongings downstairs.

Major Harrison stood in the hall, greeting those who arrived early for breakfast. Ruth stopped and set the suitcase down. "I can never repay the Salvation Army and you, Major, for all you have done. Thank you for everything."

Major Harrison smiled broadly. "Your job is going well?"

"I love my job at Sartori's. And Sarah and I have rented a room, so I guess this frees a couple beds for you to take in others."

Major Harrison took her hand. "I'm proud of you, Ruth. You have worked hard to get on your feet. I pray God continues to bless and guide you. Is there anything else we can do for you?"

Ruth nodded. "I need to pick up my sewing machine from your office."

"Certainly. Follow me." The Major walked to his office and unlocked the door. A paper sack lay across the top of the machine and he scooped it up. "This is for you. Edna found it in the donations and felt it should go to you as gratitude for all the mending and alterations you have done for everyone here."

Speechless, Ruth took the sack he held out and peeked into it. Folded inside were several yards of a beautiful light blue fabric with white polka dots. Enough for a new dress.

"Thank you. Oh, thank you. This is a wonderful gift." She clutched the fabric to her chest and hefted the sewing machine. As she turned to leave, tears sprang to her eyes. Major Harrison had been the closest to a father she'd ever known. "Can we come back for services on Sundays?"

"Of course." The Major's voice boomed. "You are always welcome here."

In the dining hall, Ruth set her suitcase and sewing machine down at a table close to the kitchen but kept the sack of fabric with her as she searched for Edna.

The diminutive woman scurried about the kitchen, checking on the meal and the workers. Ruth waited until she noticed her standing in the doorway.

"Thank you, Edna." Ruth held up the sack.

"Oh, I'm so glad you didn't forget to say goodbye. Sometimes our residents are so happy to move on, they leave without saying a word." Edna gave Ruth a warm hug. "I knew you could put that material to good use. I don't know why someone would purchase something, and then not make use of it."

"I will certainly use it. There's enough for at least one dress. I'll make it and wear it when I come back to see you."

"That's a deal. You take care, now." Edna gave her one more short hug, then hurried off to oversee the kitchen.

Excitement kept Ruth's stomach in a whirl, so she only nibbled on her piece of toast and drank a cup of coffee. The anticipation buoyed her all the way to the streetcar stop, despite her heavy baggage, but by the time she arrived at Sartori's she felt her arms had been pulled out of their sockets.

"*Buongiorno*, Mr. Sartori." Ruth greeted the store owner as he fed meat into the sausage grinder.

His bushy eyebrows rose. "Are you moving into the store?"

Ruth giggled. "No, I have rented a room from Beatrice Gallo, only a few blocks from here. I can walk to work from now on. Is it all right to put these things in the back room until I'm finished today?"

"*Certamente*. Put them against the wall. You're going to live with Beatrice, huh? She'll turn you into a real Italian." Mr. Sartori smiled and resumed his sausage making.

As the day went on, Ruth spoke to every customer she saw. These people were now her neighbors. By the time Mr. Sartori took the brass key out of his pocket, locked the front door and flipped the sign to *Closed*, Ruth was itching to see how Sarah had arranged their room, and she was even more excited to put her own things away.

Even though she had both her suitcase and the sewing machine, the walk to Beatrice Gallo's seemed short. She stood across the street and gazed at her new residence. Roses bloomed by the front door and a huge garden filled the backyard. Ruth could see lettuce plants, ripe red tomatoes, and green beans hanging from a vine.

The door at the top of the stairs opened and Sarah looked down and waved before descending. "Here, let me carry something."

"Thanks." Ruth handed her the suitcase, and then hefted

the sewing machine for what she hoped would be the last time for a long while. In the spacious upstairs room, Sarah set the suitcase on the bed by the window. She pointed to the bed on the opposite wall. "I took that bed and gave you this one. Is that okay?"

"Are you sure? This one will get more of the breeze from the window."

"I'm sure." Sarah opened a drawer in the chest. "This room is huge. I used only one drawer, so you can fill the others."

Ruth unfastened the closures on the suitcase, pulled out her dresses, shook them, and hung them on one of the pegs next to her bed. She placed the rest of her clothes in the drawer Sarah had opened. In another empty drawer, she put the polka-dot fabric. She slid the empty suitcase underneath, sat on the bed, and looked around with a sigh of contentment. "Home."

Sarah grinned from her perch on the opposite bed. "We have fifteen minutes until dinner. I filled the pitcher if you want to wash up." They'd decided their budget allowed for them to eat dinners with the family. Ruth, especially, liked the idea of learning Italian from the Gallos.

Ruth used a soft worn cloth to wipe her face, then brushed her curls back. Sarah led the way through the upstairs hall and down the main stairway. Smells of warm pasta and marinara sauce drifted up.

The girls paused at the bottom of the stairs. To their right, pocket doors stood open enough to reveal a parlor with couches and chairs trimmed with wood and upholstered in a rich red velvety fabric. Heavy red and gold drapes covered the windows.

Beatrice Gallo appeared suddenly, holding a wooden spoon and chattering in Italian. She motioned to their left, where a large table had been set for dinner. Ruth and Sarah sat where she indicated, and then the room filled with people, all of them greeting the girls and talking loudly to each other. Ruth could only grasp fragments of what they were saying, as they talked over one another and shouted across the table.

Viola sat across from her, beside another woman with two children who sat and stared at Ruth and Sarah. A gray-haired man stood by his chair at the head of the table with Beatrice, still holding the spoon. He removed a rumpled hat, and the group fell silent as he prayed.

After the *amen,* the only part of the prayer Ruth understood, everyone made the sign of the cross, then the table erupted in talk again. Beatrice brought in bowls of steaming pasta, a salad made of greens that Ruth guessed were picked from the garden that morning, and a loaf of focaccia bread that Ruth was certain she'd baked at Sartori's.

Viola waved her hands. "*Silenzioso,*" she shouted. When the talk died down, she motioned at Ruth and Sarah. "Let me introduce you to the family." She pointed first to Ruth, then to Sarah, saying their names clearly. Next, she introduced the people at the table. The older man at the head of the table was Beatrice's husband, Roberto, the young woman, was Viola's sister, Maria. Her husband and children were to her left. Viola's older brother, Antonio, sat beside his mother. Everyone said, "Hello," or, "*Benvenuto,*" when they were introduced, except for the smallest girl, Giana. She gave Ruth a shy smile and hid behind Maria's arm. Then the boisterous talk resumed.

Ruth ate quietly, enjoying the food and trying to catch snatches of what was being said. When the meal was finished, she waited until others began carrying dirty plates and dishes into the kitchen. Then she stood and said to Beatrice, "*Grazie.*" Turning to Viola, she asked, "May I help with the dishes?"

"That's not at all necessary. Maria and I and the kids are all here to help out. You just get settled in. We aren't all here for dinner every night, and I'm sure Mama would appreciate help when we're not." Viola took the dirty plate Ruth held and turned toward the crowded kitchen.

Ruth and Sarah walked up the stairs and into the bedroom. Ruth sat on her bed and leaned back against the pillow. "What a wonderful meal. I feel like I've eaten enough for a week."

Sarah groaned softly. "If I eat like that every night, you'll have to make me a new wardrobe."

Ruth looked around their room. "Where can I put my sewing machine?" The two women discussed possibilities, but never made a final decision.

Sara spun around in the open space at the foot of her bed. "I love it here! I want to work for a few years, and just have fun —go to every hop I can. Then I can look for Mr. Right."

Ruth leaned back against her pillow and thought about the sock of money. "I want to save some money. I don't want to rely on others to take care of me ever again."

Sara sat down and lifted her feet. "And I'll buy as many shoes as I want."

Both girls collapsed in giggles.

As the summer sun slipped below the rooftops of the little Italian community, they spun more dreams of their futures. When they pulled down the window shades and changed into their nightgowns, Ruth lay down feeling like she'd found a home where she belonged at last.

38

Sunshine streamed through the window. Ruth blinked and glanced over at Sarah, who still slept. She tried to lie quietly, but she was too excited about her day off.

She eased out of bed and gazed out the window. A mist rose from the river and drifted over the garden. The hot sun would soon burn it away. Far in the distance, she could see the gleam of the golden dome of the capitol.

"What are you looking at?" Sarah, propped up on her elbow, spoke from her bed.

"The morning. It's beautiful."

"And we don't have to fight the crowd for the bathroom. Or listen to Nellie's complaints about the food."

Ruth giggled. "Or work in the hot kitchen for hours preparing breakfast."

"So, what's the plan for our day off?"

"Do you want to go to church at the Citadel? If we hurry, I think we can make it."

Sarah swung her legs over and sat up. "I suppose we could.

It would give us a chance to see everyone, but it will be a long walk."

"I won't be carrying a suitcase and sewing machine, though." Ruth looked at her dresses on the hook. "I wish I had something new and fashionable to wear." She pulled one of them down. "This one is clean. I'll wear it."

The girls used the bathroom and dressed. The Gallos had left for early Mass at their church. Ruth watched them from the window as they walked down the sidewalk. Mr. Gallo wore a clean felt hat and Mrs. Gallo, in a flowered print dress and a hat with a feather, held his arm. Ruth could tell she was talking to him. He smiled down at her.

Ruth turned away and moved to the inside door. "I'll go slice some bread for us."

After their breakfast of coffee and Italian bread, they left, crossing the river on the bridge and walking through the quiet downtown area until they reached the Citadel. As they walked in the door, Edna greeted them. "Good morning, girls. Did you get moved in okay? Is it suitable?"

Ruth hugged Edna's petite frame. "Yes. We have a wonderful place to live. The Gallos treat us like family."

Edna smiled, and Ruth knew she felt sincerely happy for them. "Great. Are you here for the service?"

Ruth nodded. "We are. We just wanted to come back and see everyone today."

"Major Harrison will be delighted. Most of our residents move on and want to forget about the time they spent here." Edna gave Sarah a hug before bustling off toward the kitchen.

The two girls found a seat in the chapel area. Enos sat in his regular spot near the front. Ruth waved a little, but he didn't see her. Major Harrison walked down the aisle. He smiled at Ruth and Sarah but didn't stop to greet them. When he reached Enos, the Major bent down and spoke to him. Enos shook his head, the Major spoke again and Enos stood, reluctantly it seemed, and walked to the piano.

Ruth and Sarah looked at each other in astonishment. *Enos plays the piano?*

Soon lively strains of music resounded through the chapel. Major Harrison held out his hands and gestured for the congregation to rise. *"What a wonderful change in my life has been wrought, since Jesus came into my heart."*

How did Jesus come into your heart? That seemed like a nice idea. Maybe she would ask Enos sometime. *"I have ceased from my wand'ring and going astray, since Jesus came into my heart. And my sins which are many were all washed away, since Jesus came into my heart."*

Ruth watched Major Harrison as they sang. She thought, *sure, Jesus washed away his sin. But not mine. Mine are too many.*

After the service, Ruth and Sarah stayed for the noon meal, visiting with numerous residents. Sarah stood first and reached for Ruth's dishes. "We have a long walk," she reminded Ruth.

"I want to speak to one more person, and then I'll be ready." Ruth hurried into the kitchen and found Enos washing dishes.

"I can't believe you play the piano too. Is there nothing you can't do?"

Enos chuckled softly. "Miss Ruth, sometimes I wish I could speak God's word with authority the way Major does. But then God reminds me, He wants me to use the gifts He's given me to serve Him." He rubbed his knuckles. "I like to play, but my hands aren't so young anymore."

"I thought you did well. I liked the song about Jesus coming into your heart."

"Glad you enjoyed it. I like the fact that Jesus came in and changed this old man into a new creation."

Ruth wanted to hear more, but the woman who was working with Enos brought another pile of dishes, and he turned back to the sink. "I need to get back to my dishes. God be with you."

Sarah stood by the door waiting for her, and they left among a chorus of "goodbyes."

———

The next morning at work, Ruth found a crate in the back room that could easily be used for a sewing table. They'd received a shipment of produce in it, but it wouldn't be used again, so Mr. Sartori was happy to let her have it, along with a wide board she could use for a top. He even offered to haul them to the Gallos in his battered truck.

Beatrice saw them unloading it, and when she understood what the crate was to be used for, she carried a straight back chair up the main stairs to Ruth's room. Ruth could hardly contain her excitement. She could start on a new dress the next day.

As a thank you, Ruth bought a loaf of focaccia bread, carried it home, and gave it to Beatrice. The old woman's wrinkled face beamed as she patted Ruth's cheek. Unexpected tears sprang up in Ruth's eyes, and she had to look away for a moment. It had been so long since she had been the recipient of such tender treatment.

Every night, it was a surprise to see who sat down for dinner. Beatrice, Roberto, and Viola were always present. Maria and her family, and other members of the Italian community were often extras at the table. Sarah sometimes chose to eat downtown with others from her office, but

Ruth looked forward to the noisy meals and rarely missed one.

One evening, a young man, Leonardo, came for dinner. He ate without much conversation, but he cast frequent glances in Viola's direction. When dinner was over, he asked in Italian if she wanted to take a walk.

Viola peered into the kitchen at the piles of dirty dishes. Before she could answer him, Ruth laid a hand on her arm. "Go with Leonardo. It's a lovely evening. I'll help your mother do the dishes."

Viola hesitated briefly, then smiled up at Leonardo as she took his arm. "*Si*, I will walk."

While they did dishes, Beatrice kept up a steady stream of conversation. Ruth focused on her words and was able to understand most of it. The older woman told her that Roberto and Leonardo both worked for the railroad. Roberto invited Leonardo for dinner because he had no family close. He was a good man, and she could not understand why Viola didn't take more interest in him. The girl was not getting any younger, and she couldn't live with her *madre* and *padre* forever.

Ruth didn't trust her own Italian enough to make lengthy responses. An occasional, "*Si*" and freqent nods let Beatrice know she was listening. When the last dish was dried and Beatrice hung up the towel, she opened a cannister on the counter, took out two pizzella, wrapped them in a napkin and pressed them into Ruth's hand.

"A little snack for later," she said in Italian.

"*Grazie*." Ruth almost wished there were more dishes, so the time in the kitchen with Beatrice could last longer. Instead, she climbed the stairs to her sewing machine.

The polka dot dress slowly took shape. Ruth made a pattern using one of her old dresses but altered it to make it more fashionable. She'd found some left-over material to make a white collar and cuffs on the short sleeves. The dress should be a going-out-on-a-Friday-night dress. Or even a church dress. Not an Italian bread-baker's dress.

Ruth baked bread, had dinner with the Gallo's, and either sewed in the evening, visited with Sarah, or just went to bed. Sarah liked to go out in the evening, meeting friends or going to dances. Maybe, when the dress was finished, she would let Sarah borrow it.

She was stitching the second cuff on, when she ran out of white thread. She looked in her supplies, and saw the dark blue thread was low as well. And she needed buttons to finish the dress.

The next morning, she found her opportunity to shop. Mr. Sartori told her that the store would be closed Thursday, August 15, for *Ferragosto*, or Assumption Day. Although the Gallos might prefer she go to church with them, Ruth planned to take the streetcar downtown, where the stores would not be celebrating the Italian holiday.

Thursday morning, Ruth woke before the sun had peeked over the capitol building. She tiptoed downstairs and made a cup of tea. She chewed on a piece of ciabatta bread as she sipped her tea. The morning was sticky and warm, promising nearly unbearable heat for the afternoon. She'd been smart to get up early.

When she left the house, Sarah had gone to work, but Beatrice bustled about the kitchen. She asked Ruth if she wanted to join them for a big breakfast, but Ruth declined, knowing it would be late in the morning if she waited.

The streetcar dropped her off near Woolworths. As she walked to the store, a flood of memories surfaced. She wondered if Jack had graduated and if he was working full time at the law firm. She wondered who he took for automobile rides and who held his arm in Union Park. Tears filled her eyes, but she blinked them away. She refused to cry over something that was in the past.

She spent a long time choosing out her thread, buttons, and a few other sewing items. She picked up a bar of soap she and Sarah could use at their washstand. Looking at all the items on display, she wondered how it would feel to have her own house with dishes and towels and sheets and ... Ruth turned into an aisle with diapers, baby clothes, and toys.

The wave of grief nearly caused her to stumble and fall. She grabbed a shelf to steady herself, then walked to the front, paid for her purchases, and left the store.

When she was back on the street, Ruth turned to go to the streetcar, but changed her mind. There was no reason to hurry back. The Gallos would be at the *Ferragosto* celebration. She strolled by the storefronts, window shopping and ogling all the displays. A little boy in a stroller caught her eye. She smiled at him and he smiled back, waving the rattle clutched in a chubby fist.

When she passed Rizzo's, she paused, memories flooding her mind as the familiar smells filled her nose. She knew the restaurant owners. They shopped regularly at Sartori's. She saw the owner inside and gave him a brief wave before moving on. When she'd walked almost the entire length of the sidewalk, she crossed the street, and walked leisurely down the opposite side. This area had fewer shops and more offices. One large brick building had a sign that hung above the door. *Law Offices of Martin and Brown, Attorneys at Law.*

On the door itself was a small sign listing the available lawyers. And there in gold paint was his name, *John Walter Meyer.* A lawyer. He'd achieved his dream. A bubble of happiness rose, then burst suddenly as she realized she couldn't congratulate him, couldn't share in his joy. She was an orphan, but he belonged here, in Des Moines, with his name in gold paint on the door of a law firm. Her finger touched the gold lettering, then she jerked her hand away as if the letters were on fire. She moved on, but the bright shining day felt like a cloud had moved across it. She trudged to the nearest streetcar stop and started her journey home.

39

R uth stacked fresh-baked loaves of ciabatta bread on the shelves at the front of the store. No matter what time of day, the warm bread always made her mouth water. The bell dinged when a customer entered. Ruth didn't look up as the footsteps headed directly down the aisle toward the meat counter. She finished arranging the bread and wiped the crumbs off her fingers onto her apron.

"I'd like a half pound of the salami, please. And a quarter pound of provolone, sliced."

She knew that voice as well as her own—Jack Meyer was in Sartori's, and she had no place to hide. He stood between her and the entrance to her back-room bakery. She peered around the corner of a display of packaged Jell-O. Maybe someone with an identical voice had just requested salami.

She would recognize that lanky broad-shouldered frame anywhere. Those arms had held her. She'd tenderly touched the hair that insisted on curling at his hairline.

"Thank you, sir." Jack reached for a package and turned back toward the front.

As Ruth ducked back out of the aisle, her foot caught the edge of the stacks of Jell-O and small cardboard boxes tumbled everywhere. She tried frantically to restack them as Jack walked closer. He reached for a box that had skittered down the aisle.

"Here you go, ma'am." He held out the box of strawberry Jell-O.

When Ruth looked up, Jack's eyes widened. "Ruth."

"Hello, Jack," she answered softly. "Can I get you some bread for your sandwiches? Or some Jell-O?" She looked down at the scattered boxes.

Jack closed the distance remaining between them in two gigantic steps. His face flamed red, and his voice held more than a little anger. "Where have you been? Do you realize I have been looking everywhere for you? I began to think you'd disappeared into thin air. Every Saturday, I waited outside Woolworths, hoping, somehow, you'd turn up. Is it me? My Aunt Nancy? Mildred said you'd quit suddenly, leaving them without help, and she didn't know where you had gone."

"Oh, Jack." Ruth reached for him, longing for his strong arms to hold and shelter her.

Jack stepped back. "I need some answers, Ruth. What you did was unforgivable."

The bell dinged as another customer arrived, and Ruth suddenly remembered the mess of Jell-O boxes on the floor. She laid her hand on Jack's arm. "Can you come back at six? The store closes then, and we can talk. I need to get this cleaned up and back to my job."

Jack's steady gaze caused emotions she thought she'd buried to suddenly rise to the surface. "I'll be here. I never left. It's you who always disappears."

Ruth attempted a tiny smile. "I won't disappear." She began restacking the Jell-O display as Jack carried his package of salami and cheese to the cash register where Mr. Sartori waited.

After Jack left, Mr. Sartori poked his head in the back room. "Is everything okay? Did you know that man?"

Ruth gave a final knead to the dough and set it in a bowl to rise. "Yes, I'm okay. He's an old school chum. I knocked over a stack of Jell-O boxes, and he helped me pick them up."

For the rest of the day, Ruth had difficulty focusing on her duties. When Mr. Sartori locked up, she looked for Jack's car. He was parked on the street, and, as Ruth walked toward him, he remained in the car. She opened the passenger door. "May I sit in here?"

"Of course." Jack wasn't going to make this conversation any easier.

Ruth waited for a moment, but it appeared he wanted her to do the talking. "What do you want to know?"

Jack turned to face her. "I want to know why. Why did you just leave and not tell me where you were going?"

Jack's bewildered and wounded face broke the pieces of Ruth's heart that hadn't already been shattered. In seeking to spare him, she had been the one to deliver the wound. "I'm so sorry, Jack. It just seemed like the only thing I could do. Your aunt told Mrs. Irvine to let me go. They said I was only an 'interesting diversion' for you, and I wasn't fit to be with a lawyer. They didn't want someone like me around Bobby."

"Why not?" Jack looked confused.

"Because I ... I'm damaged goods." Ruth whispered.

Jack's hand came down hard on the steering wheel. "And you believed them over me?"

Ruth shivered at his tone. "I didn't want to stand in your way. I wanted you to have someone," she searched for the right word, "who is not an orphan."

"But what about me? Did you ever ask me what I wanted?"

Ruth shook her head, not trusting her voice for a moment. "No. I didn't. Can you forgive me, Jack?"

Jack looked out the window. When he turned back to her, his face seemed hard, like one of the statues at the capitol. "I need to think, Ruth. And I need to go. I have a dinner meeting tonight with a client."

Ruth swallowed. "Okay. Do you want to see me again?"

Jack looked long and hard at her. "If I want to see you, I will meet you here. How do you get home? Where is home?"

Ruth opened the door. "I have rented a room just a few blocks that direction. I need to go too. The Gallos will be expecting me for dinner."

Jack nodded, and after she closed the door, the Model A sped away. Ruth stood watching, even after the car turned the corner and disappeared.

All the next day she hoped. When Mr. Sartori turned the sign to *Closed*, she hurried out the door, but there was no Model A in sight. She trudged home and spent the evening sewing, but the satisfaction she usually received when creating new clothing eluded her.

Three long days passed. Ruth slogged through her work, weighed down with guilt and sorrow. After eating dinner with the Gallos, she spent evenings sewing frantically, trying not to think about Jack.

On the fourth day, a Friday, she decided Jack could not forgive her, and she probably would never see him again. She simply must move on—be that "new creation" Enos had talked about. She focused on her bread baking, visited with all the customers, and attempted to be more cheerful with Mr. Sartori.

Shortly after five o'clock, Mr. Sartori asked, "Do you know anything about that green Ford that has been parked outside most of the afternoon?"

Green Ford? It must be Jack. Ruth looked out the window in the front door and saw the car parked under the elm tree across the street. Suddenly she felt lighter. Her cheeks warmed. "Umm. He's a friend."

"Well, young lady, when a friend is as persistent as he is, you'd better not keep him waiting. Take off your apron and go."

"Oh, no, Mr. Sartori. We're still open."

He waved his hand at her. "It's a slow day. Go and enjoy the evening. But watch out for storms. This heat will bring a thunderstorm."

"Thank you." After Ruth hung up her apron, she finger-combed her curls, wet from the heat of the back room, then picked up the day-old ciabatta loaf she'd purchased. Jack leaned out the open window of his car and watched the front door. When he saw her, he straightened up.

She could hardly keep her feet from skipping as she made her way to the car. "You need this for your salami." She handed him the loaf of bread through the window.

"Thank you." He held the loaf to his nose and inhaled the fragrance.

Ruth stood by the car for a moment. *Had he only come for bread?* She took a step back.

After a moment that seemed much longer, Jack cleared his throat. "Is it okay for you to leave now?"

"Yes. Mr. Sartori let me go early today. I think he noticed your car."

"Do you want to go somewhere? I have salami and cheese with me; we can go for a picnic and talk."

Ruth smiled. "A picnic sounds lovely. We need to go by the house where I board, though, so I can let them know I won't be there for dinner."

Jack reached across and opened the passenger door for her.

She slid onto the warm seat, breathing in the familiar scents of leather and gasoline.

"Where do you live?" Jack started the familiar *chug, chug, chug* of the motor.

"Three blocks down this street," Ruth directed him. When he pulled up in front of the Gallos', Ruth didn't wait for him to open the door. She slipped out and trotted inside. Beatrice stood in front of the big black stove, stirring marinara sauce. She looked up in surprise.

Ruth quickly explained. "I'm early. Mr. Sartori let me go before we closed tonight. I'm with a friend and wanted to let you know I won't be here for dinner."

Beatrice nodded. Then, in Italian, she asked if the friend was a boy, if he knew how to behave, and if he was Italian.

Ruth chuckled. "He is a perfect gentleman. I'm afraid he is not Italian, but that is his only flaw."

Beatrice reached out and patted Ruth's cheek. "Go and have fun, *bambina*. He is a lucky gentleman to have a date with you."

Ruth went up the inside flight of stairs, washed herself, combed her hair, and changed to the blue polka-dotted dress she had just finished. Then she left by the outside entrance.

Jack circled the front of the car to open the passenger door. He bowed as he opened it. "My lady."

Ruth giggled as she slid in. "I told Mrs. Gallo you were a perfect gentleman. Were you listening?"

"No, I wasn't listening. But only a cad would not treat a beautiful woman with respect."

They drove for a bit in a comfortable silence. The sun was still warm, but the breeze through the windows cooled their cheeks and sent Ruth's curls flying around her face. At Greenwood Park, Jack pulled a blanket from the trunk. He spread it on the grass overlooking the lagoon. Ruth carried the sack containing the bread, salami and cheese.

"Oh, look, a family of ducks." Ruth pointed. For a while they watched the ducks paddle around, occasionally bobbing under the water for a bite to eat. Then Jack reached for her hand. "I can't take finding you and losing you again. I agreed to just be your friend for a while, but I didn't know that entailed not knowing where you were."

"After the Irvines told me to leave, I couldn't find another job." Ruth stared ahead at the pond, the pain of being rejected overflowing her again. "I lived at the Salvation Army shelter for women."

"Ruth, why didn't you let me know? I could have helped." Jack's voice was laced with anger, but she knew it wasn't directed to her.

"I couldn't. Not with the way your family felt about me."

"Aunt Nancy and Mildred felt that way," Jack growled. "Not my parents. And certainly not me."

Ruth looked away, struggling with all that was in her to believe him.

Jack reached out and tenderly brushed her hair from her face. "So how did you get the job at Sartori's?"

"The Salvation Army helped me get an interview. At first, it was supposed to only be a couple weeks before the Italian Fest. But Mr. Sartori's baker quit, and he asked me to take her place."

"Well, I'm glad I had a hankering for some salami last week." Jack squeezed Ruth's hand, and she turned to him. "Please, promise you won't take flight again. At least not without letting me know."

"I promise, Jack. I thought about you every day. I just believed you would be better off without me."

Jack leaned forward and kissed her. A kiss that took her

breath away and left her heart pounding, a kiss that promised more. "I am better *with* you, Ruth, and I plan to spend every day of my life proving that to you." He kissed her again. "Now, can we eat sandwiches?"

Ruth used a knife Jack had brought to cut thick slices of bread, then layered them with generous amounts of salami and cheese. Jack unscrewed the top of a Thermos bottle, and they shared the cup, marveling at how cold and refreshing the iced tea was. After they ate, they put the sack and the blanket in the trunk and walked around the park.

Jack talked about his last semester at Drake and getting the position at the law firm downtown. Ruth told him about Mr. Sartori and the store. The sun slipped away and darkness crept in. A round full moon and thousands of stars lit the path where they walked hand in hand.

"I need to be at the store early to bake bread," Ruth reminded him gently.

Jack turned back to the car, still holding her hand. "I'm sorry, I should have taken you home earlier. Now your landlady won't believe that I'm a gentleman."

Ruth stopped suddenly. "Jack, why don't you come for supper some night? I'd love for you to meet the Gallos. And my friend, Sarah too. Of course, I'll need to ask Beatrice."

Jack grinned. "As long as I get to sit at the table by the prettiest girl in Des Moines."

"I'll ask her if you can come next week. We eat about six-thirty. I'll drop you a note to let you know if it's okay."

When Jack pulled up to the Gallos', he hopped out and held the door for Ruth. She stepped out slowly, reluctant to end the evening.

"I'll see you next week." She climbed a few steps, then turned and watched Jack drive away.

40

R uth approached Mrs. Gallo after dinner. "My friend, the one who is not Italian, loves Italian food. May I ask him for dinner Saturday evening? Take this to pay for his meal." Ruth tried to hand her the change she had counted out.

Beatrice brushed her hand away as she spoke in rapid Italian. "No. Your friend will be our guest. He is welcome, but you cannot pay for his meal."

"May I bring a loaf of bread?" Ruth asked.

"*Si*. You may bring the ciabatta bread." The older woman's face creased in a grin.

Ruth mailed a note to Jack, formally inviting him to dinner at the Gallos on Saturday. She felt giddy with excitement all week. Mr. Sartori must have been aware of the upcoming dinner, because he shooed her out the door early on Saturday, telling her she had been at the store early all week and she deserved an afternoon off.

Ruth had time to take a quick bath, comb her hair, and put on her polka-dot dress before she heard the motorcar outside. She hurried down the inside stairs. Viola, Leonardo, Maria, and

Maria's family had all come for the dinner. Even Sarah decided to eat with the family instead of going out dancing. When Jack knocked, Ruth opened the door and drew him inside to the commotion of the Italian family. Maria's children chased each other through the house, Leonardo and Roberto were in a friendly, but heated argument, and Viola and Maria laughed at a shared joke.

For a moment, Jack looked panic stricken, then he held out a beautiful bouquet of flowers. "For Mrs. Gallo."

She beamed up at him. "*Grazie*. Our Ruth tells us you are a gentleman, but not Italian. That's too bad."

The room erupted in laughter, and Jack looked befuddled. "What did she say?"

Ruth patted his arm. "She said it's too bad you're not Italian."

Beatrice took the flowers to the kitchen, and Viola returned with them in a large vase, which she set in the middle of the table.

"Do you work on the railroad?" Viola asked Jack. When he responded that he worked for a law firm, she began to quiz him. Ruth knew she was practicing her English, so she remained quiet. When Roberto pulled out his chair, the family moved to the table.

Roberto removed his hat, held it to his chest, and looked at those gathered around the table. "*Benvenuto in casa mia.*" Then he translated in heavily accented English, "Welcome to my home." He prayed a lengthy prayer in Italian asking a blessing not only on the food, but the friends and family. Ruth tried to concentrate on the prayer, but she was very conscious of Jack's presence, his knee almost touching hers under the table, and his strong hands clasped in his lap.

Roberto concluded his prayer, and they made the sign of the cross, even Jack, who looked a little befuddled. The talk rose again, amongst the sound of utensils on plates. Most of the conversation was in Italian.

"Can you understand them?" Jack asked between bites of cavatelli made with sausage Mr. Sartori had ground that morning.

Ruth laid down her fork and smiled. "Mostly. Sometimes I need to ask someone to slow down. They all talk so fast."

"Did you always speak Italian? I should have let you order when we went to Rizzo's."

"No. My mom rarely spoke her native language, and I was so young when she died, I never learned. But I've picked it up from the store and from living here."

Jack reached for another piece of ciabatta bread and sopped up the sauce on his plate. "I feel like I'm in another country. I'm so glad you invited me."

After eating, Jack thanked both Beatrice and Roberto for the meal, and Ruth translated. When Ruth asked if she could help with the dishes, Beatrice sent her out of the kitchen with a wave of the dishtowel. "Go be with your nice young man," she said in Italian.

Roberto and Leonardo wanted to see Jack's Model A. They spent a long time looking at the engine and the interior of the car. Both asked lots of questions which Jack patiently answered, using Ruth as a translator.

Finally, Roberto and Leonardo returned to the house, and they were alone. Ruth showed Jack the vegetable garden. "I bet Beatrice's sauce was made from tomatoes picked from these plants this morning."

Jack took her hand as they walked through the yard. "I should go, but after finding you again, I have a hard time leaving. I'm afraid you will disappear."

"I promised, remember?"

Jack stopped and swung around to face her. "You have tomorrow off, right?"

"Yes."

"Let's go to the Iowa State Fair. It's the last day this year."

Ruth couldn't help herself. She clapped her hands and twirled like a small child. She'd gone to the county fair with Thelma and Otto, but she'd never been to the State Fair. "Yes, let's do. Would you like me to bring a picnic?"

"Sure. It will be colossal." He swung her hand until she giggled then his arm went around her, he pulled her close, and kissed her soundly. "And we'll do that on top of the Ferris wheel," he announced. "I'll pick you up at seven."

After watching Jack drive away, Ruth climbed the stairs. Sarah laid down the *McCall's* magazine which she had been reading. "Finally. I thought he'd never leave so we could talk. Who is this handsome man?"

Ruth giggled. "His name is Jack."

"Why have I never heard of Jack?"

"He's an old school friend."

Sarah laughed. "I have a lot of old school friends. I don't kiss them like you kissed Jack."

"Were you spying on me?" Ruth lay back on her bed, her face flaming. "Jack and I were good friends, but when I went to the shelter, I didn't tell him where I was."

"Why?"

"I was ashamed. I didn't think I was good enough for him. I still don't."

"Apparently, he thinks you are. That was some kiss."

Ruth aimed her pillow at Sarah, but she laughed and dodged it. "We're going to the Iowa State Fair tomorrow."

"Oh, you lucky duck. What are you wearing?"

Ruth tipped her head back and sighed. Her only choices

were the faded dresses she wore to work, or the new polka-dot dress. She held up one corner of the skirt. "This, I guess."

"You can't wear the same thing. And besides, that one is too dressy." Sarah bounced up and plucked a new dress off the hook. "How about this one? We're close enough in size, I'm sure it would fit. The white stripes will make you look real tall and thin."

"Sarah, that's kind of you to offer, but I can't wear your new dress. You bought that for work."

"Nonsense." Sarah tossed the dress on Ruth's bed. "I'm not wearing it tomorrow."

"I've never had a best friend like you," Ruth choked out.

"It goes both ways. Just remember every detail of the Fair, so you can tell me when you come home."

41

Ruth tiptoed into the kitchen, wondering what she could take for the picnic and why she had volunteered, when Beatrice came through the back door wearing a bright, flowered-print church dress and a hat with real feathers. Her apron, held up by one hand, overflowed with ripe red tomatoes.

The screen door banged shut behind her as she looked up, her face crinkling in a smile. "Look. Look at all the tomatoes," she said in Italian as she eased them onto the table. Then she cocked her head at Ruth. "You're up early on your day off. Are you coming to Mass with me?"

Ruth explained about the fair and that she was taking a picnic.

"Oh, we know how to pack a lunch." Beatrice pulled a ragged basket from the porch. She added bread, cheese, fresh tomatoes. Then she found a battered Thermos and told Ruth to fill it with cold water. She slipped in several Italian cookies and covered the basket with a clean towel.

"*Grazie.*" The word hardly expressed what she felt for the

Gallo family. Yes, she paid them rent, but they had embraced both her and Sarah as part of their family. "I'm not sure what time I'll return. Please don't count on me for dinner."

She carried the basket and Thermos outside and waited for the familiar rumble of Jack's car. She didn't have to wait long before the Model A chugged down the street. Ruth's heart lifted in anticipation. Jack took their picnic and the Thermos, put them into the trunk, then drew her into his arms for a hug.

"You look lovely," he whispered into her hair. Then he opened the door for her, and she slid into the car, feeling like a carefree child on a holiday.

When they got to the fairgrounds, the parking area was nearly full. Jack parked underneath the shade of a giant oak. It would be a perfect place to lay the blanket out for lunch.

Jack bought tickets at the entrance, then took her hand as they entered. "Where do you want to go first?"

Ruth stood, her mouth agape, her head swiveling in all directions. An assault of sounds, smells, and sights left her breathless. Streams of fairgoers passed them, heading in all directions. Two men on horseback trotted toward a barn. A pickup truck with a crate full of squealing pigs inched its way through the crowds. A man selling breakfast plates from a stand shouted, "Hot breakfast. Get your eggs and bacon here." In the distance, the Ferris wheel spun slowly.

Ruth turned to face Jack and shook her head. "I want to see it all."

Jack tipped his head back and laughed. "Come on."

They strolled through three barns, looking at all the animals. Ruth stroked a baby lamb, watched a cow being milked, guessed the weight of a huge hog, and marveled at the show horses, hooves polished and manes braided.

They bought a bottle of root beer and stopped outside the agriculture building to sip the sweet drink from two straws and watch the other fairgoers. Then they went into the building and marveled at the life-sized cow carved entirely from butter. They spent the remainder of the morning looking at the displays of fresh vegetables and watching cakes and cookies being judged.

When they stopped for lunch, Ruth sank down on the blanket with a sigh, slipped off her shoes and rubbed the back of her heel where a blister was forming.

Jack pulled the contents of the basket and arranged them on the blanket. "Are you sure Mrs. Gallo packed all of this for just the two of us?"

Ruth laughed. "What can I say? She's an Italian mama."

"So, if we got married, I could expect to eat like this all the time?"

Ruth stopped midchew, her piece of focaccia bread poised at her mouth. She must not have heard him correctly. *What was he saying? How should she respond?* She swallowed the lump of bread. "What did you say?"

Jack leaned forward, his eyes dark and serious. "Surely you know how I feel about you, Ruth. But you keep disappearing from my life. If I marry you, maybe I can keep track of you."

"I'm not sure that is a good reason to marry someone," Ruth whispered.

"I would marry you because I love you." Jack's eyes never wavered. They pinned her, holding her helpless.

She moved her foot, and the Thermos tipped. In the ensuing scramble to save the water, Ruth was spared from a reply. A reply that needed thought before she spoke. Ruth packed the remaining food into the basket and Jack shook the crumbs off the blanket before they stored them in the trunk. Then they headed back to the fairgrounds for their afternoon.

Jack held Ruth's hand and led her to a ride, *Ye Olde Mill.*

Boats for two floated through a long, winding tunnel. He pulled her close and kissed her in the dark enclosure.

Then they watched hog-calling, ate funnel cake, saw the elephant named Baby Mine, and rode the merry-go-round. At the grandstand, they stood outside the track and listened to the sound of the horses' hooves pounding the dirt as they raced around the track. The sun slid behind the capitol and tall buildings of downtown, casting a warm light over the fair.

"What did you want to see or do that we haven't?" Jack asked.

Ruth gazed around. The day had been perfect. Her eyes lit on the Ferris wheel, still spinning its passengers up into the sky and down.

Jack reached for her hand. "Let's ride the Ferris wheel." They stood in line to buy the tickets, and by the time they had them, the attendant was unloading passengers from the previous ride. He beckoned to them, Jack gave him their tickets, and they climbed in. The seat rose slightly, then stopped as they filled the next car. They rose again and swayed gently. Then they climbed slowly, up to the top, followed by a heart-stopping drop to the bottom. Ruth clutched Jack with both hands, holding her breath as they rose, and letting it out as they descended. Jack pointed out the building that housed his law firm and the Equitable building.

Ruth tried to spot Sartori's, but her stomach lurched as she looked over the edge of the car. Finally, she focused on the beauty of the setting sun and the warmth of Jack's arm around her. Then the giant wheel slowed and stopped for passengers to disembark. When the ticket taker lifted the bar on their car and they stepped out, her legs wobbled, and she thought she would tip over like the Thermos. But Jack's strong arms went around her and held her until she was steady.

By the time they arrived at the Gallos', the moon had risen

and the house was surrounded by shadows, but lights glowed in the kitchen. Jack helped Ruth get the basket and Thermos out of the trunk, then carried them to the foot of the stairs.

"You never responded to our lunch discussion." His voice was soft as the moonlight.

"I need to think, Jack."

He set the basket and Thermos on the stairs and drew her into an embrace. "Don't keep me waiting too long." He kissed her, leaving her knees as weak as if she had just stepped off the Ferris wheel.

Ruth took the basket upstairs. She would unload it tomorrow. Right now, she wanted to hold and treasure all the moments of the day. Grateful that Sarah was already asleep, Ruth slipped into her nightgown, lay on her bed, and lost herself in a swirl of State Fair memories.

T uesday evening, Beatrice gave Ruth a note that had come in the mail.

I am missing you. Is it okay if I come by Wednesday? I will take you to dinner.

Jack

Ruth held the note close, as if a part of Jack had slipped into the envelope.

"From your young man?" Beatrice asked.

"*Si.*" Ruth smiled. "He is coming tomorrow, so I won't be here for dinner."

"Doesn't he know he is welcome at our table?" Beatrice scolded. "Ahh! He must not like Italian food. Or maybe it's me."

"He loves your food, Mrs. Gallo. He just doesn't want to impose."

"Who is this Mrs. Gallo? You call me Beatrice, or Mama, *la ragazza.*" Beatrice folded her into a hug before hurrying back to the kitchen.

Later, Ruth pulled a coffee can out from under her bed. When the sock that held her money frayed and threatened to split open, Beatrice had given her a coffee can without even asking what it was for. Every week she'd worked at Sartori's, she'd managed to put some change away in her coin purse. When the purse was full, she emptied it into the can. Now, she poured the contents onto her bed and counted. Over five dollars. Surely, that would be enough.

Sarah looked up from her fashion magazine. "What are you saving your money for?"

Ruth fastened the lid on the can and put it back under her bed. "Nothing in particular." There were some things she could not share, even with her best friend and roommate.

"Well, I wouldn't be worried about saving money. You're going to marry Jack and be a rich lawyer's wife."

Ruth threw her pillow across the room at Sarah, who simply ducked and continued. "You'll have two kids, but they'll be raised by your maid, because you'll take up golf and be gone everyday practicing. Except for the days you have to get your hair waved or your nails done."

Both girls laughed until breathless, then spent the evening talking.

Wednesday, Ruth had trouble concentrating on her job. She nearly added salt twice to the first batch of bread. And when she was filling in for the cashier, she forgot a customer's change until the woman shook her cane and scolded her.

When it was close to five, Ruth hurried with her chores, so the minute Mr. Sartori flipped the sign on the door, she could leave.

"I am thinking of making *buccellato*, maybe for the

holidays, something special." Mr. Sartori seemed in no hurry to close the store.

Ruth bit her lip. "Whatever you choose is fine with me. I just need the recipe." She removed her apron, hoping that would prompt him to lock up.

"A bread that costs a bit more, when the money is tight, do you think it will sell?"

She took a deep breath. "Our customers choose how to spend their money, and sometimes they buy special treats. Especially during the holidays."

Mr. Sartori's face lit up. "You're right. Let's do it." He glanced at the apron still in her hand. "Well, I guess it is time to call it a day. I'll close up."

With a sigh of relief, Ruth hung up her apron and picked up her bag. "*Buona notte*, Mr. Sartori," she called as she sped out the door. When she got to the Gallos', Jack's car was already parked out front. He spotted her and came across the yard.

"I'm sorry I'm early. I just couldn't wait to see you." His grin reminded her of a little boy trying to escape a scolding.

Ruth looped her hand through his arm. "Mr. Sartori kept me later than usual to talk about a new bread he wants to carry. Please give me a few minutes to freshen up."

"Sure. I'll be here waiting."

Ruth skipped up the stairs. She washed her face, combed her hair, and added a touch of pink lipstick Sarah had given her. She wished she could change clothes, but she had only the polka-dot dress to change into, and it needed to be washed and ironed. She brushed the skirt of her faded dress free of crumbs.

Jack turned as soon as her door opened, and his smile lit her descent. When she reached the bottom step, he held out his hand. She took it and stepped into his arms for a quick embrace.

Jack spoke first. "Let's go to Rizzo's. I know you don't get enough Italian food."

Ruth laughed. "Okay, but you mustn't tell Beatrice. She thinks you don't like her food."

Jack looked hurt. "It's not that at all. I just want you to myself sometimes. She has a lot of family."

"I understand." Ruth slid into the car and waited until Jack climbed in. "I'm grateful I'm learning and don't have to translate every word in my head. I rarely have to ask Mr. Sartori what a customer is saying anymore."

At Rizzo's, the waiter seated them in a secluded booth, and Jack ordered spaghetti for both of them. Jack asked about Ruth's day and she told him about almost adding double the salt to the bread. He shared the details of an important court case he was handling. When the food arrived, their conversation turned to the delicious pasta, and how lucky they were to have plenty to eat. Ruth thought about the line of weary people waiting for food at the Salvation Army, but she didn't speak of it to Jack.

After the waiter cleared away their plates, Jack reached for her hand across the table, but Ruth tucked both hands in her lap. "I need to ask you something."

"Sure, honey." Jack leaned back. "Ask away."

Ruth wiggled a little, trying to think of the right words to make him understand. "I have some money saved up. I can pay."

Jack's face wrinkled in confusion. "Oh no, I pay for dinner when I take my girl out."

Ruth shook her head. "No, not dinner. Lawyer services. I need a lawyer."

"Darling girl, if you need a lawyer, you don't need to pay me."

Ruth twisted her napkin, knotting and unknotting it.

Slowly she raised her eyes to meet Jack's. "I want to find my baby. I didn't give her up for adoption. They took her. I promised her she would not be an orphan, yet she is." The tears spilled over, trickling over her cheeks, and dropping on the napkin in her lap.

In one fluid motion, Jack rose from his seat, came around the table and slid in beside her. He put his arm around her, and his spotless white handkerchief appeared. Ruth took it and dabbed at her eyes. She gave a little laugh—more snuffle than laugh. "I don't know why I always end up needing your handkerchiefs. I really am not this weepy."

"Maybe you care enough about me to let your feelings show?" Jack's finger lifted her chin, so she looked at him. "I will help you look for her, Ruth, but I can't promise anything. Those records are sealed, and just because I'm a lawyer doesn't mean I have access to all legal documents. Don't even think about paying me. But I do need to know all the details."

The waiter walked by, and Jack waved at him. "Could we have two cups of coffee with cream, please?"

Jack moved back to his side of the booth and pulled a pen and a tiny notepad from his shirt pocket. "Good thing I came prepared. Start at the beginning. I need names, date of her birth, details of the adoption, anything you know that might help me track down your baby."

Ruth wiped her eyes one more time, then leaned forward. "I arrived at the home in September. Mother Superior took charge of everything. She kept all the records ..."

For over an hour, Ruth talked. Occasionally, Jack asked a question or paused her narration so he could write it all down. The waiter refilled their coffee cups once.

"... and I went to work for the Irvines. And ran into you in front of Woolworths." Ruth finished with a smile.

Jack closed the notebook and slipped it and the pen back

into his pocket. "I will start tomorrow. But, Ruth, please don't get your hopes up. We're treading on thin ice here, and I don't want to jeopardize my job."

Ruth nodded. "I understand. I don't want that either." She reached across the table and Jack laid his hand over hers. Her voice trembled a little as she added, "I need to find her, my baby girl, before I can answer your questions about us."

Jack nodded and tightened his grip on her hand. "Then I'll do my best to find her."

When the waiter swished by with a broom and dustpan in hand, Jack rose. "Looks like they're preparing to close. Ready to go?"

As they walked out of Rizzo's she felt lighter than she had for years. She threaded her arm though Jack's. "Let's not go back yet. I've never been downtown at night."

They strolled the streets, peeking into windows of darkened storefronts, and watching streetlights wink on. A few stars poked the sky, and a round full moon rose behind the dome of the capitol. Ruth felt no need for conversation, just the quiet strength of the man beside her, and the fragile hope that she might find the baby she'd lost.

43

For the next few weeks, Ruth held her breath every time she saw Jack, but when he saw the questions in her eyes, he reminded her, "These things take time. Be patient."

She'd waited nine months for her baby to be born. Now, it had been nearly a year since they'd been separated. She was tired of being patient. But what could she do?

Sarah attributed all her jumpiness to being in love and teased her about it. Ruth teased her as well. Sarah talked continuously about one of the young men at the canning factory. It seemed Chester made all sorts of excuses to come into the office and visit with the new secretary.

Ruth sat on her bed and watched Sarah shake the wrinkles out of another new dress. Sarah held it up to her shoulders. "Do you think this would look best with blue pumps or white sandals?"

"I think it will look best with the one pair of black pumps you already own."

Sarah sighed. "You're right. I don't need another pair of shoes. These are perfectly fine." She grinned. "But Brown's

Shoes is having a sale, and if I got a new pair, I could give you these."

Ruth laughed. "Your feet are bigger than mine. If I wore those, I'd fall down and probably knock over another display. You really don't think Chester cares what shoes you wear, do you?"

Sarah twisted a loop of hair around her finger. "I hope he does. I hope he notices everything about me."

Ruth sniffed. "I'm sure he does notice. But I meant, he should like you for other reasons besides the way you look or dress." She glanced at her hand-me-down dresses on the hook, and knew she was speaking for herself as well. "Now, when are you going to turn off the light so we can get some sleep?"

Sarah scooped up the clothes, put them back on the hooks, and pulled the chain. It made a quiet clink as the lightbulb swung back and forth in the darkened room. Yet, for nearly an hour, the two girls continued their conversation about the men who held their hearts.

———

Ruth wasn't surprised when Sarah began spending evenings and her days off with Chester. He didn't have an automobile, so they met and rode the streetcars to a park or to the river to fish. And then came the night when Sarah wasn't yet home and Ruth had gone to sleep, leaving a candle burning for her friend.

"Ruth, you aren't sleeping yet, are you? Wake up." Sarah shook her shoulder slightly.

Ruth sat up with a little shriek, clutching the sheet to her chin.

Sarah held her finger to her lips. "Shhh. You'll wake Beatrice, and she'll come up the stairs with her iron skillet."

Ruth managed a giggle at the image. "What are you doing? Did you just get home? What time is it?"

"It's nearly midnight."

Even though Ruth whispered, her words came with a yelp. "Midnight? What are you thinking, Sarah?"

"I couldn't wait until morning. I had to tell you. Chester asked me to marry him."

Ruth pulled her friend into a tight hug. "Congratulations, Sarah. What wonderful news. Okay, sit here and tell me all the details." Ruth slid over and patted the bed beside her.

Sarah sat on the edge of Ruth's bed. "He took me to eat at a little restaurant near the factory. After we ate, he suggested a walk on the bridge. And while we were there, he asked me to marry him. He said I was the best thing that ever happened to him. He can't afford a ring, but he's going to quit the factory and go to work for the railroad. That's good money."

"So, when will the wedding be?"

Sarah giggled. "We're going to the courthouse on Saturday."

Ruth gasped. "You're getting married on Saturday? This Saturday?"

"Yep. Chester is taking a job with the railroad in Nebraska. We're moving to North Platte in two weeks."

"But ... but ..." Ruth felt she was on the Ferris wheel, only spinning so fast that everything was a blur. "I'm happy for you. You'll have family again. You and Chester, you'll be a family."

Sarah pursed her lips and blinked. "We will. I wish my mom could be here, then maybe I'd have a real wedding, in a church, with guests and all."

"Would you like me to ask Mr. Sartori for the morning off so I could stand up with you?"

Sarah's grin returned. "That would be super keen if you could be there."

"I'll ask him tomorrow."

"I'd better let you get back to sleep." Sarah stood and blew out the candle.

Ruth slid down in her bed and pulled the quilt up. "Thanks for waking me with your news."

The next morning, Ruth greeted her employer as she slipped on her apron. "*Buongiorno*, Mr. Sartori."

"And good morning to you. I am putting in an order to our supplier this morning. Would you check on the flour?"

"*Certemente*. And Mr. Sartori?"

He paused mid-step on his way to unlock the front door. "Yes?"

"My roommate is getting married Saturday. Could I have the morning off to attend?"

"Ack. Saturday. Our busy day. Surely she could get married on another day?" Ruth's face must have registered her disappointment, because Mr. Sartori chuckled. "Of course, you may have the morning off. I will get my cousin to help. We must celebrate the important times, yes?"

Sarah shared the news with the Gallos at dinner that night. Immediately the table erupted in typical Italian fashion, congratulations coming from those who understood her English, and Beatrice, who never could tolerate not knowing what was going on, pummeling Viola with pleas to translate.

For the rest of the dinner there were questions in Italian, answers in English and translations back to Italian. Ruth left the table when Beatrice did, to help in the kitchen. When Beatrice waved her apron to shoo her out, Ruth waved the dishtowel back, causing both women to laugh.

While she dried the dishes Beatrice washed, Ruth searched for the correct words in Italian. "After she's married, Sarah will be moving out. I don't have another roommate, so I will pay her rent as well as mine."

Beatrice stopped washing and turned to face her, wet hands on her ample hips, "You'll do no such thing. Your rent will remain the same." When Ruth began to protest, she held up a finger. "Not a word. I'm the mama, I decide."

"Thank you, Beatrice. You are so good to me."

At that moment, Viola and Sarah entered the kitchen. Beatrice turned to Sarah, "Go on upstairs, we don't need your help here. You must have much to do." Turning to Ruth, she added, "You go, too, and help your friend."

Ruth handed the towel to Viola and followed Sarah up the stairs. A beautiful floral print dress lay draped across Sarah's bed.

"Ohhh." Ruth squealed. "Did you buy this to wear Saturday?"

Sarah's grin was as bright as the dome of the capitol lit by the setting sun. "Do you like it?"

"Try it on." Ruth sat on her bed and waited while Sarah changed. The dress had short sleeves, a fitted bodice, a tiny matching belt at the waist, and a full skirt. Sarah looked beautiful.

Sarah spent the rest of the evening sorting through her clothes and other possessions. She packed a few things in her suitcase and offered Ruth a dress she no longer wore. When everything was ready, they sat on their beds and talked until the moonlight peeked through the curtains.

44

Saturday morning, both girls woke before the sun's first rays crept in the window. Sarah bathed, then Ruth helped her shape finger waves in her normally straight blond hair. Once her hair was styled, Sarah slipped into her dress and the new two-tone shoes she had purchased from Brown's. Ruth wore her polka-dot dress and a new hat Sarah had bought for her.

Chester's brother, Fredrick, arrived to pick the girls up in his automobile. Just before they climbed into the car, Beatrice hurried across the yard with a colorful arrangement of fall flowers from her garden. "A beautiful bride deserves a beautiful bouquet," she said as she laid them in Sarah's arms. Sarah reached out for one of Beatrice's famous hugs.

At the courthouse, Chester paced the sidewalk. When he spotted the car, he waved, and as soon as his brother parked, Chester opened the back door. Ruth stepped out first. Then Sarah followed, and Chester caught his breath.

"You're beautiful," he whispered. She slipped her arm into

his and gazed up at him. Ruth felt a flood of joy for her friend. And a tiny pang of envy. Would she ever be Jack's wife?

They walked into the courthouse, and all four gazed upward and marveled at the ornate architecture of the building. Chester led the way up the wide stairway to the second floor, room 204.

The judge introduced himself, and the ceremony began. The entire service lasted no more than a few minutes. No vowing to love, honor and obey. No solemn homily. But when the judge ended with, "You are now husband and wife," and Chester pulled Sarah close and kissed her, Ruth found herself wiping tears away. She could barely see to sign the marriage certificate as a witness. The judge presented the document to Sarah, and she flashed it at Ruth and Fredrick. "It's for real. We're married."

Ruth wrapped her arms around Sarah and hugged her tightly. "Thanks for being the sister I never had. Let's not lose touch, even when you move to Nebraska."

Sarah drew back and Ruth saw her eyes were also wet. "You have been my sister too. And the best of all friends. You'll see me before we leave for Nebraska. I have to pick up the rest of my things from our room at the Gallo's. Wow, think of all the space you'll have." Ruth laughed and let go of her friend.

Fredrick smiled brightly at Ruth. "I'll give you a ride back to your house. We could maybe stop for some coffee?"

"No, thank you. I will take the streetcar." Ruth declined politely. She would go straight to Sartori's and hope her apron would protect her good dress.

At the store, Ruth jumped into the routine. Mr. Sartori's cousin had made bread for the day, but the tiny bakery area was a mess. Ruth put things away, returning order to the back room. She straightened the loaves on the shelves and restocked the entire bakery section. She took over for the cashier, Theresa, so the woman could leave early. And then, Mr. Sartori flipped the sign on the door to closed.

Ruth removed her apron and hung it on the hook. It seemed a very long time ago she had stood beside Sarah as she said, "I do." She imagined Chester and Sarah sharing supper, then returning to Chester's apartment that the two of them would share until they left for Nebraska.

As Ruth trudged the two blocks to the Gallo's, every step felt as though she were pulling her feet through thick Iowa mud.

She remained quiet through dinner, listening to the ebb and flow of the family's chatter. Viola asked about the wedding, and Ruth shared briefly. She helped clear the table and do dishes before escaping upstairs. She'd hoped Jack would stop by, and maybe bring the information for finding her baby. But the street remained quiet and empty, just like her room. She mended a tear in one of her dresses, turned out the light, and went to bed.

Sunday morning, a cold rain blew against the window. Ruth pulled the blankets up and tried to go back to sleep. But her stomach rumbled, and her thoughts tumbled. With a sigh she threw off the blanket and dressed. The Gallos had all left for early morning Mass. Ruth made herself a cup of tea and cut a slice of bread. She nibbled it and watched raindrops making tiny rivers down the windowpanes. The sound of a motor outside continued for a while before it registered in her brain. She ran to the door and peered through the deluge. Jack's car sat in the street.

Ruth had no shoes on, no jacket, but without pause, she threw open the door and ran outside. Jack jumped out of the car, and his hug lifted her up and whirled her around.

"You crazy lady. What are you doing out here without a coat?" Jack removed his trenchcoat and wrapped it around her. When she looked up at him, laughing, he bent and kissed her. Taking her hand, they ran together to the house. Inside, Ruth had a moment of panic. What would the Gallos say if she entertained a man in the house when they were gone? But as hard as it was raining, it didn't seem there was an alternative.

They shook the rain from their clothes, and Ruth slipped out of the trenchcoat and hung it on the coat tree in the hall. Jack removed his shoes. Then they sat on the stiff horsehair sofa in the parlor.

Jack stretched out his arm along the back of the couch. "How was the wedding yesterday?"

"Sarah made a beautiful bride."

"I would have had eyes only for the girl who was standing up with her."

"Oh, Jack." Ruth giggled. Then she shared all the details of the short ceremony.

"You'll miss her, won't you?"

Ruth nodded, her throat suddenly thick with emotion. "She and I were in the Salvation Army shelter together. Sharing that experience—created a bond."

Jack nodded. "I'm sure it did." He paused, then said, "I do have some news." His face was so solemn that Ruth's heart dropped, and she clutched the arm of the couch.

"I think I have the name of the family who adopted your baby."

Ruth gasped. "Jack, that's great news. Do you have an address? Can we go see her? Today?"

"Hold on, darling. We can't just go barge in on someone and disrupt their life, telling them about something they thought was sealed in the records."

"But she's my baby."

"No. Her adoption is legal. According to the law, she belongs to the Andersens."

"Andersen? That's their name? Please, Jack, I have to see her."

Jack frowned. "We could, maybe, just drive by their house."

Ruth leaped to her feet. "I'll get my shoes and a jacket."

Jack stood and took a long look outside. "The rain is letting up some. I think we can get through in the car."

Ruth took the stairs two at a time, put on stockings and her shoes, grabbed her coat from the peg and raced back downstairs. "I'm ready."

Jack helped her on with her coat, retrieved his from the hall tree, and slipped his shoes back on. They sloshed through the wet yard to the car.

Ruth didn't even wait for Jack to open the car door, but yanked it open herself. Jack stood bewildered for a moment, before going around to the driver's side and climbing in.

The familiar *chug chug* of the motor usually brought a thrill of excitement to Ruth. The car meant adventures with Jack. But not today. Today, she wanted only to see where her daughter lived. She imagined various scenarios—parents overwhelmed with a baby, or somewhat disinterested as the Irvines were, and more than willing to annul the adoption and return the infant to her mother, the one who loved her.

She sat perched on the edge of the leather seat, wishing she could somehow move the car faster. Jack drove without his usual banter, as if he knew she needed to be alone with her thoughts. They traveled through downtown, swerving to avoid puddles and flooded areas. When they reached the north side, Jack turned into a neighborhood with wide streets lined with trees. The houses were big, but not as stately as those near the

Irvines. Most were boxy two-stories, with wide lawns sprinkled with flowers, and welcoming front porches with swings or chairs. Jack pulled to the curb, turned off the car, and took Ruth's hand.

She wondered if it was his usual affectionate gesture, or simply to restrain her from leaping from the car and running to the house.

He pointed to a gleaming white house with red geraniums in pots on the porch steps. "That's where the Andersens live."

Ruth stared with longing, trying to imagine the people within. Were they older? Were they kind? Hardworking? Did they laugh? She imagined a newborn, red and squalling. But eight months had passed. Her baby would be laughing, babbling, holding toys, sitting in a highchair, maybe even walking.

They sat in front of the house, not talking, for several minutes. Finally, Jack broke the silence. "Are you ready to leave yet?"

Before Ruth could answer, the front door swung open. A short, slender woman emerged holding a baby who wore a mint green dress and a white bonnet. Dark curls poked out from underneath the cap. She clutched a flannel blanket in one chubby fist, her other hand clung to the woman's shoulder.

Ruth could barely breathe. "My baby girl," she whispered.

A man held the door for his wife and baby, then turned and locked it. Both the man and the woman were dressed like they were going to church. He wore a suit, and she had on a striped dress, a wide-brimmed hat, and gloves.

A stroller sat on the porch. The man carried it down the steps, then he lifted the baby from the woman's arms. As he turned, Ruth could see a leather and metal brace engulfing the baby's leg.

Ruth grabbed Jack's arm. "What's wrong with her leg? Why is she wearing a brace?"

Jack sighed. "She was born with a club foot. She had surgery to correct it."

The man slid the baby into the seat of the stroller and tucked the blanket around her. She looked up at him, laughing. He bent and kissed her forehead, then began pushing the stroller as the family made their way down the sidewalk. Church bells chimed somewhere close.

As they passed Jack's car, Ruth watched—without moving, without breathing—until they turned a corner and were out of sight.

She didn't even realize tears were running down her cheeks until Jack, without a word, handed her his clean handkerchief.

"She's my baby. I know it. Those curls ..." Ruth touched her own dark curls and burst into sobs.

Jack put his arm around her and drew her close, but he still didn't say anything.

Ruth lifted her head to look at him. "What caused her club foot? Was it something I did?"

"No, darling. Some babies are born that way."

"Will she be okay? Will she walk?"

"According to what I read, she should be able to walk and run. The surgery corrected the problem. I think the brace is just temporary."

Ruth bit her lip. "I couldn't have paid for surgery. She would have been crippled."

Jack's silence affirmed her, and she sobbed on his shoulder for a moment. Then, she looked up at him. "They love her very much, don't they?"

"It seems they do. I can't imagine anyone going to all the work to adopt a child, especially one with a handicap, and then not loving the child."

"They're the only parents she knows."

Jack nodded. "Yes, I imagine so."

Ruth straightened up in her seat. "We can go now," she said, her voice only quivering slightly.

The bells chimed again. Ruth stared at the house as they pulled from the curb into the street. "They were on their way to church, Jack. Maybe we should go to one sometime?"

45

Fall dressed Iowa in yellow, red, and orange. Round pumpkins sat on the porches. Johnson vine wrapped scarlet around the trees. Sunflowers bloomed in the garden, drooping their yellow faces over back fences as if they were peeking on the neighbors.

Jack came often, a welcomed guest for the evening meal at the Gallos'. He never failed to bring a loaf or two of bread, a basket of fruit, or a generous package of the famous Sartori sausage. His attempts at conversations in Italian brought friendly laughter and jokes.

Sundays became their days for just the two of them. They picnicked in the parks, took drives in the Iowa countryside, or sat in the parlor and played *Uncle Wiggly* or *Finch*.

Amidst all this happiness, a day never passed that Ruth didn't think of her little dark-haired baby girl. But she reminded herself of the adoptive parents' tender care, and that eased the ache in her heart.

One warm Sunday in mid-October, Ruth peeked out the bedroom window, but no Model A sat in the drive yet. She could finish the seam of her new dress. After seeing the baby with the Andersens, Ruth used some of her savings to buy fabric and was finishing up her second dress. She could finally throw away the worn-out hand-me-downs from Thelma.

She cut and knotted the thread at the end of the seam, then hung the dress on a peg. After sewing on the buttons tonight, it would be finished. She heard Jack's car turn in the drive, so she grabbed her cardigan and straw hat and hurried down the outside steps. He stood at the passenger side, holding the door for her. After she slid onto the seat, he leaned in for a quick kiss before closing the door.

Jack slid behind the wheel and started the motor. "Let's go to Union Park. We haven't been there for a long time."

"Okay with me."

"Maybe we could get tickets and go for a boat ride on the river."

"Sounds lovely, Jack." Ruth thought he seemed rather tense and hurried today. Perhaps he needed to get back early to prepare for court on Monday.

Jack remained quiet on the short ride to Union Park. Ruth filled the silence with chatter about customers at the store and her sewing projects.

At the park, she slipped her arm in Jack's as they walked toward the ticket booth for the boat ride. "Do you remember the first time you brought me here?"

Jack stopped and turned to face her. "I remember everything. I think I fell in love with you under that tree by the river." He pointed to the willow, now dropping yellow leaves into the water.

"And I fell in love with you when I won the spelling bee, because you were such a good sport. You told me I was the best speller in the state. And asked me if you could walk with me at recess."

"I did?"

Ruth nodded as they approached the ticket booth. She added mournfully, "I don't think we ever got that walk. Otto took me out of school that day because Thelma had taken a turn for the worse."

"Two tickets for the boat ride, please." Jack said to the attendant in the tiny white booth.

"Sorry. We're sold out for today's ride. I can sell you one for next Saturday or Sunday."

Jack's face flushed. "Sold out? What do you mean?"

"I mean exactly what I said. We're sold out of tickets for today's ride. An entire Sunday school came." He pointed toward a large, noisy group of adults and children milling toward the waiting paddle boat.

"Well, that's just dandy," Jack exploded. He grabbed the money he'd lain down and stuffed it in his pocket. Then he stomped down the sidewalk, not even waiting for Ruth.

When she caught up with him, she laid a gentle hand on his arm. "Jack, it's okay. We don't have to go on a boat ride. We can do something else." When she glanced out on the river, something caught her eye and she had an idea. "We can rent a canoe. I've always wanted to ride in a canoe."

The tension in Jack's arm began to lessen. "You have? What if we tip over?"

Ruth laughed. "I can swim. A little, I guess. Just don't rock the canoe."

"Come on." Jack hurried back to the ticket booth.

When the attendant saw Jack, he stepped backward, bumping the back wall of the booth. "I'm sorry sir, we're still sold out."

"I understand. We'd like to rent a canoe."

The attendant's face brightened. "That will be twenty-five

cents, sir. You may take canoe number twelve. It must be returned by five p.m."

Jack handed him the money, grabbed Ruth's hand and made their way to the river's edge where the canoes were tied.

Ruth eyed the narrow boat with the two wooden seats. "How do I get in?"

"Let me get it in the water first. Then, I'll hold your hand and you can step in. But you have to be careful."

Jack held the rope and pulled the canoe into the shallows. He lifted out the short wooden oars and laid them by his feet. Then he reached out with his other hand to Ruth.

She took his hand and put one tentative foot into the canoe. When it rocked back and forth, she withdrew her foot and looked up at Jack. He steadied the canoe with his hand. "Come on. You can do it."

Taking a deep breath, she stepped in again and sat quickly on the wooden seat. Jack handed her the paddles and climbed in. He sat facing her and used one paddle to push them away from the shore. Ruth gripped the sides of the canoe, trying not to shriek as it rocked from the wake of passing boats. Jack paddled, first on one side, then the other, maneuvering the boat in the river. Suddenly a little current caught them and carried them more swiftly than Ruth would have liked. At the same moment, a breeze stirred through the trees and over the water. It caught her hat and sent it sailing into the river where it floated toward the shore.

"My hat." Ruth cried as she lunged for it. The canoe rocked wildly.

"Ruth. No." Jack reached for her.

The canoe tipped, spilling both occupants into the muddy river. Ruth came up, gasping from the chilly water. She grabbed the overturned canoe beside her and held on with both hands. Jack popped out of the water on the opposite side.

"Are you okay? Hold on, I'll get us to shore." Pushing the canoe ahead of him, Jack kicked his strong legs and propelled them the few feet to shallow water. They stood, and Jack righted the canoe. One oar still lay under the front seat of the canoe, but the other oar and Ruth's hat floated away downstream.

Water streamed from Ruth's hair and clothes. "I'm so sorry. The wind blew my hat away and—"

Jack interrupted. "It was my fault. I never should have taken you in a canoe. Neither of us has spent a lot of time canoeing."

Jack grabbed the rope, and they slogged through the mud and thick algae to the river's edge. When they reached shore, Jack climbed onto the bank and held out his hand for Ruth to hold as she stepped over the rocks. She looked in dismay at her shoes, wet and covered with the muck. "I don't think they'll ever be wearable again."

"I wanted today to be perfect and instead everything has gone wrong." Jack scowled and his hands fisted.

Ruth looked at him in amazement. "It's just an accident. We can dry off, clean up, and try it again sometime. Someday we may even laugh about it."

Jack relaxed slightly. "I'm sorry. But I don't think I'll ever laugh about this day." They started off upstream, dragging the canoe through the grass. When they reached the dock, Jack tied the boat. He went to the ticket booth and handed some bills to the attendant, probably for the lost paddle. The man took the money and seemed not to care that his customers had obviously taken an unintended swim.

At the Model A, Ruth looked in dismay at her wet skirts and ruined shoes. "We can't get into your car like this."

"The car will clean up. I just hope you will."

Ruth laughed. "I'm washable."

By the time they got to the house, they were both

shivering. A big group of the Gallo family sat outside, using any available device for a seat. Leonardo sat on an overturned wheelbarrow. Roberto sat on a bucket. The group greeted them and asked in Italian why they were wet.

Jack shrugged. "A canoe ride went badly." Ruth interpreted, then laid a gentle hand on his arm. "Will you give me time to clean the mud off and change clothes?"

"Take as long as you like. I'll sit here and see if I can learn some Italian."

When Ruth returned, she wore one of the new dresses she'd made. Her hair was brushed and held back with combs, and she'd changed shoes. She hung her wet dress on the clothesline.

A casual shirt and pants bagged around Jack's slender frame. "Roberto offered me some dry clothes. And, I've accepted an invitation from Beatrice for dinner. Is that okay with you?"

"Oh, yes. I'll go in and see what I can do to help."

For the next couple hours, Ruth barely spoke to Jack as she helped with the meal and joined in the banter with the spirited Gallo family.

As the afternoon shadows began to lengthen, Jack found Ruth in the kitchen, a dishtowel in her hand. "Care to go for a walk with me?"

"Just let me finish—"

Beatrice snatched the towel from Ruth and gently, but firmly, pushed her toward Jack. "Go, be with your young man," she admonished in Italian.

Ruth smiled and took Jack's arm as they left the kitchen. They strolled down the sidewalk a while without conversation, as if to clear their minds from the noisy confusion of the afternoon.

"I'm sorry—" Jack began, but Ruth put a finger on his lips.

"It has been a wonderful day. And we will have a story to laugh about."

"To tell our grandchildren?" Jack teased.

They'd reached the end of the street, a few feet away from the river. Jack took her hand and led her toward the bank. Suddenly he was on his knees, a ring box had materialized from somewhere, and he held out a gorgeous, sparkling diamond ring. "Ruth Russo, would you do me the honor of becoming Mrs. Jack Meyer, my wife?"

"Oh, Jack," were the only words Ruth could squeak out.

"This is not how I planned today. I wanted to be on the boat, not in the river, dressed in my stylish clothes, not these baggy loaners. But despite everything that has gone wrong, you can make it all right by saying 'Yes.'"

Ruth gazed at him, sure her heart would burst with the love she felt. "Jack, yes, yes, I will be your wife."

Jack stood, placed the ring on her finger, and tenderly kissed her. A kiss full of promise and longing and love.

46

The next few weeks flew by in a whirlwind of activity. Ruth and Jack planned to have the wedding in late November. Nearly every minute Ruth was not at Sartori's, she worked on her wedding dress. She chose a sheer fabric in pale orange, to be lined with a linen fabric of the same shade. The sleeves were long and loose, and the skirt hung mid-calf.

Jack spent evenings looking for a house to buy. He told Ruth, "I don't want my wife to live in that little apartment I'm renting." Finally, he found what he thought was suitable, a white stucco bungalow near downtown, and he took Ruth to look at it.

The owner unlocked the door, and Jack led the way inside. He led her from room to room, describing how "we'll put a sofa here" and "this is the spot for our table." Upstairs were two bedrooms, and Ruth poked her head in quickly and then hurried back downstairs, not wanting Jack to say, "this is where our bed will be," in front of the seller.

When she told Jack that it was perfect, the seller pulled papers out of his briefcase and Jack signed everything to make the house their own. As they walked out to the car, Ruth spotted a little brick church down the street. "Oh, look. Let's check out the church."

They thanked the seller and walked the short distance to the church. Ruth tried the door, and found it unlocked. They slipped inside. The last rays of the setting sun lit stained glass windows. One window had a scene with Jesus holding a lamb, and Ruth remembered the sermon when she'd gone to church with Donna. She looked at the wooden pews facing a simple stage with a wooden cross as the only decoration. "I feel," Ruth turned in a circle. "I feel like I'm home."

Jack laughed. "In a church? Your home is the bungalow I just took out a mortgage on."

"Let's get married here, Jack," Ruth pleaded.

Jack looked around, then back to Ruth. "Whatever you want, my love. I can come here on my lunch time and see if it's available." He held the door open for her. "Maybe we should attend next Sunday?"

Ruth followed slowly, glancing behind her. "I'd like that, Jack."

The next Sunday, Jack's Model A chugged down the road past the bungalow and pulled up in front of the church. The bells began to chime just as Ruth stepped out of the car. She followed Jack up the stairs and through the open doors.

A couple greeted them just inside the door, the man in a pinstriped suit and the woman in a soft floral print dress and a cute pillbox hat with flowers on top. "Welcome to Shady Grove Church. Is this your first time with us?" the man asked as he grasped Jack's hand.

Jack nodded. "Yes, sir, it is. We're buying the white bungalow across the street, and we'll be moving in after we're married. I'm Jack Meyer and this is my fiancée, Ruth Russo."

The woman squealed and grasped Ruth's gloved hand with

both of hers. "That's wonderful. We live in the green house, so we'll be neighbors."

Her husband grinned. "I'm Elden, and this is my wife, Wilma."

More people were entering the church, and Jack moved over to let them pass. He patted Ruth's hand on his arm. "We should find a seat."

"I'll walk you in." Eldon led them down the carpeted aisle, stopped about midway, and gestured. "Is this pew all right?"

"Perfect." Jack waited for Ruth to slide toward the middle, then he sat next to her. "This reminds me of our church in Grantsville."

Ruth blinked in surprise. Would she learn new things about Jack for the rest of her life, or would the time come when she knew all there was to know?

A woman in an elaborate hat with a huge feather sat at the piano. Her hands seemed poised to make music, but she folded them in her lap as an older, gray-haired man stepped to the stage. "Welcome one and all to Shady Grove Church. I am Pastor John Freel, and it is my privilege to have you worship the Lord with us on this beautiful Sunday morning. We extend a special welcome to Jack Meyer and Ruth Russo who are with us for the first time." He held out his arm and gestured for them to stand as the congregation clapped. "I understand that Jack and Ruth are buying Oscar Canfield's home across the street, so welcome to the neighborhood as well. Now, let's praise God in song."

Jack held a hymn book for both of them as the pianist called out the number of the page they were to sing. Ruth tried hard to follow the unfamiliar tunes and lyrics, but Jack seemed to almost know them by heart. When they finished singing, she sat with relief.

Pastor John moved behind a simple wooden pulpit and led

SUSAN R. LAWRENCE

them in prayer, opening with, "Our Gracious Heavenly Father …"

Ruth had never thought of God as a father. Fathers held their children on their lap. Fathers taught their children things. Fathers loved their children and took care of them. Fathers forgave their children. Could God really be her Father?

Pastor John opened a large Bible and began to preach. Ruth tried to focus her mind on his words. Her world was changing too fast. It seemed she had been in flight from one place to another for most of her life. Now, she was marrying Jack and would live in a house—her new home. Would she still feel like an orphan?

Her eyes lit on the window with the scene of Jesus holding a lamb, and like the sunbeam gleaming through the window, the light pierced her heart and soul. And she knew. She wasn't the shepherd looking for the lost lamb, her baby girl. God was the Shepherd, and the lost lamb, the one without a family, was her. God wanted to hold her, teach her, and love her. He wanted to be the Father she'd never had.

A Shepherd like Jesus she could believe, she could trust, she could follow.

Tears spilled from her eyes, and she bowed to pray. She didn't deserve His love, she'd been untruthful to others, she'd run from her problems, and hurt others. And yet His love filled all the empty places in her heart.

She pulled herself back to Pastor John's words as he wrapped up his sermon and prayed for the congregation. When he lifted his head, it seemed he looked right at her, his eyes both kind and compelling.

The congregation stood and the words of "Just As I Am" floated around Ruth. Jack nudged her and held out his handkerchief. She smiled at him as she wiped tears from her cheeks.

As they exited the sanctuary, Pastor John shook her hand. "Ruth, I noticed you seemed moved by the message."

Her words came in a rush. "I want to belong to God's family. I don't want to be an orphan anymore. I want to belong to Him."

"Wonderful news." Pastor John exclaimed. "And can I ask what part of the sermon convicted you?"

"Oh, not the sermon. It was the picture in the window." Ruth pointed to the Good Shepherd glass.

Pastor John erupted in laughter. "Well, young lady, you know how to humble a man of God."

Ruth took Jack's familiar, steadying arm and they made their way through the stream of people, many of them greeting and welcoming them.

At the car, Jack held the door for Ruth. She snuffled softly as she slid in.

"Are you crying? What's the matter?" Jack leaned over to her; his eyes dark with concern.

"I'm just so happy." Ruth mopped more tears from her cheek.

"I'll never understand women crying when they're happy." Jack leaned back in his seat and sighed.

"We not only have a home here," Ruth pointed to the bungalow, "we have a church home too. And the two of us will be a family, but now we also have a church family." Ruth smiled through her tears. "And best of all, I belong."

47

P astor John beamed at Jack's request. "Why, I would be honored to marry you two kids. And of course you can use the church. Did you have a date picked out?"

"The end of November." Jack looked at Ruth and she squeezed his hand.

Pastor John checked his calendar while Ruth and Jack grinned at each other. "How about after the service on November 26?"

After Ruth confirmed with a nod, Jack replied. "Super keen." Then he stood and reached across the desk to shake Pastor John's hand.

"Now, Alice insists that I bring you over to the house for dinner. We live in the parsonage next door." Pastor John motioned out the window.

"We'd love to come, wouldn't we, Jack?" Ruth rose and smoothed out her skirt. She'd put a basket with lunch into the automobile, but it could be for their supper.

The parsonage, built from the same dark red brick as the church, was a Tudor style with two dormer windows. Large pots of blooming mums graced the front entryway. Pastor John held the door for them as he called, "Alice, honey, our guests are here."

Alice came down the hallway, wearing an apron that was both floured and flowered. Her round face was flushed red and her arms were speckled with flour. She dusted her hands before reaching out and pulling Ruth into a warm hug. "I'm so glad you could come. I just popped the biscuits into the oven, so it will be a few minutes. Let me hang up your jackets. Why don't you take them into the parlor, John? I'll finish up in the kitchen."

Pastor John led the way to a small but comfortable parlor with turn-of-the-century furnishings and heavy draperies, all in a warm maroon. Soon, he and Jack were deep in conversation about President Roosevelt and his New Deal. Ruth listened, but her eyes roved around the room and her mind wandered to her home down the street. How would she decorate her parlor? She decided she would not have heavy drapes—she wanted sunlight in her house. And the furniture would be less stiff and formal.

"What do you think, Ruth?" Pastor John asked.

She had no idea what they were discussing. "I think, umm, President Roosevelt ..."

Alice saved her from embarrassment by appearing in the parlor doorway. "Dinner is ready. Let's move to the dining room."

The dining room opened off the kitchen and was just large enough for the oak table and four chairs. Alice directed Ruth and Jack to sit together on the side farthest from the kitchen, then she and Pastor John sat opposite them.

Pastor John cleared his throat. "I'll say grace." His prayer was eloquent, asking God's blessing on the meal, but also on Jack and Ruth as they joined their lives together. Ruth struggled to focus on the prayer as she wondered what she and Jack would use for dishes and silverware.

For the next several minutes, they were all busy filling their plates with roast beef, potatoes, carrots, biscuits, and Jell-O salad.

"Save room for chocolate cake." Alice's cheerful voice warned them as they ate. Then she leaned toward Ruth. "Do you need any help with your wedding preparations?"

Ruth laid down her forkful of potatoes. "I'm not sure. I don't even know what I should be doing."

During the remainder of the meal, Ruth attempted to answer Alice's questions concerning the details of the wedding.

When she brought in plates of warm chocolate cake, Alice asked, "Are you having a reception? A cake?"

Ruth looked up in surprise. "I hadn't thought of that. I haven't been to many weddings. Just one, really. My best friend, but she married at the courthouse. I guess they don't do receptions there." She looked at Jack. "Do you want a reception?"

Jack scooped a forkful of chocolate cake in his mouth, chewed, and swallowed. "Honey, if you want to plan a reception afterward, go ahead. I think it's usually done. I had a couple friends at Drake that married, and they had receptions."

Ruth's cake sat untouched. She twisted the linen napkin lying in her lap. "I don't have the money to pay for a reception." She felt terrible, but it was true. Any extra money from her job had gone to purchase material for her dress and a new nightgown for her wedding night.

Alice exchanged a long look with her husband, and when Pastor John nodded slightly, she reached across the table toward Ruth. "Let us give you a reception. I can make the cake, and we'll have some mints and nuts. We can hold it in the church basement. It's small, but there are tables and dishes. And we'll make coffee. It can be our wedding present to you."

Ruth's eyes widened and her fork dropped to her plate. "I can't let you do that. It's too much." She looked to Jack for support.

Jack wiped his mouth with his napkin and smiled at her. "I think we should say 'Thank you,' and accept Alice's generous gift." He looked across the table. "That cake was wonderful. And I would marry Ruth just to get another piece of one of your cakes."

Everyone laughed, and Ruth reached across the table to squeeze Alice's hand. "Thank you, both of you, for the offer of this marvelous gift."

After dinner, Ruth helped Alice with the dishes, and the men retired to the parlor. When the two women joined them, Jack scooted over to make room for Ruth on the couch. They visited until the sun shone through the west window.

Ruth nudged Jack. "I think it's time to go." The young couple said their goodbyes and left.

After Jack dropped Ruth off at the Gallos' and gave her a long, sweet kiss, she walked slowly up the stairs, watching the Model A go down the road and turn the corner. Only a few weeks left until she would be Mrs. Jack Meyer. Her life was perfect.

48

"No, Jack. I can't do it." Ruth turned to face him, tears streaming down her face. They were seated in the Model A, parked at the newly constructed Des Moines airport hoping to see one of the flying machines take off or land.

Jack's mouth tightened into a grimace. He stared at the empty runway. "They're my parents. I can't not invite them to our wedding. They just want to meet and get to know you." He turned to her with a pleading look in his eyes. "If I have to choose, Ruth, I will always choose you. But please, don't force me to make that choice."

It was Ruth's turn to stare out the window. "Maybe we should just go to the courthouse like Sarah and Chester."

"You know we can't. We've reserved the church. Alice is baking us a cake. I've invited everyone from the office."

Ruth's head whipped around. "Everyone from the office?"

"Well, yeah. I couldn't invite one and not all. You invited the entire Gallo clan."

"They're like my family."

Jack didn't speak for a moment. When he did, his voice was soft and low. "My parents *are* my family."

Ruth caught the sob before it escaped her lips, and it subsided to a whisper. "Okay." But the image of Mrs. Nelson, Jack's aunt, hissing, "You must never see him again. He deserves better than you," burned in her mind. What if his mother thought the same as her sister? What if she tried to stop the wedding?

Jack's arm went around her and pulled her close. "Please don't worry about Mama. She'll love you. And Papa will finally have a girl to spoil. They're coming to Des Moines a week before the wedding, not just to meet you, but because they want to take us to Poulson's to buy bedroom furniture. That will be their wedding gift to us."

Conflicting emotions warred within Ruth until she felt she would explode. She sat up straight, pulling herself from Jack's embrace. "What a wonderful gift! Now we won't have to sleep in your twin bed."

Jack didn't answer, but his eyes had a twinkle that made her cheeks warm. "So, what day can we go shopping? When is your last day at Sartori's?"

Ruth frowned. "I hadn't thought about my last day. I've been training Maria to do the baking. She'll help out only as long as she isn't in, you know—in a family way." Ruth finished in a rush.

And then she thought of having a baby with Jack—his blue eyes and her dark curls—and she melted back into his arms.

At that moment they heard the drone of a motor, and both of them threw open the car doors and peered up into the brilliant blue Sunday afternoon sky. Jack spotted the plane first and pointed, "There! Look! She's coming in for a landing."

They hopped out and watched as the tiny silver dot grew

larger, angled down, and then coasted past them on the runway.

"That's a Tin Goose. A Ford trimotor. It's probably carrying passengers." Jack's excitement chased away Ruth's clouds of worry. She stood beside him and put her arm around his back. The plane was far down the runway, but they watched as men ran out to chock the wheels. The door opened, steps appeared, and several people emerged to the tarmac.

Jack whirled Ruth around in an impromptu dance. "Someday, we'll take a ride on an airplane."

Ruth laughed. "With all six of our children?"

"Six? We're going to have six? Three boys and three girls?"

Ruth nodded solemnly.

Jack bent and kissed her tenderly before they returned to the car.

———

Mr. Sartori's mouth drooped. "Ah, Ruth. I'm so happy for you, but so sad for me."

Ruth felt like hugging the man who had been so kind to her when she was at her lowest. The man who was like a father. "Maria will do a great job for you. She's a quick learner and already knows how to make all of the breads."

"*Si*, she has been mixing up dough with her mama since she could stand on a stool and help. But it won't be the same."

"I'll still come into the store. Rather frequently, I think. Jack loves your homemade sausage."

"Perhaps we'll make him an Italian yet, huh?" Mr. Sartori chuckled. "Now, go on, get out of here. I'll see you a week from Sunday." He pulled a long white envelope from his pocket and handed it to her. "Your last paycheck. It's a little bigger than usual, and that's your wedding present. I figure you'll need it to stock your pantry and ice box."

Ruth pulled the check from the envelope and gasped. "This is too much."

Mr. Sartori's smile was gentle. "No, young lady. You've not only been a good employee, you always lift my spirits. Now, go on."

Ruth removed her apron for the last time and hung it up. Then she pulled on her jacket and slipped the envelope into her handbag. As she left the store, the sturdy screen door banged behind her.

Tomorrow, she and Jack would attend church at Shady Grove, then meet his parents for dinner.

The cloud of worry descended again as she trudged to the Gallos's.

49

S unday morning, a steady rain beat against her window.
Ruth peeked outside at the dark clouds and shivered. She
dressed carefully in her blue polka dot dress, pulled on her
white gloves, and placed her new pillbox hat over her curls.
Then she picked up her umbrella and opened the door. Jack
waited in the Model A on the street.

She started slowly down the stairs. When she crossed the
yard, Jack hopped out, held her umbrella, and helped her into
the car. Then he hurried around to the driver's side, scrunched
in behind the steering wheel and shook his head like a dog,
spraying rainwater over Ruth, the dashboard, and the seat.

"Nice day, huh?" Jack leaned over to kiss Ruth's cheek.
"Sorry about the water." He wiped a drop off her nose. "My
father telephoned yesterday morning, and they came a day
early. They decided to stay with my cousin."

"The Irvines?" Ruth struggled to breathe. Just when she
thought things could not get worse, they did.

"Yeah. My parents couldn't stay with me, because my
apartment's too small. And the new house has no furniture yet.

So, they stayed with Mildred and Frank. They'll meet us for church, and then we're all invited to Mildred's for dinner. You'll get to see Bobby again." Without waiting for her to respond, Jack backed out into the street.

Ruth emotions swirled around her, imprisoning her behind the familiar walls. The only consolation was Bobby. She'd missed him terribly. Would he even remember her?

The rain let up slightly by the time they got to Shady Grove Church. Jack parked in the new gravel parking lot. As he held the door for Ruth, he waved. "There's Mother and Papa now." He grasped her elbow and steered her across the lot.

Jack's father was an older version of his son—the same blue eyes that crinkled as he smiled, the same mop of unruly hair, only Mr. Meyer's had streaks of gray at the edges. The woman beside him bore no resemblance to her sister, Mrs. Nelson. She was taller, with gray hair swept up under a lovely hat with pheasant feathers.

"Mama, Papa, this is Ruth." Jack nudged her forward.

Ruth resisted the urge to flee—to the car, to the Gallos', where could she go? She forced herself to stand and held out one gloved hand.

Mrs. Meyer brushed aside Ruth's hand and drew her into a warm hug. "You're going to be my daughter in a week. My first daughter. I don't shake a daughter's hand like a stranger."

Mrs. Meyer no sooner let her go, than her husband gave Ruth a huge bear-like hug. Then he slapped Jack on the back. "My boy. A lawyer and a married man. Hard to believe."

Several of the Shady Grove congregation greeted Ruth and Jack by name. An usher led them to an empty pew near the front. Ruth's mood lifted when Alice began playing, softly at first, then louder as voices quieted for the service. At least she wouldn't have to make conversation for the next hour.

The music, Pastor John's message, and even the reminder

of her Shepherd from the stained-glass window, all served to calm Ruth's raging emotions. But as Alice played the final strains of the last hymn and the people moved toward the aisle, panic rose again. How would she ever get through the next few hours? Jack reached for her hand and tucked it under his arm. He bent and whispered, "I'm right here. Hang on tight." She gave him a grateful smile and they walked behind his parents to the car.

Jack's dad loosened his tie. "I'll follow you, son. You know Des Moines better than I do. Just give me a minute to get that cantankerous old truck started."

A few minutes later, Jack parked in front of the Irvines'. The view of the house she had lived in for three months brought back a flood of memories. And a wave of panic. "I don't think I can do this, Jack. You don't know how they feel about me. How they feel about us being together."

Jack's hand grasped hers. "Look at me." When Ruth raised her eyes to his, he continued. "I love you. I chose you. I asked you to be my wife. I don't care what others think about us being together. I want you to hold up your head, walk into that house, and not feel anything less than the most beautiful, most-loved woman in the world. Can you do that?"

Ruth's objections crumbled in the wave of Jack's love for her. She nodded. "I will try."

Jack opened the car door and they followed his parents, who had parked the farm truck behind them, up the wide steps to the Irvine's home.

Mrs. Irvine opened the door. "Jack. Finally getting married, huh? Congratulations. Hello, Ruth. Nice to see you. You won't believe how Bobby has grown." As they stepped into the house, Bobby toddled down the hall. Walking. And carrying his rabbit, by now a bit ragged.

Ruth bent down. "Hello, Bobby. I see you still have Bunny. How has he been? Are you feeding him carrots?"

Bobby stared at her for a long moment, then lifted his hands to Mrs. Irvine. "Mama."

She hoisted him to her hip. "I'm going to put Bobby down for a nap, so we can eat without interruptions. He's already had his meal. Go ahead into the dining room. I think dinner is ready."

Mr. Irvine rose from his chair in the parlor, folding the Sunday paper he'd been reading and laying it on the seat. "Come on in. I hope you're hungry. Adella's a great cook."

He led the way to the dining room. The table had been set, and smells of food wafted from the kitchen. Jack pulled out a chair for Ruth and sat next to her, giving her hand a quick squeeze before she laid it in her lap. His mother and father sat on the opposite side of the table.

"How's the new lawyer?" Mr. Irving asked Jack, as he took the chair at the head of the table.

Jack responded, and the conversation slowly shifted from the courtroom to politics. Ruth listened but didn't join in. When Mrs. Irvine took the chair opposite her husband, he asked, "Is Adella ready to serve?"

Mrs. Irvine nodded. "Yes, everything's ready. Would you say grace?"

After Mr. Irvine's prayer, a stout woman entered carrying a platter of sliced roast beef surrounded with steaming carrots and potatoes. She handed the platter to Mr. Irvine, slipped back into the kitchen, and returned with a Jell-O salad and basket of freshly baked biscuits.

As they passed the food around the table, Ruth took a small serving of each, and when everyone began eating, she took a few bites. She laid her fork down and took a sip from the water goblet—a goblet she had filled many times. The meal smelled delicious, but when she chewed and tried to swallow, it stuck in her throat. She pushed the food around her plate and tried to concentrate on the conversation.

Jack's mother leaned toward him. "Did I tell you that Suzanne Krantz is marrying the Johnson boy? What is his name?"

Jack held a bite of roast poised on his fork. "Raymond?"

"Yes. That's the one. They're planning a spring wedding ..."

Ruth tuned out her future mother-in-law's voice as she chattered on about various people from Grantsville.

"And did I tell you what happened to Otto Schmidt?"

Jack's fork clattered to his plate. He glanced sideways at Ruth, shaking his head. "Mama, no ..."

His mother forged ahead as if Jack had said "Please tell me," rather than trying to stop her. "He had a heart attack. He was in the barn and just keeled over. The neighbors to the east found him, but it was too late. He was gone."

Ruth sat, frozen. The few bites she'd eaten churned in her stomach. She tried to breathe, but could only manage a stuttering gasp.

Jack's mother's hand flew to cover her mouth. "Oh Ruth, I'm so sorry. I forgot that's where you lived—with the Schmidts."

Jack reached for Ruth's hand, and she grasped it as if it were the rope that would pull her to safety. "Ruth? Ruth? Are you okay?"

"Excuse me," Ruth mumbled. She pulled her hand out of Jack's grasp and stumbled upstairs to the bathroom. Emotions raged like flames through her.

Otto, dead? Had she somehow wished this on him? Would his death bring an end to her nightmares?

After several moments, she splashed water on her face, then walked slowly back to the dining room table.

Jack stood and pulled her chair out for her. "Are you okay?" he asked again.

"Yes," she said firmly. "The news shocked me, but I'm okay."

Slowly, talk resumed around table.

"I didn't mean to shock you, but I'm curious. May I ask you a question?" Mrs. Meyer's eyes were riveted on Ruth.

Ruth looked up from her plate, the waves of nausea turning to icy fear. She glanced at Jack, but he was deep in conversation with Mr. Irvine. She swallowed, even though there was no food in her mouth, and looked directly at Jack's mother. "Certainly."

"Why did you leave Grantsville so suddenly? We know Otto Schmidt was rather rough around the edges, but he had no idea where you had gone—or why. He seemed rather bereft."

The room swirled around Ruth and the waves were sucking her under. For some reason, the other people in the room had ceased talking.

Jack's arm went around the back of her chair, his strong hands steadying her. "That question is out of line, Mother. Ruth had her reasons for leaving as she did. She did nothing wrong. And she doesn't have to explain herself."

Ruth glanced up at him, drawing strength from his love. She reminded herself that she was no longer an orphan, she had a Heavenly Father who loved her and forgave her. She no longer needed to take flight.

She took a deep breath. "Thank you, Jack. But a good friend told me once that the Bible says, 'the truth shall make you free.' Your mom will be my only mother here on earth. I don't want to marry you without her knowing who I am and what was done to me." She looked back at Mrs. Meyer.

"Otto Schmidt was an evil man who took advantage of a young orphan. I left Grantsville pregnant with Otto's child. I spent five months in the Sisters of Mercy Home for Unwed

Mothers. My baby was adopted, then the Irvines gave me a chance and offered me employment, even though they knew I had given birth to a child. I will always be grateful to them for that. After a long time, Jack convinced me that what happened had not been my fault. I hope you can believe that, too, and if not love me, at least respect me as your son's wife."

Ruth heard a quick intake of breath. Jack's mother held her hand to her mouth and her cheeks flushed red as the strawberry Jell-O. No one spoke. Jack's arm tightened around her, and when she looked up, his eyes were filled with love and maybe admiration.

Mr. Irvine cleared his throat. "So, do you follow the Chicago Bears, Jack? They play today, and we should be able to hear it on the RCA. Want to have dessert in the parlor and listen?"

Jack looked down at Ruth, who nodded, grateful to Mr. Irvine for the distraction. Jack scooted his chair back and stood. "Sure. I'd like a chance to hear the game. How about you, Papa?"

Mr. Meyer laid down his napkin. "I can't ever get the games to come in on our radio at the farm. I'd like to hear it too." As he passed Ruth's chair, he patted her shoulder. Her eyes filled with tears at his loving touch.

A sudden loud shriek came from upstairs. "Bobby's awake." Mrs. Irvine sighed.

"Please, let me go up and get him." Ruth asked.

"Sure. You know where the nursery is."

Ruth skipped up the stairs, listening as Bobby crooned to himself. She pushed open the door. "Hello, buddy. How are you? Will you let me get you out of bed?"

Bobby stared at her for a moment. Then he stood and raised his arms to her. She lifted him out, noting how much he had grown. Then she changed his wet diaper.

She sat a moment in the rocking chair with Bobby on her lap. When she left the Irvines', she'd worried about Bobby, but his parents had taken good care of him. Like her daughter, he had a loving mother and father. And she and Jack would soon have their own family. She smiled at Bobby and carried him downstairs.

Halfway down, Bobby burrowed his head into her shoulder and tightened his grip. When they got to the dining room, Adella had cleared the table and Mrs. Irvine and Jack's mom sat in the dining room visiting. Ruth attempted to set Bobby down, but he only clung tighter. So, she pulled a few toys out of the playpen and sat with him on her lap.

"He remembers you, doesn't he?" Mrs. Irvine mused as she watched them. "He missed you when you left. And he still won't let Adella do anything for him. I end up with most of his care."

Ruth smiled at the toddler and spoke softly. "I can't imagine a better thing to be doing."

After Adella served a wonderful lemon meringue pie and coffee, Jack left the parlor and the game, and came to find Ruth. "Are you ready to go? I need to look over some briefs before court this week. And you need to rest up for our big shopping day tomorrow. Right, Mama?"

Mrs. Meyer beamed up at her son. "That's right. We're going to see if we can get that lovely little house outfitted in style." She looked across the table at Ruth. "I'm looking forward to it. And after we get the furniture, I can help you do some cleaning at your new house."

"Thank you, that's very kind. It would be nice to have everything all clean before we move in." Ruth tried to hand Bobby to his mother, but he wrapped both arms around her neck and hung on. "I have to go. But if your mother says it's okay, I'll come back and see you sometime."

"Of course, any time. Will you have a phone at your house? You could call and see if we're here."

She peeled Bobby off and set him on his mother's lap. Mrs. Irvine offered him a bite of meringue, and Ruth and Jack slipped out the front door.

50

S arah lifted the veil and attached it to Ruth's curls with a few discreetly placed hairpins. She stood back and surveyed the results. "There. The crowning touch. You look simply beautiful. Your dress is new, the veil is borrowed. Do you have something old? And something blue?"

Ruth pointed to her bouquet. "There are some blue asters in the flowers Mrs. Gallo gave me. But nothing old. It doesn't matter. It's just a silly rhyme for good luck."

"And you don't need good luck?" Sarah tilted her head, her eyes sparkling as she regarded her friend.

"No. I have God as my Father and Jack as my husband. We can survive anything life throws at us."

Sarah reached out and gave Ruth a quick hug. "I hope life doesn't throw you anything too big. You and I have already survived a lot."

"We certainly have," Ruth agreed. "Is it time to leave for the church?"

Sarah looked out the window. "Chester's waiting for us."

When they got down the stairs, the entire Gallo family was

watching. Mrs. Gallo gave Ruth a hug and one last admonition in Italian. "We will be at the church, but I want to tell you now that you have become like another daughter to me. So, when you're all settled in that fine house, don't forget about your Italian family over on the south side. You and your man will always have a chair at our table."

Ruth pressed her cheek to Beatrice's wrinkled one. "I could never forget you—how kind you've been to me, how you made me feel like family. Jack and I will visit often."

Then Sarah helped her into the car, handing her the bouquet to hold on her lap. A short time later, Chester pulled up in front of the church.

When Ruth walked in, Alice greeted her. "There's our bride. Come, you can sit in John's office until it's time. And someone has been waiting to see you."

Ruth gasped. "Jack's not supposed to see me."

"It's not Jack. It's his mother."

Ruth's joy evaporated as quickly as the steam from a boiling pot of pasta. In the few minutes it took to walk down the hall to Pastor John's office, she imagined several scenarios, all of which featured Mrs. Meyer demanding that her wedding be called off immediately.

She had been with Jack and his parents all week. They'd shopped for furniture and cleaned the new house. But she'd never been alone with Jack's mother, and Mrs. Meyer had said very little to Ruth. Nothing that didn't pertain to the furniture or house. What could she have to say now? By the time she pushed the door open and entered the office, Ruth was close to tears.

Mrs. Meyer stood as she entered. "Oh, Ruth. You look so lovely. I wanted to visit with you a minute before you walk down that aisle."

Ruth tried to interrupt with *Nothing you have to say will*

make me change my mind. I will marry Jack but when she opened her mouth, Mrs. Meyer held up her hand and continued. "I thought you were very brave when you shared your misfortunes with us last Sunday. But I wasn't sure how to respond. I didn't know you very well, and I have to admit, my sister had put some questions in my mind. I apologize for that. I have watched you all week long—when you were so grateful for the furniture, when you worked hard cleaning your house, when you put all of our needs above yours, when I saw how you loved your church and our Lord, but above all that, when I saw how much you love my son. My heart breaks at all you had to endure, but if I had looked this whole world over, I could never have found a woman more worthy of being Jack's wife. This isn't my wedding, but I want to ask you, Ruth soon-to-be Meyers, will you be my daughter?"

Relief gushed over Ruth. Jack's mom wasn't objecting, she was giving her blessing. "Yes, oh, yes. I will be honored to be your daughter."

Mrs. Meyers reached into her bag and pulled out a delicate golden chain with an engraved locket with the initials *RM*. When Ruth looked up in confusion, she explained. "My given name is Rachel. Jack's dad gave me this locket, and I hoped someday to pass it on to my daughter. I've had to wait longer than I thought, but it's yours if you want it."

Ruth reached for the locket and clutched it to her heart. "It's lovely. Thank you. May I call you Mother now?" Tears pooled in her eyes and spilled down her cheeks.

Mrs. Meyer rushed to her side. "Oh no, you mustn't cry. Your face will be all blotchy and Jack will never forgive me." She wiped Ruth's face carefully with a lace edged handkerchief.

Ruth held up the locket. "Will you put it on for me? I'd like to wear it." She lifted her hair from her neck as Rachel fastened the chain and kissed Ruth's cheek.

"I would love for you to call me Mother."

Just then, Alice opened the office door. "Are you ready, Ruth?"

"I've never been more ready for anything in my life." Ruth followed Alice to the back of the church. Alice hurried to her place at the piano and began to play softly. Sarah and the best man, Jack's friend from the law firm, strolled to the front and turned to watch her. Ruth took Mr. Sartori's arm. He leaned down and whispered, "You are a vision. That Jack is one lucky man." He patted her hand. Ruth glanced up to the stained-glass *Good Shepherd* and knew her Shepherd accompanied them as well. As the strains of Mendelssohn's "Wedding March" filled the church, Ruth floated down the aisle to Jack.

The End

DISCUSSION QUESTIONS

Part One

1. In the first chapter, Ruth takes flight away from an abusive situation. Flight is a theme throughout the book until Ruth flies toward a better life. What is a flight you have taken in your life—either away from something or toward something?

2. Ruth begins life at Sisters of Mercy by hiding her past and taking a false identity which causes problems and later has severe consequences. Share a time you haven't spoken the truth. What repercussions did you experience?

3. Which of the girls living at the Sisters of Mercy Home do you empathize most with? Why?

4. The adoption of Ruth's baby is a heartbreaking loss for her, yet the nuns felt they were making the right and ethical decision. Have you ever experienced a heartbreaking loss? Did anyone tell you it was for the best?

Part Two

5. Working for the Irvines is Ruth's first paying job. What was your first job? How was it like Ruth's? How was it different? How did the culture affect Ruth's job? How does the current culture affect your job?

6. When Ruth attends church with Donna, she hears the story of the Good Shepherd, but misinterprets its meaning. If you knew Ruth, would you correct her? Why or why not?

7. Why do you think Ruth is drawn to Jack, yet continues to push him away?

8. Do you think Mrs. Irvine felt caught between her mother's opinions and her need for Ruth's help? Do you feel sorry for her? Have you ever been caught between conflicting views? What did you choose?

Part Three

9. When Ruth moves to the shelter, she is required to attend church services. Does she show spiritual growth? Why or why not?

10. Why do you think Ruth could not tell Jack she moved to the shelter? What implications could have resulted from her secrets? What secrets have you kept from loved ones and why?

11. Ruth saves money to search for her daughter. Would you help her or discourage her? Why?

Part Four

12. In Part Four, Ruth lands with people who care for her. Which of these—Mr. Sartori, the Gallos, Pastor John and Alice, or Sarah—was your favorite and why?

13. Throughout the book, Jack tries to help Ruth see that

her abuse and pregnancy were not her fault. Do you think she comes to believe this? Why or why not? Have you had something in your life you had to learn was not your fault?

14. How is the sewing machine like a character in the story? What role does it play in Ruth's life?

15. Ruth and Jack's mother did not initially connect. What do you think was the primary cause of this? Tell us about meeting your mother-in-law. Was it uncomfortable? Did you feel welcomed?

16. If you were a guest at Ruth and Jack's wedding, what advice would you give them?

17. When Ruth attends Shady Grove Church, she finally understands God is her Shepherd and chooses to trust Him. How has her spiritual journey up to this point led to her epiphany? What other factors played a part?

18. How has God been the Good Shepherd in your life?

AUTHOR'S NOTE

To my readers:

I pray that *Flight of the Red-winged Blackbird* blessed you. If you purchased this book, you have blessed others as well. All my author's proceeds from this book go to Pour International to build and maintain homes for abandoned and orphaned babies and children in eSwatini, Africa. For more information on this organization go to:

www.info@pourinternational.org

> *For I will pour water on the thirsty land,*
> *And streams on the dry ground.*
> *I will pour out my Spirit on your offspring*
> *And my blessing on your descendants.*
> (Isaiah 44:3)

ABOUT SUSAN R. LAWRENCE

Susan R. Lawrence is a speaker, an author, and a storyteller. She grew up on a farm in the heart of Iowa. As a child, she learned to love country life, writing stories, and her Savior, Jesus Christ.

She graduated from Kansas State Teacher's College and taught special needs children for twenty-six years before putting away the chalkboard to devote more time to writing, speaking, and storytelling.

Susan lives and travels with Gary, her husband and best friend for fifty-one years, and their rescue pup, Maggie. She has three adult children and seven brilliant and beautiful grandchildren who love to hear her stories.

When Susan is not writing, she enjoys spending time with her family, hiking in the woods, bicycling, and traveling. But most of all, she loves to tell the story, the good news of Jesus Christ, in writing, speaking, and living.

Her previously published works include two family

devotion books; two novels, *Atonement for Emily Adams* and *Restoration at River's Edge;* and two middle grades novels, *The Blue Marble* and *The Long Ride Home.* She has also contributed to three anthologies and has written numerous articles for various Christian publications.

MORE HISTORICAL FICTION FROM SCRIVENINGS PRESS

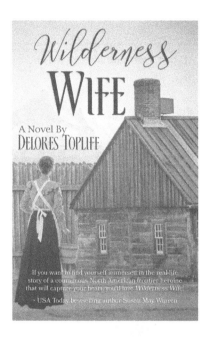

Wilderness Wife
by Delores Topliff

Marguerite Wadin MacKay believes her 17-year marriage to explorer Alex MacKay is strong-until his sudden fame destroys it. When he returns from a cross-Canada expedition, he announces their frontier marriage is void in Montréal where he plans to find a society wife-not one with native blood. Taking their son, MacKay sends Marguerite and their three daughters to a trading post where she lived as a child. Deeply shamed, she arrives in time to assist young Doctor John McLoughlin with a medical emergency.

Marguerite now lives only for her girls. When Fort William on Lake Superior opens a school, Marguerite moves there for her daughters' sake and rekindles her friendship with Doctor McLoughlin. When he declares his love, she dissuades him from a match harmful to his career. She's mixed blood and nine years older. But he will have no one else.

After abandonment, can a woman love again and fulfill a key role in North American History?

———

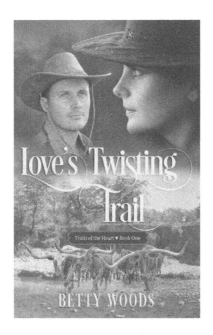

Love's Twisting Trail
by Betty Woods

Stampedes, wild animals, and renegade Comanches make a cattle drive dangerous for any man. The risks multiply when Charlotte Grimes goes up the trail disguised as Charlie, a fourteen year-old boy. She promised her dying father she'd save their ranch after her brother, Tobias, mismanages their money. To keep her vow, she rides the trail with the brother she can't trust.

David Shepherd needs one more successful drive to finish buying the ranch he's prayed for. He partners with Tobias to travel safely through Indian Territory. David detests the hateful way Tobias treats his younger brother, Charlie. He could easily love the boy like the brother he's always wanted. But what does he do when he discovers Charlie's secret? What kind of woman would do what she's done?

The trail takes an unexpected twist when Charlotte falls in love with David. She's afraid to tell him of her deception. Such a God-fearing, honest gentleman is bound to despise the kind of woman who dares to wear a man's trousers and venture on a cattle drive. Since her father left her half the ranch, she intends to continue working the land like any other man after she returns to Texas. David would never accept her as she is.

Choosing between keeping her promise to her father or being with the man she loves may put Charlotte's heart in more danger than any of the hazards on the trail can.

———

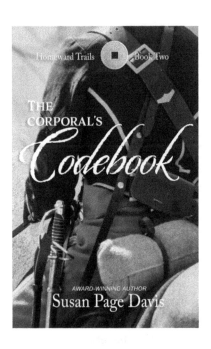

The Corporal's Codebook

by Susan Page Davis

Homeward Trails Series

Book Two

Jack Miller stumbles through the Civil War, winding up a telegrapher and cryptographer for the army. In the field with General Sherman in Georgia, he is captured along with his precious cipher key.

His captor, Hamilton Buckley, thinks he should have been president of the Confederacy, not Jefferson Davis. Jack doubts Buckley's sanity and longs to escape. Buckley's kindhearted niece, Marilla, might help him—but only if Jack helps her achieve her own goal.

Meanwhile, a private investigator, stymied by the difficulty of travel and communication in wartime, is trying his best to locate Jack for the grandmother he longs to see again but can barely remember.

Stay up-to-date on your favorite books and authors with our free e-newsletters.

ScriveningsPress.com

CPSIA information can be obtained
at www.ICGtesting.com
Printed in the USA
JSHW030630180222
22959JS00004B/21